CATCH
HER
DEATH

ALSO BY MELINDA LEIGH

BREE TAGGERT NOVELS

Cross Her Heart

See Her Die

Drown Her Sorrows

Right Behind Her

"Her Second Death" (A Prequel Short Story)

Dead Against Her

Lie to Her

MORGAN DANE NOVELS

Say You're Sorry

Her Last Goodbye

Bones Don't Lie

What I've Done

Secrets Never Die

Save Your Breath

SCARLET FALLS NOVELS

Hour of Need

Minutes to Kill

Seconds to Live

SHE CAN SERIES

She Can Run

She Can Tell

CATCH HER DEATH

MELINDA LEIGH

Montlake

Published by Montlake, Seattle

www.apub.com

Amazon, the Amazon logo, and Montlake are trademarks of Amazon.com, Inc., or its affiliates.

ISBN-13: 9781542038645 (hardcover)
ISBN-13: 9781542038652 (paperback)
ISBN-13: 9781542038669 (digital)

Cover design by Shasti O'Leary Soudant
Cover images: © Maria Heyens / ArcAngel; © Wendy Stevenson / ArcAngel;
© Tavarius / Shutterstock; © Maleo / Shutterstock

Printed in the United States of America
First edition

For Annie and Jason:
may you live happily ever after

CHAPTER ONE

"That dog sounds pissed," a slurred voice said. "Gonna take a chunk out of somebody."

Sheriff Bree Taggert closed the door of her official SUV and located the source of the voice on the sagging front porch of a three-story house. In the dim glow of a dirty porch light, a group of college-age males clustered, commenting on the police activity and gesturing with red plastic cups. Empty cans and bottles ringed the yard like soap scum in a bathtub.

They must be too drunk to feel the cold.

Bree stepped onto the sidewalk and tugged a knit cap over her ears just as the brand-new K-9 unit cruised to a stop at the curb. In the back of the specialized vehicle, a black German shepherd barked. Two weeks before, Deputy Laurie Collins and Greta had passed their certification, and the team was officially part of the Randolph County Sheriff's Department. So far, they'd helped find a couple of drug stashes. But this would be Greta's first real manhunt.

One of the drunk guys said something Bree didn't catch.

Another replied, "Dude, I dare you."

She crossed the lawn and pointed at the intoxicated young men. "Do not come off that porch." Young drunks made stupid decisions. Bree would not allow one of those stupid decisions to get a bystander or deputy killed tonight.

"You can't make us do anything." A blond guy wearing a *My daddy's a lawyer* sneer crossed his arms over his chest.

Bree had no time for his insolence. "If you leave that porch, I will arrest you for public drunkenness." She spotted a pimply-faced younger man vomiting over the porch railing. "Is everyone in that building over twenty-one? Underage drinking is against the law—as is serving alcohol to anyone not of legal age."

"This is private property." The blond's smug look faded to contempt. "If you put me in jail, my father will hand you your ass."

"You'll still spend the night there." Bree held his gaze with her own unwavering one.

Party Boy must have recognized Bree's no-bullshit glare because he backed down with a final, bitter glower. After he broke eye contact, she returned to her vehicle. Except for the party house, the street was quiet on an early Monday evening. People in this neighborhood were survivors. They excelled at not getting involved. As soon as the police cars rolled in, residents hustled into their homes. Mothers called their children inside. Doors were shut. Dead bolts thrown. But Bree had no doubt the neighborhood was watching from behind their drawn curtains.

She turned back to the job at hand.

Bree's chief deputy, Todd Harvey, approached with Deputy Juarez. They gathered at the back of the K-9 unit.

"We're here to serve an arrest warrant on Travis Ekin. Travis is currently living at his mother's house, that ramshackle two-story down the block." Bree double-checked the address on the warrant. Every line on the paperwork had to be perfect.

Travis was the worst of the worst. He was wanted for the rape and murder of fifty-three-year-old Tamara Jenkins. The week before the murder, Travis had assaulted the victim's daughter, twenty-two-year-old Emma Jenkins, and attempted to force her into his car. She'd barely gotten away. Her mother had called 911.

Travis had committed most of his crimes before Bree's tenure as sheriff, but his rap sheet read like an episode of *Justified*. He had two previous drug convictions, for which he'd served barely a year in jail. He'd been arrested three times for sexual assault, but the charges had been dropped every time when the victims refused to testify. No one could prove witness intimidation, but Travis's violent, drug-dealing family had a reputation in the area. Everyone knew not to cross them, and if someone broke that rule, they paid, dearly.

Mrs. Jenkins served as the latest example.

Bree had Travis cold this time. The dumbass had worn a condom and gloves but left his DNA on a glass of lemonade he'd taken from the victim's fridge. Crumbs on the corpse indicated he'd eaten the woman's homemade oatmeal cookies over her violated body. Additional DNA on the plate suggested he'd licked it clean. This DNA had been matched to Travis via CODIS, the FBI's Combined DNA Index System. The daughter had seen Travis leaving the house through the back door as she circled the block looking for a parking spot. She'd picked out his mug shot from a photo array. Then she'd gotten on a plane to California to stay with a friend. The sheriff's department had presented the evidence to the DA with a metaphorical bow. The entire investigation had been too quick and clean for a TV show. In Bree's opinion, the one aspect fictional crime got wrong was that most criminals were generally not masterminds of anything.

Todd circled a finger in the air. "Patrol units established a perimeter around the block. If Travis runs, he won't get far."

"Do we have eyes on the back door?" Bree asked. The Ekin house was in the middle of the block. The property backed to the rear yard of the house behind it. Bree did not want Travis to end up in a neighbor's house with a hostage.

"We do," Todd assured her. "There's one exit, and it's covered."

She studied the house. Blinds drawn. Windowless garage doors. No lights. No vehicles parked outside. No signs of life at all. Travis was hunkered down, hiding, likely armed in a big, old house with plenty of hiding places, which was where the dog came in.

She glanced at the K-9 unit. A good dog could be worth a dozen men in a situation like this, but the risk to the dog was very real. Dogs were stabbed and shot. They died in training accidents and were hit by cars. Greta's canine bulletproof vest would help, but there was plenty of her body still exposed.

A slight ripple of discomfort rolled through her. Before she'd moved to upstate New York to raise her sister's kids, Bree had served in the Philadelphia PD, from patrol up to homicide. She'd worked with K-9s, but they'd always intimidated her. While she'd appreciated K-9 abilities, she'd had no love for dogs in general.

As a young child, she'd been mauled by her father's dog. She touched her shoulder at the phantom slice of pain. She'd covered her scars with tattoos, but she could still feel them, the unnatural tautness of her skin. But over the past year, she'd formed a bond of sorts with the retired patrol dog that belonged to her criminal investigator—and boyfriend—Matt Flynn. Unlike most of the K-9s she'd worked with back in Philly, Brody was calm. He didn't get riled up, didn't bark or lunge. He loved the kids. Bree was sure he'd give his life to protect them.

Then Matt had sweet-talked Bree into adopting Ladybug from his sister's canine rescue. But did Ladybug even count as a dog? She was more Pillow Pet or couch potato than canine. Bree had learned to accept—even love—Brody and Ladybug.

Bree and Greta didn't have the same relationship—yet—but instead of fearing the K-9, Bree feared getting the dog killed. The reversal of perspective was unexpected.

They had no idea what weapons Travis possessed, nor could they assess his frame of mind. But Bree doubted he'd walk out the door with his hands in the air. Travis was going to state prison for this crime, and he knew it.

She swallowed her indecision. The K-9 was a tool, one that the sheriff's department sorely needed. Police dogs saved lives, both officer and civilian. It was their purpose.

"Let's do this," Bree said.

Collins popped the cargo door, and Greta leaped out into the ankle-deep snow. The dog knew something big was going down. Her hackles were lifted, making her black ruff seem thicker and her body larger. She was on the small side for a German shepherd, with a lean body and sleek coat. Could she take down a large man? Travis wasn't particularly tall, but he was built like a refrigerator.

Bree would keep her reservations to herself. Collins and the dog needed confidence.

"We'll give him a chance to surrender first," Bree said.

"Yes, ma'am." Collins looped the long line around her hand several times to hold the dog back. Greta pressed forward, sniffing the air, her tail held high and waving. Most canines Bree had observed looked vicious when they were excited. They scared the hell out of suspects. But Greta looked like she wanted to play. Would she bite?

The dog surged forward and let out a quick series of loud, excited barks. Collins leaned into the leash, using her body weight as leverage. The dog was ready to work, no doubt about that, but whether she was aggressive enough remained to be determined.

Todd and Deputy Juarez held their AR-15s. They followed Bree up the front walk of Travis's mother's house. The walkway hadn't been shoveled, and snow found its way into Bree's boots. Her breath fogged in the evening air, but adrenaline kept her warm. She moved ahead to knock, standing to the side to avoid the dead zone, where a potential gunshot could come through the door. With one hand on her sidearm, she rapped on the door. No one answered. She knocked again, harder, calling, "Sheriff's department! We have a warrant. Open the door or we will break it down."

Sweat trickled down Bree's back under her vest. She wiped a damp palm on her thigh, drew her sidearm, and listened. Footsteps approached the door. They sounded too soft to be Travis's. She braced as the door opened.

The woman who faced her was a hard fiftysomething. Stout and sallow, with bloodshot eyes and a meth mouth, she stuck her face through the six-inch gap. "What?"

"Mrs. Ekin?" Bree asked, hoping she'd open the door wider so Bree could get a look inside the house.

But the woman just squinted at her and didn't budge. Mrs. Ekin had small, beady eyes full of resentment. "What's it to you?"

"I'm Sheriff Taggert." Bree identified herself even though she was wearing her uniform. She pulled the warrant from her pocket. "I have an arrest warrant for Travis Ekin and a search warrant for the premises."

"He's not here." Mrs. Ekin pulled her head back, and moved like she was going to close the door.

As if Bree would just take her word for it. Didn't matter. Bree knew this woman would lie herself blind to protect her precious, murdering son.

"We're going to search the house." Bree lifted the warrant. "I need you to step outside. Is anyone else inside?"

"No," Mrs. Ekin said. "Travis is innocent. He didn't do nothing."

Bree ignored her comment. "Where are your other sons?" Travis had two brothers. All three young men were regularly in and out of trouble.

"They ain't here either," Mrs. Ekin spit out. "I didn't know the sheriff's department had a dog."

Bree ignored her comment. "Does Travis have a weapon?"

Mrs. Ekin gave her a smug *You can't trick me* look. "I already told you. He ain't here." But nothing Mrs. Ekin said meant anything. They would have to assume he had some kind of weapon. But Bree liked to get statements and lies on record. Her patrol deputies wore body cameras, and tonight, so did she.

Bree stepped back and motioned for Mrs. Ekin to come out.

"I'm grabbing my coat. Don't shoot me. You cops shoot everybody." Mrs. Ekin leaned sideways and emerged with a gray parka. As she put it on, she shuffled onto the front stoop in a pair of dirty sheepskin booties, muttering, "Fucking bitch" under her breath. She shot Bree the evil eye, but gave the dog a respectful, wide berth. Greta was staring at the woman with an uncanny intensity.

Bree waved for another deputy to escort Travis's mother to a safe position. Someone would need to keep her from interfering. Then Bree shouted into the house, "Travis Ekin, this is the county sheriff. I have a warrant for your arrest. Come out of the house with your hands in the air immediately or I'm sending in the K-9. The dog will find you and bite you."

The house was dark inside. Bree reached in and swept a hand on the wall. She felt a light switch and flipped it. Dim light blinked on, illuminating a narrow hallway. The rooms beyond were shadowed. She didn't want to wait and give Travis any more time to prepare. Bree stepped out of the way and signaled to Collins.

Collins paused at the door. Greta lunged against her working harness. The dog was fearless, but then, she didn't comprehend the danger. Not knowing the floor plan of the house made the search unpredictable and risky. Travis could be anywhere.

Collins stopped in the doorway and yelled a second warning into the house. "K-9 entering the premises. Surrender right now or my dog will bite you." Greta let out a string of barks to punctuate Collins's statement. It sounded as if the dog were cursing out Travis.

After three heartbeats of silence, Collins moved forward. Bree, Todd, and Juarez gave the K-9 team room to work but followed them as backup. Bree held her sidearm in one hand, her flashlight in the other. Todd and Juarez used the lights mounted on their rifles.

Collins let out some leash, and Greta sniffed her way down the hall. She passed a dark room with barely a quick sniff and glance. Bree shined her light into each corner, but the Ekins were hoarders. Boxes and junk were piled everywhere, casting deep shadows. Without Greta, the search would have taken hours.

In a mud/laundry room at the back of the house, the dog spent a few minutes checking out a pile of dirty laundry before moving on. Greta went through the kitchen and paused at the bottom of the stairs. Bree passed an overflowing garbage can, thankful it was winter.

Greta lifted her nose and inhaled deeply. With a snort, she charged up the steps. Collins gave her more line and jogged behind her.

Bree and her men followed. Stairwells were fatal funnels with blind spots. The dog, though, made all the difference. While humans relied on their eyes and ears, the dog could smell the suspect. Humans guessed. The dog *knew*.

Head down and leaning into her harness, Greta plowed down the hall. Six doors lined the corridor. Four stood open. Two were closed. Todd, Juarez, and Bree shined lights into the open rooms as they passed them. Greta didn't pause until she reached the last, closed door.

Travis was in there. The dog's posture made that clear. Bree and her deputies stayed away from the center of the door. If Travis had a gun, he might fire through the wood. Greta pressed her nose to the bottom of the door and sniffed, her lips quivering, as if she could already taste her quarry. Her lips lifted in a snarl. Fixating on the door, she barked once.

Bree and Collins exchanged silent communication. Collins put her hand on the leash clasp. Bree shoved her flashlight into her pocket, reached forward, and opened the door while Collins turned the dog loose.

Bree held her breath as Greta streaked into the dark room. A frantic scream—Travis?—pealed through the house. Something thudded, and the dog growled. More terrified screaming, then begging followed. "Help! Fuck! Help!"

Todd and Juarez charged through the doorway, sweeping the space with their lights and ARs. Bree flipped the wall switch, turning on a lamp on a nightstand. They were in a bedroom. Greta was pulling a man out of a closet. A knobby fleece blanket designed to look like sheepskin partially covered him, as if he'd been trying to hide under it. She'd bitten him right through the blanket, high on the thigh, and held on. If she'd shifted her teeth an inch or so, she'd have bitten his groin. She had to be close to his femoral artery. Travis screamed again. He was a solid man, with dark hair, sharp features, and abundant tattoos. The high-pitched and panicked tone seemed incongruent with his size and tough-looking exterior.

The dog whipped her head back and forth, dug her feet into the worn hardwood, and shifted her weight backward, dragging Travis a few inches toward them. With three weapons trained on the suspect, Collins moved forward, straddled the dog, and yelled out a command in German. The dog didn't want to release, but as Collins lifted her front feet off the ground, Greta spit out Travis's leg. Bright-red blood stained the cream-colored fleece blanket. Bloody spittle trailed across the floorboards and dripped from the dog's jaws.

Hanging over Travis, Greta looked like a wolf dining on a lamb.

Todd moved in, handcuffed Travis, and patted him down, and it was over. Bree and her deputies blinked at each other for a few seconds.

"Good girl," Collins crooned, pride filling her voice.

Greta barked, her attention still focused on Travis.

"Get it away from me!" he cried. Tears and snot ran down his face.

Todd tossed the blanket aside. Blood soaked Travis's gray sweatpants. He sobbed, his words indecipherable. If Bree hadn't known the details of Travis's cold-blooded crime, she would have felt bad for him. But she'd been to the murder scene, and there were things she could not unsee. Mrs. Jenkins's murder would haunt Bree for the rest of her life.

Bree scanned the room. A butcher knife lay on the hardwood. She turned to Collins. "Check Greta for injuries."

Collins spotted the knife. Her eyes widened. She ran her hands over the parts of the dog not covered by her vest. "She has blood on her neck, but I don't feel any cuts. I need better light. I'm taking her out." Collins stood and commanded the dog to heel. *"Fuss."*

Greta obeyed, reluctantly, her eyes fixed on Travis until she was out of sight.

CHAPTER TWO

Dana Romano felt naked without her 9mm strapped to her ankle as she steered her SUV into Dr. Kent McFadden's driveway. While she normally considered her Glock to be a very versatile fashion accessory, it didn't fit under the boots she'd bought for her date.

Ice and rock salt crunched under her tires as she brought the vehicle to a stop and shifted into park. She grabbed her purse from the passenger seat, feeling the reassuring weight of the gun inside the special concealed-carry pouch. After twenty-five years on the police force, wearing a gun was as natural as underwear. Now that she was retired and playing nanny to two kids, she usually opted for an ankle holster for discretion. Leaving the gun at home was an adjustment she wasn't ready to make, but she wondered what Kent would think of it. They had been dating only a month. At what point should she reveal she was always armed?

It was too early to say whether their attraction would grow or ebb. Kent was the first man she'd felt a good heady sexual chemistry with in a very long time, but she didn't have any illusions.

Still, she hoped tonight would end in a second round of quality sex. Otherwise, she'd shaved her legs for nothing. They had a nice friends-with-benefits vibe happening, and she didn't want to blow it. Dating in your fifties was like juggling a lit torch, a chain saw, and a bag of dog poop. Drop one ball and everything went to shit.

She turned off the engine and opened the vehicle door. Swinging her legs out from under the steering wheel, she admired the knee-high black suede and skinny heels in the dome light.

The boots were badass.

She slid her phone into her jacket pocket, lifted the container of lemon bars from the console, and stepped out of her vehicle.

At seven in the evening, the January night was crisp and clear. She didn't bother zipping her jacket for the short walk to the front door. Stars twinkled above her head. Snow blanketed the ground. She picked her way up the driveway, watchful for icy patches, but the paved areas had been neatly shoveled.

Kent lived in a big-ass house on a big-ass lot in Redhaven, one town over from Grey's Hollow, where Dana lived. His closest neighbor was a football field away. Most people would have considered the winter evening lovely, but she was a transplanted Philadelphia girl still acclimating to country life. Waking to bird sounds instead of sirens was nice, and clean air beat inhaling bus exhaust every day. But Dana wasn't quite at home here yet. The empty land was too dark, too desolate for her comfort. There were coyotes. Lately, they'd been picking off neighbors' chickens and cats.

A roaming, bold pack of travel-size predators was one more reason she liked to keep her Glock handy. She was fond of their new barn cats, rescues too feral and aggressive for traditional adoptions.

Just a year before, Dana's homicide detective partner and best friend, Bree Taggert, had moved to upstate New York to raise her niece and nephew after their mother was killed. After solving her sister's murder, Bree had accidentally become sheriff. Dana, poised on the brink of a terrifyingly aimless retirement, had offered to play nanny. Her all-encompassing law enforcement career had left her with two divorces, a family disappointed in her failure to reproduce, and a deep distrust of her fellow man.

The move had been a relief. As much as Bree said Dana saved her butt by taking over the daily domestic duties, the truth was that Bree and the kids had given Dana the fresh start she'd needed. She loved her family, but if her mother commented one more time on how sad it was that Dana hadn't had kids while she'd had the chance, Dana would lose her frigging mind. And there was no way in hell she was taking a fucking job as a fucking night security guard at her cousin's fucking flooring store.

The kids were easy. Dana had plenty of time to cook, attend spin classes, and decompress from all those years in law enforcement. If she could round things out with a romantic relationship, her life would feel complete. Hefting the lemon bars, she walked toward Kent's house. The screech of an owl carried on the wind, and in the distance, she heard a smaller squeal. The sounds of predator and prey lifted goose bumps on her arms.

Dana quickened her steps to the front door and rang the bell. The chime echoed inside, but no one answered. She pushed the button again. When Kent didn't appear, she tried a hard knock.

She tested the doorknob. Like last time, it was unlocked. She pushed open the door and leaned in. "Kent?"

But no one answered. Maybe he hadn't heard the doorbell. Music played in the back of the house—Sam Cooke's "Bring It On Home." She listened for Kent's tenor voice singing along the way he did in the car but didn't hear him.

Dana stepped inside. On one side of the foyer, the double doors to Kent's home office stood open, the room dark and empty. On the other side, a staircase curved to the second-story landing. Dana continued straight down the hall to the huge kitchen.

The smell of cooking meat filled the room and made her stomach rumble as she set down her purse and container. A slow cooker sat in the middle of the giant island. She lifted the lid. Carrots and potatoes surrounded a simmering beef brisket. She replaced the lid. On a cutting board next to the pot, a small pile of garlic cloves waited, half chopped. A knife rested on its side next to them. A baking pan sitting on the stove held a split loaf of french bread. Kent was in the middle of making garlic bread.

Where is he?

She was tempted to finish chopping the garlic while she waited, but *he* wanted to make dinner for *her*. Resisting the urge to cook, Dana turned away from the food and strolled into the breakfast nook. On three walls, windows overlooked the snowy yard. A bottle of pinot, two glasses, and a plate of cheese and olives sat on the table. She reached for an olive.

The music paused between songs. A groan sounded from upstairs. She froze, listening over the first few lines of Percy Sledge singing "When A Man Loves A Woman." Something scraped overhead.

Was something wrong? Had Kent become ill or fallen and hit his head?

She hurried around the corner, passed the back door, and started up the U-shaped back stairs. As she turned the first corner, a dark shape hurtled toward her. She barely recognized the figure as a man in a ski mask before his shoulder rammed into her ribs, knocking the wind from her lungs and sending her flying backward. She toppled down three steps and hit the hardwood floor flat on her back. Her head struck the corner of the baseboard, and her vision dimmed.

He landed on top of her, his weight crushing her solar plexus. Fear, anger, and shock—and the inability to inflate her lungs—paralyzed Dana for a few seconds.

She wheezed and wriggled her body sideways a few inches. With the pressure on her lungs eased, she sucked in a deep breath, then another. Oxygen flooded in, and her vision began to clear.

He recovered first. Shoving himself into a sitting position, he strad-dled her waist and wrapped both hands around her throat. But Dana's long career as a homicide detective had required countless hours of tactical self-defense training. She'd supplemented with private martial arts instruction. Muscle memory kicked in. She crossed her arms on top of his, then levered her elbows downward, forcing his elbows to bend and relieving the pressure on her windpipe.

Her foot snaked behind his ankle, trapping it. Then she bridged upward and flipped over, reversing their positions. He flopped onto his back.

Dana landed on her knees between his legs. She raised her arm to drive an elbow into his groin, but he scrambled backward a few inches. The point of her elbow hit the floor. Electric-like nerve currents numbed her arm. Her attacker flipped onto his belly, got his feet under his body, and stumbled toward the back door. Dana lurched to her feet. Her head throbbed, the room spun, and nausea swirled in her belly. She reached for the wall to steady herself before staggering a step in pursuit.

Another moan from upstairs stopped her cold.

Kent!

She couldn't help Kent and chase the intruder. She had to choose. Still wobbly, she turned toward the stairway. She heard the back door open and felt a rush of cold air as she went up the steps. The main bedroom suite was on the right. She paused in the doorway.

Kent lay sprawled on his back, his bent arms spread like a giant cactus. A bloody circle the size of a basketball stained the front of his white shirt. His eyes were closed, and Dana could hear the raspy rattle of his breaths from across the room.

Digging her phone from the pocket of her jacket, she detoured to the attached bathroom and snatched a small stack of hand towels from the linen closet. She rushed back to him, dropped to her knees, and ripped open his shirt. She tossed the phone onto the floor. Blood flowed from a bullet hole near the center of his chest.

Fuck fuck *fuck*.

She placed a folded towel over the wound and leaned on it with both hands while she used voice commands to call 911 and request police and an ambulance. She gave the address. "Chest wound, GSW, male victim, forty-seven years old." Warmth soaked the knees of her jeans. She looked down to see a red stain spreading on the pale-gray carpet. "He's bleeding heavily."

"Dispatching an ambulance to your location. Stay on the line," the 911 operator instructed.

Kent's breath rattled, and the wet sound brought fresh fear bubbling into Dana's throat.

"Kent?" She leaned closer. "Open your eyes. Come back to me."

His arms began to flail. A fist struck her jaw. His hands grabbed her wrists.

Still fighting his attacker.

Dana ignored the attempts to push her away. She needed both hands to keep pressure on his wound. If she didn't stop the bleeding, he'd be dead before the ambulance arrived. "Kent, it's Dana. It's OK. I've got you."

His eyes fluttered open, circled wildly, then focused on her. He went still. The pain and panic on his face twisted in her gut. Blood soaked through the towel, and fear clawed at her. His body was pumping out blood at an alarming rate. She leaned all her weight on her hands. "Stay with me, OK?"

With a small nod, his body relaxed, and weakness clouded his eyes.

"Do you know who did this?" she asked.

His lips moved, forming a silent "No."

The 911 operator said something Dana didn't hear. She shouted at her phone, "What's the ETA of the ambulance?"

"Three minutes," the 911 operator answered. "Is the door unlocked?"

"Yes. We're upstairs."

Minutes ticked by in slow motion. Blood seeped between Dana's fingers. Finally, the wail of a siren approached.

"Kent?" Dana bent close to his face. "Help is here."

"Are the EMTs at your location?" the 911 operator asked.

"I hear someone," Dana answered.

Kent squinted at her, his gaze bleary. His eyes were losing focus.

She kissed him on the lips. "Hang on."

But his eyes rolled back, and he stopped breathing.

"No!" Dana started CPR. "Come back." She gave him two rescue breaths.

The front door opened, and a male voice shouted, "Police!"

Dana shifted to chest compressions. She yelled, "Up here!"

Feet thundered on the steps. Two Redhaven uniforms burst in, guns drawn.

Dana kept up with the chest compressions. "I didn't have time to clear the scene." She could hear more activity downstairs. "But I think I heard him go out the back door."

The cops spoke into their lapel mics. Dana ignored them. After twenty-five years on the Philly PD, she knew what was happening. They were checking the house before they'd let the EMTs inside. Best leave them to their job.

They were quick about it. Maybe two minutes passed, then two EMTs rushed in, carrying med bags. Dana lurched to her feet and moved out of the way, and they deftly took over. On autopilot, she wiped her hands on her thighs and shoved her hair out of her face. She snagged her phone from the floor as she stepped backward a few feet.

The floor pitched, and she leaned on the wall for support. She looked down at her shaking hands. They were smeared in blood. Her heartbeat thudded in her ears, her pulse drowning out the sound of the EMTs.

So much blood.

She'd seen many crime scenes in her career, but this seemed different. She knew this man intimately. She'd spoken with him just a couple of hours before. Yes, even with her personal connection to the victim, she felt the gears shifting in her brain, compartmentalizing her emotions as she scanned the room, taking in the details. A handgun lay on the floor between the bed and the wall.

"Pulse!" an EMT announced.

She watched the EMTs working on Kent, hooking up an IV and oxygen. Her pulse thrummed, echoing as if she were in a tunnel. Ambulance attendants brought a gurney. They loaded Kent onto it and hurried out without wasting any time. With a gunshot wound to the chest, the only chance of survival was getting to an OR—fast. Her vision went blurry. She felt herself slide down the wall like an out-of-body experience.

"Ma'am?" A cop's voice broke through the rush of blood in her ears. She blinked. The cop squatted next to her, his face at her eye level. "Were you hit?"

"No. I'm not shot," Dana said. Pain was building in the back of her head and, with it, nausea. She pointed out the gun on the floor.

With a quick glance at it, the cop scanned her. "Are you sure you're OK?"

Dana looked at her clothes. It wasn't just her hands that were covered in blood. It was everywhere. Red stains soaked the knees of her jeans, streaked her open jacket, and stained the front of her white sweater. She'd gotten it in her hair and on her face too.

"Yes." She gestured to her body. "Pretty sure it's Kent's blood."

"What's your name?"

"Dana Romano." She recited her address.

"OK. Let's get you out of here." The cop steered her out of the room.

Her knees wobbled as they went down the stairs. He kept a firm grip on her elbow. She spotted a few uniforms downstairs. "Stand By Me" played from the kitchen, the smooth notes sounding surreal. Outside, lights swirled from patrol vehicles lining the street. She inhaled the cold night air in grateful gulps, hoping it would clear her head. But the warm, bloody wetness of her clothes turned cold almost instantly, and she began to shiver.

They went down the driveway, and he stopped her next to the first patrol vehicle. "Can you tell me what happened, Ms. Romano?"

Up close, the swirling lights made Dana dizzy. She turned away from them, then took a few seconds to gather her thoughts. "Kent was cooking me dinner."

"Kent is the victim?"

"Yes. Dr. Kent McFadden. I walked into the house and couldn't find him. Then I heard a noise upstairs. I thought maybe he fell or something. I started up the stairs, and a man came running down." The images flashed through her head in strobe-light fashion. The impact of his body with hers. The smack of her head hitting the baseboard. "He tackled me. We went down. He tried to choke me." She slowed her breaths, which slowed her mind. As she recalled the hands squeezing, her throat began to ache.

The cop shined his flashlight on her neck and made an empathetic noise.

"I got him off me. He ran for the door. I was going to go after him, but I heard Kent moaning upstairs." The memory seemed fuzzy. All her thoughts felt fuzzy.

"Can you describe the man you fought?" The cop opened a notebook.

Despite her confusion, her training kicked in. She'd automatically noticed the necessary descriptive details. "Five ten to six feet tall, one eighty, fit. Dressed in jeans, a black jacket, and a black ski mask. Blue disposable gloves. I couldn't see the color of his eyes." The flash of images made her light-headed. She closed her eyes.

"Good details." The cop looked up from his notes, his eyes almost suspicious.

"I'm a retired cop," Dana explained. "Philly homicide."

He nodded and wrote down her description. His phone trilled. He tilted it on his belt, glanced at the screen, and frowned.

"Any update on Kent's condition?" she asked.

Instead of answering, he asked, "Can you give me any other details on the attacker?"

"Not at this time." The ache in Dana's head was expanding. All she wanted to do was lie down and close her eyes.

He closed his notebook.

Dana added, "My weapon is in my purse in the kitchen." Better she tell them before they found it. She should have kept her piece on her body. She'd gotten complacent living in the country.

"We'll need to take it in to ballistics." He reached for his lapel mic.

"Understood." Dana blinked hard, but the stars in her field of vision remained. "I need to make a call. And wash my hands."

But she knew he wasn't going to let her wash up right away.

"Sure, we'll get you cleaned up, but first we need to scrape under your nails and swab you for gunpowder residue." He turned away. "Wait here."

Dana leaned on the car. Pain roared through the back of her skull as she pulled out her phone.

Was Kent still alive?

CHAPTER THREE

Bree turned and walked out of Travis's bedroom. Her deputies would take the prisoner to the ER for treatment for the bite before transporting him to the county jail. She headed down the stairs and out of the dank house. Outside, she breathed in the crisp night air. As she walked down the street, she green-lighted the waiting CSI team.

"I won't forget what you did to my son," someone whispered.

Bree spun around and caught sight of Mrs. Ekin hunched on the sidewalk about twenty feet away. A young man stood next to her. He was average height and a little stocky. Probably one of Travis's brothers. Bree could feel their focus—and their hostility.

"An Ekin don't ever forget," the son echoed.

"Is that a threat?" Bree faced them squarely. The image of Mrs. Jenkins's body was fresh in her mind, and she had to suppress a burst of rage.

Neither responded, and Bree turned away. Her boot slid on a patch of black ice. She wobbled but didn't go down. By the time she'd righted herself, Mrs. Ekin and her son had moved away. But Bree swore the air still smelled of their animosity. With a quick shudder, she continued to the K-9 unit.

Collins was at the back, the hatch open, half-inside the vehicle. Greta sat in the cargo area. The dog seemed calmer, but her tail remained stiff. Collins had removed the dog's vest and was using wipes to clean blood from her fur. Holding a small flashlight in her teeth, she parted the dog's thick fur.

"Is she OK?"

"Her undercoat makes it hard to see her skin, but I don't see a mark on her." Collins sat back and handed Greta a stuffed hedgehog. She snapped it up and chewed hard. The toy emitted a high-pitched squeak with every grind of the dog's powerful jaws.

"How long does one of those last?" Bree asked. Her radio crackled with chatter on a shooting in the neighboring town of Redhaven. She and Collins both went quiet for a minute, listening for any request for assistance. When none came, they continued.

"She disembowels one a week." Collins grinned. "I buy them by the case. All the other dogs in the class had tug ropes and rubber balls, but not her. She has to have a toy that sounds like a small animal being murdered."

"Good job tonight, both of you." Bree did not reach toward the dog. Greta's adrenaline was still running high. Accidental bites were a risk when working with some K-9s.

Collins closed the door. "I'm going to take her to the field to let off some steam before I start my report." She'd been using an empty field down the street from the sheriff's station to let Greta stretch her legs.

Bree nodded. "Personnel first, paperwork second. Always." Greta might be a dog, but she was part of the team.

The K-9 unit drove away. Bree spotted a black Suburban at the curb. Despite the stressful op she'd just finished, she felt the corner of her mouth turn up as she approached the vehicle. Matt stepped out. At six three, he wasn't just tall, but big-boned. The body armor he wore under his clothes added more bulk to his frame. With short reddish-brown hair and a tight, trimmed beard, he looked like he should be swinging a Viking battle-ax. He wore a sheriff's department jacket over a long-sleeve polo shirt with the sheriff's department logo. As a civilian consultant, Matt didn't wear a full uniform.

"I thought you were going to stay away." The winter wind gusted down the street, and Bree shivered. The damp sweat under her body armor chilled her.

"I didn't want to confuse her." Matt had pulled Greta from his sister's canine rescue. "She seems bonded with Collins, but still . . ." He'd fostered the dog until she'd been old enough for official K-9 training. "How did it go?"

"She took Travis out in about five seconds. It was over so fast; it was actually kind of stunning."

"Yes!" Matt pumped a fist in the air before shoving his hands into his pockets. "I knew she could do it." From the beginning, Matt had said the same qualities that made her a difficult family placement would also make her a great K-9.

"I was worried. She seemed almost playful going in. She kept wagging her tail. But as soon as she found Travis, she wanted to eat him."

"That's my girl." Matt grinned. "FYI, a wagging tail signals excitement. It's not an indication of friendliness."

"Good to know," Bree said. "She's a lot stronger than she looks."

"Fun fact: dogs pull with three times their body weight."

"Well, she and Collins impressed me tonight." Bree's phone vibrated in the pocket of her barn coat. She drew it out and read the screen.

Dana? She'd specifically told Bree not to wait up.

Bree answered the call. "You just got there. Did he do something shitty? Do you need an excuse to leave?"

"Someone shot Kent," Dana said in a flat tone.

Bree must have misunderstood. "Wait. What?"

"I must have walked in right after he was shot."

"Matt is here. I'm putting you on speaker." Bree lowered the phone and pressed the button. "How bad is it?"

"Bad." Dana's voice broke. "It's a chest wound. I called 911. He's on the way to the hospital. The Redhaven cops are here." Redhaven was within Bree's jurisdiction as sheriff of Randolph County, but the small town also had its own police department.

"Where's the shooter?" Bree asked.

"He got away." Dana paused for a shaky breath.

Bree paused, scenarios racing through her mind. "Are you OK?"

"I think so." Dana huffed, as if she were out of breath. She didn't sound OK. She sounded stressed. Dana had put gang members and drug dealers in prison. She'd seen murder scenes that could only be described as horrific. Not much freaked her out.

"Where are you now?" Bree asked, meeting Matt's concerned gaze.

Dana read off a house number and street located in the neighboring town.

"We're on the way," Bree said.

Matt turned to his own vehicle. "Meet you there."

Bree hurried to her SUV. She called Todd to let him know she was leaving and why. "You're in charge here."

"Yes, ma'am."

Bree ended that call. Behind the wheel, she drove away from the scene and called home, where her nephew, sixteen-year-old Luke, was babysitting his nine-year-old sister, Kayla.

"You're on speaker," Luke warned.

"When are you coming home?" Kayla asked.

"I have another call. I'm going to be later than I thought." Bree stopped herself. She shouldn't lie to them. "It's actually Dana. She's OK, but something happened to the man she's dating."

"What happened?" Luke asked.

"I don't know the details," Bree said. "But I'm going to find out."

Kayla's tone held just a little bit of whine. "You were going to help me study for my spelling test."

"It's OK," Luke said. "I'll quiz you." His voice tensed. He knew something was up. Bree didn't want to alarm him until she knew more, and he wouldn't ask—not when his sister was listening.

"Thanks, Luke," Bree said. "I don't know how late I'll be. I'll text you, but don't wait up."

Before she could give any further instructions, Luke said, "I'll get Kayla to bed by nine. I've got this, Aunt Bree." Over the past year, he'd become a man. Bree was proud of him but sad for the reason for his abrupt transition to adulthood. Having your mother murdered aged a person.

"Thanks, Luke. Make sure the alarm is set. I love you both." Bree ended the call and roared toward the scene with lights and sirens.

The radio crackled and dispatch relayed a BOLO for the potentially armed and dangerous shooter at large. Bree grabbed the mic and responded, coordinating her own department's assistance with the search. There was too much geography for the Redhaven PD to cover on its own. Plus, a fleeing suspect would likely put some distance between himself and the scene. Local PDs would cover their own townships. Her deputies on patrol focused on the municipalities that didn't maintain their own law enforcement. State troopers patrolled the interstates.

She called the Redhaven police chief, Colin Hanover, to let him know she was en route and would offer her assistance. Hanover was curt. Bree didn't know him well enough to determine whether his brusque response was due to the urgent situation or her call. They'd met a few times at professional functions, but they'd never worked closely together.

A half mile from the address, Bree could see the emergency lights of responding vehicles. She drove on, then slowed as she spotted Matt's Suburban pulling onto the shoulder of the road. She parked behind him, and they got out of their vehicles.

Falling into step beside her, he zipped his jacket. Together, they walked toward what appeared to be the hub of scene coordination, a cluster of uniforms in the street at the base of the driveway.

"There's Hanover." Bree nodded toward the center of the group, where Chief Hanover was clearly issuing instructions. She knew the moment he spotted her because his posture stiffened.

Bree made a beeline for the Redhaven chief. Hanover was somewhere in his late forties. Stress, too much sun exposure, and overall leanness made him appear older. He had a runner's body. His short brown hair was generously shot with gray, and deep lines fanned out from the corners of his eyes and mouth.

As Bree and Matt approached, Hanover stepped toward them, away from the uniforms. He held out a hand. "Sheriff Taggert."

She shook his hand and introduced Matt. She wanted to find Dana ASAP, but considering Hanover's potential prickliness, she'd give him a few minutes first.

Hanover gave Matt the same wary look. Perhaps that was just his personality, but Bree would tread carefully. Making him an enemy would serve no one's best interest.

"Any word on the homeowner?" she asked in a low voice.

Hanover shook his head. "No update on Dr. McFadden's condition yet."

"How about the shooter?" Matt asked.

"No sign of him." Hanover squinted at Matt, then turned back to Bree. "Do you intend to take over the investigation, Sheriff?"

At least he was direct. She'd take honest distrust over a fake-friendly backstabber any day.

Considering Bree's personal relationship with Dana, forcing herself onto the scene would be inappropriate, but she sensed that ceding complete control to Hanover would also be the wrong move. She skirted his question with one of her own. "Do you want me to?"

Hanover tilted his head back and stared down at her as if surprised by her answer. Had he expected her to kick him off the scene? "No."

"Then my department is available for whatever assistance you might need." She added, "**And I would** like to be kept in the loop."

26

"Of course." Hanover seemed satisfied with the compromise.

Bree glanced at the house. Lights blazed. Uniforms were everywhere. She'd heard more units over the radio chatter. Redhaven wasn't a big department. He must have called in half his men, but he seemed to have the situation under control. "My deputies are actively looking for the shooter, of course."

"It's going to be hard to find him," Hanover said. "Ms. Romano didn't see his face."

"Do you have a description of his vehicle?" Matt asked.

Hanover shook his head. "Dr. McFadden has a basic security system but no cameras. We are checking with the neighbors. The houses are too far apart for a neighbor to capture the McFadden house, but maybe we'll get lucky and someone's camera has a view of the street." Hanover tilted his head toward Bree. "Ms. Romano says she's your former partner."

"That's correct," Bree said. "We worked homicide together back in Philly." She met his direct gaze with her own. "Do you know how the shooter got in?"

"We haven't found any sign of forced entry," Hanover said. "But I called for a crime scene unit."

"Let me know if you need deputies for a ground search," Bree offered. "Where is Ms. Romano?"

Hanover nodded, then moved aside and gestured to a patrol car parked on the shoulder of the road fifty feet away. Now that the crowd of uniforms had dispersed, Bree could see that the rear door stood open. Dana sat sideways with her feet planted on the street and her head between her knees. Worry rose in Bree's gut.

Hanover said, "We may have more questions once I've walked through the scene, and she'll need to sign a formal statement." With a nod, he turned back to his men.

With Matt at her side, Bree crossed the street to Dana. In the wash of the vehicle's dome light, she could see dark stains all over Dana's clothes. Her blonde and gray hair was streaked with red. A small container of hand wipes and a plastic bag full of used—bloody—ones sat at her feet. Concern amplified through Bree. "Hey."

Dana raised her head. Her body sagged with relief. "I'm so glad you're both here."

"How do you feel?" Bree crouched and scanned her friend's pale face.

"My head hurts some," Dana admitted, one hand cupping the back of her head. "I smacked it when he tackled me."

"Who tackled you?" Bree asked.

"The shooter," Dana said.

Shock rippled through Bree as she absorbed the implications of those two words.

Matt muttered a curse. "The shooter was still here when you arrived?"

"Yeah. We tangled. He got away." Dana pressed a hand to her forehead. "I left my gun in my purse. Stupid."

"Lean forward," Matt said.

Dana bowed her head, and Matt shined his flashlight on it.

"There's blood in your hair," he said.

"Could be Kent's." Dana lifted her hands. There was still blood under her nails.

Bree pulled a glove out of her pocket. After tugging it on, she carefully parted Dana's tousled shag. "Nope. You have a gash and a goose egg." The back of Dana's sweater was soaked, but the bleeding had slowed to a trickle. How did she not feel it?

"You need a few stitches." Matt's exhale sounded angry. "Didn't the EMTs check you for injuries?"

"Not their fault." Dana held up a hand. "I told them I wasn't hurt. I didn't realize . . ." She spread her fingers in front of her face. "I thought I'd accidentally swiped a hand—and Kent's blood—into my hair. There was a lot of blood."

Too much, Bree thought with a fresh surge of worry.

Matt shoved his flashlight into his pocket. "Which is why they should have had the EMTs look you over."

Dana didn't comment. Her face was gray, and she looked like she was going to throw up. Bree wondered if she had any other injuries she hadn't noticed yet. Adrenaline could block a lot of pain in the moment, but later . . . Bree stood. "I'll drive you to the ER."

"I'll let Hanover know and meet you at the hospital." Matt straightened.

"Thanks," Bree said.

With a nod, Matt turned and strode away.

"Ready?" Bree offered Dana a hand up.

Dana accepted it but wobbled a little. Bree stuck close in case she went down. Dana walked to Bree's vehicle like an eighty-year-old instead of a very fit fifty-one-year-old. Bree guided her into the passenger seat. She went to the back, grabbed her first aid kit, and opened some packages of gauze. She returned to Dana and handed her a short stack. "Here."

In the passenger seat, Dana held the gauze to the back of her head and closed her eyes. "I've been wanting to do this since I called you."

"Don't go to sleep." Bree rounded the hood and slid behind the wheel.

Dana said nothing on the ride to the ER. Bree guessed she was trying not to vomit.

The ER was quiet, and a nurse took Dana into the triage area—a row of exam rooms formed with glass walls and sliding curtains. Bree paced the hall for a few seconds, then headed to the nurses' station. From here she could see into the trauma bay on the other side of the ER. Paper and plastic medical supply wrappers, gloves, and blood littered the space. Probably where Kent had been treated when he came in.

"Can I help you, Sheriff?"

Bree turned back to the nurse at the computer. "Is there an update on the shooting victim? McFadden is the name."

Instead of checking her computer, the nurse glanced down the hall, confirming Bree's guess. "He was critical when they brought him in. They took him to the OR."

"Thanks." Bree stepped back, hoping Kent pulled through and the case remained an *attempted* murder.

CHAPTER FOUR

Anger resonated in Matt as he scanned the street for Chief Hanover. The Redhaven cops had let Dana sit, injured and bleeding, with no medical attention. All responders knew that adrenaline camouflaged pain. She'd said it wasn't their fault, but Matt put the blame squarely on the responding officers.

He found the chief at the head of the driveway, just in front of the sawhorses that marked the crime scene, his phone pressed against his ear.

Matt waited at an appropriate distance until the chief lowered his phone.

Hanover turned to face him. Widening his stance, he blocked Matt from passing under the crime scene tape. "You need something, Flynn?"

"Ms. Romano has a gash on the back of her head. Sheriff Taggert is taking her to the ER."

"Is it serious?" Hanover's voice sharpened.

Matt didn't break eye contact while he sized up the chief. While he wasn't interested in a pissing contest, he wouldn't be pushed around by Hanover either. Matt raised a hand, the fingertips about an inch apart to indicate the size of the cut. "I'll bet on a concussion too."

The chief's lips flattened into an unhappy line. Was he angry that Bree had taken Dana from the scene without his permission? Or annoyed that his officers hadn't spotted the injury? The Redhaven chief was respected by his officers, and his reputation was by the book.

Matt had never heard complaints of political aspirations or rumors of corruption.

Hanover chewed his molars. "She said she was fine."

Matt didn't respond. They both knew that was inexcusable. The chief had a terrible poker face. His gaze darted to one of his uniformed officers. His jaw tightened. He was definitely irritated with the uniforms. Matt guessed the chief would publicly support his men but give them a verbal thrashing in private.

They stared at each other for a full minute, then Hanover blinked and said, "We'll take her statement at the hospital."

Matt ignored the dismissive tone. Part of him wanted to remain on scene and know what was happening.

"Can we agree you shouldn't be here?" Hanover asked, as if reading his mind. "You're personally connected to the case. If your name shows up on the crime scene log, any half-decent defense attorney will argue that your conflict of interest taints the evidence. If I have to testify under oath about our evidence-gathering procedures, I want to be able to say you didn't set foot on the property."

"You're right," Matt admitted, though he didn't like it.

"I'll update the sheriff later," Hanover assured him.

Matt nodded. "OK then. I'm leaving now."

Hanover didn't budge, and Matt felt the burn of the chief's gaze on his back as he walked to his vehicle. He slid behind the wheel and started the engine. Hanover remained in position, like a guard dog, as Matt performed a three-point turn and drove away.

At the hospital, an ER nurse directed Matt to a triage bay. The curtains were open. The gurney was missing. Bree paced the narrow space. Even if she hadn't been wearing her uniform, he would recognize her just by the way she moved—with purpose. She was average height, with an athletic body rather than a curvy one. Her wavy brown hair was bound in a professional bun. If he described her with words, she wouldn't sound special, but she turned and met his gaze with her own, and those hazel eyes—intelligent, tragic, and honest—captivated him as always.

He stepped to the opening. "Where's Dana?"

Bree paused. "Getting a CT scan."

"Is she OK?" With a quick glance around to make sure no one could see them, Matt gave her a quick kiss. Though they'd made their relationship public, Bree thought PDAs while in uniform were unprofessional. Matt didn't give a single fuck what anyone thought. But then, he'd won a huge settlement from his lawsuit with the county after the friendly-fire shooting that had damaged his hand and ended his career as a deputy. He could afford to flip off anyone he chose. It was a nice position to be in.

"She has a half dozen stitches in her head and a concussion."

"Not surprised," Matt said. "Want coffee? Seems we're going to be here awhile."

"Yes. Thanks." Bree resumed her pacing. Normally, she was not a fidgeter, so the fact that she couldn't be still told him she was struggling. Bree had only one living family member other than the kids—her younger brother. Dana was more than Bree's best friend. She was also a big-sister figure.

Matt found a coffee machine down the hall. When he handed Bree her cup, she turned and put her back to the wall. They drank their coffee and took turns pacing in silence for nearly an hour.

Clearly restless, Bree tapped a toe. "I'm going to get more coffee. Want some?"

"Sure." Matt would have offered to fetch it, but he sensed she needed the movement.

Bree strode away, turned a corner, and disappeared from sight.

A few minutes later, Dana returned, her gurney rolling into the cubicle. Her head was turned to the side, and Matt could see a shaved patch of scalp with a nasty row of black stitches. Her eyes were closed, and she didn't attempt to move as an orderly parked the bed.

"Would you mind dimming the light?" she asked.

Matt reached for the wall switch and turned off the light directly over the bed.

Dana opened her eyes. Pain shone through them.

"How's the head?" Matt asked.

"Meh." She squinted.

But her complexion was as pale as the dirty snow piled around the hospital parking lot. Her skin even had the same grayish tint. The ER staff had cleaned the area they'd stitched, but dried blood still crusted her hair, face, and neck. Bruises encircled her throat and bloomed in angry patches on her face and arms. He assumed there were more he couldn't see. She looked as if she'd gone a few rounds in a UFC fight.

"I must look like death." She grimaced. "Any update on Kent's condition?"

"He's in the OR," Matt said.

"Fuck." The expletive came out desperate and sad rather than angry. "I can't believe this is happening."

Someone cleared their throat. Chief Hanover stood just outside the curtains, a notebook tucked under one arm. "Ms. Romano?"

"She has a concussion," Matt warned, though if he were investigating a crime with an outstanding shooter, he'd want to question the witness ASAP.

Dana lifted a hand. An unconnected IV tube dangled from her wrist. "It's OK, Matt. I want them to catch this guy before he shoots someone else."

Hanover gave Matt a look, but Matt just crossed his arms and leaned on the wall. He wasn't going anywhere. Dana was normally sharp, but she was in no condition to fend for herself.

With a sigh, Hanover approached the side of the bed.

"I expected you to send a uniform," Matt said.

"They're all at the scene or out looking for the shooter." Hanover waved off his question. The truth was that the Redhaven PD was too small to have dedicated detectives. Hanover would handle the complicated cases himself. He was likely short on uniforms as well.

"Any sightings of him?" Dana asked.

"Not yet." After digging out a pair of readers, Hanover opened his notebook and skimmed the page. "How do you know Dr. McFadden?"

"We met in spinning class about a month ago." Dana gave the name and address of a gym in Scarlet Falls.

"How many times have you seen him?"

"Six or seven," Dana said.

"What kind of doctor is he?"

"Cosmetic surgeon," Dana said. "He specializes in face-lifts and eyelid surgery."

Hanover made a note. "Had you been to his home before tonight?"

"Yes. Once. Last week."

Hanover lifted his pen. "Can you take me through the events of this evening again? I know you already told my officer, but I'd like to hear the story for myself."

Dana started with her arrival at the house. She didn't flinch as she recounted her confrontation with the shooter, but when she described her attempts to save Kent, her voice cracked once. She cleared her throat and finished strong. "I called 911 and continued administering CPR until the EMTs arrived."

"Was the door locked when you arrived?"

Dana gave her head a slight shake, then winced at the movement. "Both times I went there, the door was unlocked."

"Do you have feelings for Dr. McFadden?" Hanover asked.

"Feelings?" Dana asked.

"Are you in a relationship?" he specified.

"We're dating. I like him. I assume he also likes me. That's as far as our relationship had gotten."

"Is the relationship exclusive?" Hanover pressed.

"We haven't had that discussion yet."

"But you're sleeping with him?" Hanover's question seemed almost judgmental.

But Dana didn't blink. "To be clear, we did not sleep. We had sex, but I did not spend the night."

"Why not?"

"I needed to be at home in the morning to get the kids—that's Sheriff Taggert's niece and nephew—off to school."

"You're their nanny?"

"Yes."

Hanover sniffed and made another note. "So, you had been in Dr. McFadden's bedroom before tonight?"

"Yes."

"Do you know if he owned a handgun, or did you ever see one in the house?" Hanover tilted his head.

"Not before tonight," Dana said. "Is a handgun registered to Kent?"

"No." Hanover recorded her response in his notebook. "When you arrived at Dr. McFadden's house this evening, did you see any vehicles on the street?"

Dana looked at the ceiling and concentrated for a few seconds. Then with a small shake of her head, she said, "I don't recall noticing any. The lots are big in that neighborhood. Driveways are far apart. I was focused on Kent's house. I didn't pay much attention to his neighbors."

Hanover nodded. "When you heard Dr. McFadden groan upstairs, you didn't think about retrieving your weapon from your purse?"

Dana's face tightened. "No. I thought he was ill or he fell. I never imagined . . ." Her voice trailed off. Then her shoulders gave a quick shudder. "In hindsight, I should have." She blew out a hard breath. Her nostrils flared. She closed her eyes for a second, then opened them. "If I had had my weapon on me, the shooter wouldn't have gotten away." Regret weighed heavily in her tone. She was clearly blaming herself.

"You didn't hear the gunshot?" Matt asked.

Hanover shot Matt an irritated look over his shoulder.

"No," Dana said.

Matt ignored the chief. "Then he'd already been shot when you arrived. You could not have prevented it."

Dana's gaze shifted to him, and her face softened with a hint of gratitude. "This is true."

Hanover tapped the tip of his pen on his notepad. "Do you remember anything else about the intruder?"

Dana concentrated, closing her eyes. Under her closed lids, her eyeballs flickered back and forth a few times. Then they blinked open, looking bleak. "No. Sorry. I just need a couple hours of sleep."

A doctor walked into the cubicle. Matt had been in the ER enough to know many of the staff, but he didn't recognize her. About forty-five, with short, flaming-red hair, she squinted at the chief. "Are you interrogating my patient?"

Hanover's mouth gaped before he answered, "I'm asking her a few questions."

"Well, the patient is correct. There are studies that indicate sleep helps the brain consolidate memory." The doctor pointed toward the opening in the curtain. "This interview is over. You need to leave so the patient can rest."

Hanover opened his mouth as if he wanted to argue, then closed it when the doctor stared him down.

Wise choice, thought Matt.

"Of course." Hanover closed his notebook and hooked the pen over the spiral loops. "I'll contact you for any follow-up questions."

"Not until I give permission." The doctor shot the chief a warning glare.

The chief slunk out of the cubicle like a middle schooler leaving the principal's office.

Matt didn't snicker, but he wanted to. He'd been in the same situation, balancing needing information with the patient's well-being. Detectives could get tunnel vision on their cases.

The doctor turned her laser glare on him.

Matt raised both hands in a gesture of surrender. "I'm a friend. The man who attacked Dana is armed, dangerous, and still at large. I'm not leaving."

The doctor cocked her head. "All right. But be quiet." She turned to Dana. "Are you OK with me discussing your medical condition with your friend present?"

Dana nodded.

The doctor checked the IV. "How's the pain?"

"I've felt better," Dana admitted.

The doctor sighed. "On a scale of one to ten?"

Dana blinked hard, as if focusing her eyes were painful. "Seven."

The doctor shined a penlight into her eyes, presumably checking her pupils. "I'll order something for that. Nausea?"

"Yes." Dana swallowed.

"I can help with that too." The doctor moved to a laptop computer on a wheeled cart. "You have a concussion. The good news is the CT scan shows no bleeding. We're going to keep you overnight for observation, but you should be clear to leave in the morning barring any complications. I appreciate you are former law enforcement, but please don't minimize your discomfort." The doctor turned away from the laptop, her expression softening. "You fell down multiple steps, landed on a hard floor, and suffered a violent assault. You could have injuries that aren't yet apparent. We need to know if you experience new or worsening symptoms." Clearly the doctor had experience working on cops.

"Understood," Dana said.

"Good." The doctor nodded. "I'll order something for the nausea, and you'll be moved upstairs soon." She gave instructions on using over-the-counter pain relievers. "Rest is critical for concussion recovery, especially over the next few days. In addition to the obvious physical rest, you should rest your brain. Stay away from phone and computer screens. Sleep as much as possible."

The doctor left. Dana's face was drawn and tight, as if the interview with Hanover had drained her completely. A nurse came in and injected something into the IV. A few minutes later, Dana closed her eyes, and her body finally relaxed.

Matt planted himself against the wall just outside the curtained-off cubicle and texted Bree, letting her know that Dana was being admitted and that she could go home. He'd stay and keep watch. He listened to Dana's breathing, the murmur of conversations, and the movement of ER staff. The night's events replayed in his mind.

Why would someone break into a cosmetic surgeon's house? Had Dana interrupted an attempted burglary? Why had Dr. McFadden been shot? A burglary gone sideways, maybe.

Whatever the reason for the break-in and shooting, Dana was the only witness.

Chapter Five

On the way to the coffee machine, Bree took a detour to check on Dr. McFadden's status again—unchanged—then headed for a small waiting room at the end of the hallway. The room was empty. Pulling out her phone, she called Luke and updated him. "Dana hit her head, but she's going to be fine." A text came in from Matt, and she read it. "She'll be home in the morning."

"OK," Luke said. Thankfully, he didn't ask about Dana's date.

Bree didn't like the thought of the kids being alone and asleep, which wasn't entirely rational. But then, she'd learned being rational didn't always apply to parenting worries. "I'm going to leave here soon."

"I'm finishing up my chemistry homework. Then I'm going to bed. We're fine here. You take care of Dana. She always takes care of us."

Bree's heart warmed. He was such a great kid. "Don't worry. Matt is going to stay with her."

"OK." Despite his earlier protest, he sounded relieved.

Bree ended the call. She left the room and headed down the hall toward the coffee and vending machines. Matt could use some sustenance if he was going to be on guard duty all night. She spotted Chief Hanover talking to a slim blonde woman in an alcove near the elevator. Bree stepped behind a tall plant, turned toward the vending machines, and eavesdropped while she contemplated the snack selections.

"Ms. McFadden?" Hanover introduced himself. "I'd like to ask you a few questions about your brother."

Bree glanced over her shoulder to get a glimpse at Kent's sister through the plant fronds.

"Please call me Elizabeth." The woman had been crying. Her complexion was the fairest of fair, with some freckles scattered over her nose and cheeks. Her eyes were swollen and red. She delicately dabbed the corners of her eyes with a tissue.

"Let's go somewhere more private." Hanover gestured toward the waiting room Bree had just vacated.

Elizabeth shook her head. "This is where the doctor is coming to update me. I won't walk away even for a minute."

Hanover glanced around. Bree felt his eyes land on her. She didn't blend in her uniform. Would he choose to question Kent's sister while Bree was in earshot?

"How is Kent?" Hanover asked.

Elizabeth lifted both shoulders, then let them slump again.

Bree fed a couple of dollar bills into the machine and selected a package of animal crackers, taking her time. She didn't want to miss anything.

"Do you know anyone who would want to hurt your brother?" Hanover asked.

"No. Kent isn't the kind of man who gets into arguments. He's easygoing, funny, smart. Everyone likes him." Elizabeth's description of her brother matched everything Dana had said about him over the past several weeks.

"What about his business partner, Dr. Bhatt?" Hanover asked.

Elizabeth sniffed. "Veer is Kent's closest friend."

"No professional jealousy or financial issues?"

"Not at all," she said. "They've been partners for more than a decade. Kent does facial work, and Veer specializes in breast augmentation and tummy tucks. Their skills are complementary, not competitive."

Bree smoothed out two more dollar bills and fed them into the vending machine. She selected a bag of mixed nuts and watched it fall.

Hanover continued. "Elizabeth, does your brother have a gun?"

"Yes," Elizabeth answered. "A pistol. It was our father's. After he died, Kent kept it. I didn't want it."

"Where does he keep the weapon?"

"He has a safe in his nightstand. It uses his fingerprint. He says that's the most secure way to store it."

Bree shoved the bags into her pocket and moved on to the pod-style coffee machine, turning sideways so she could watch the chief and Kent's sister in her peripheral vision. The elevator dinged, and a small group of visitors moved down the hallway.

Elizabeth gasped. "Oh, my God. He was shot with his own gun, wasn't he?"

"We don't know," Hanover said. "The gun will need to undergo ballistic testing. Do you know what kind of gun it is?"

Elizabeth shifted her weight and looked down at the tissue clutched in her hands. "I'm not a gun person. Kent said it was a Sig something."

Sig Sauer.

"We didn't find a handgun permit issued to Kent," Hanover said.

She lifted a shoulder but avoided eye contact. "I wouldn't know about that. You'll have to ask Kent."

The gun had likely been unregistered and therefore illegal, and she knew it. Bree could see the lie in her body language.

Hanover frowned. "Does Kent use the gun often?"

"He practices regularly. Kent is a very disciplined person." Elizabeth sounded proud.

"Do you know if he practiced with it recently?"

"No," she said.

"Does he go to a range?"

"Dr. Bhatt has land. Kent goes there to shoot targets."

Hanover made a note. "Has he mentioned anything concerning about his life recently?"

"He was sad about his divorce, but he's been dating again." Elizabeth sniffed. "He seems pretty happy to me."

"Did Kent mention anyone special?" Hanover asked.

"He mentioned that he'd met someone he liked when I talked to him last week, but they weren't serious. I think they'd only gone on a few dates." She paused. "I don't remember her name, but he said she was a retired policewoman." Her tone sounded disapproving. "Not that there's anything wrong with that," she blurted out quickly, as if just realizing she was speaking to a cop. "But Kent makes a lot of money, and I worry a woman might see him as financial security. Police don't make much money, do they?"

Bree almost snorted.

"Not in general. No." Hanover cleared his throat. "Has he dated any other women recently?"

"He had a couple of first, maybe second dates in the fall, but no one he was really interested in until the cop." Her tone suggested she had more to say.

Like a good investigator, Hanover waited her out.

"I'm still hoping he gets back together with Jane." Elizabeth's tone turned wistful. "I don't understand why they divorced. Until the papers were signed, I thought Kent was hoping she'd take him back too."

"Jane is his ex?" Hanover guessed.

"Yes. They were perfect for each other."

After a few beats of silence, Hanover probed for details. "Why do you say that?"

"Jane is also a plastic surgeon. She does a lot of charity work, so her income was never as high as Kent's, but she had the potential. Plus, she understood his job. They have a lot in common besides work too. They both like running and tennis." Elizabeth clearly liked the ex.

"So why did they get a divorce?" Hanover asked.

"I don't know. Kent wouldn't discuss it with me." Elizabeth sounded almost petulant that her brother refused to discuss the intimate details of his marriage breakup. "But I have the impression that the divorce was Jane's doing. She was always traveling. He never specifically said so, but I don't think he wanted to split up. He'd seemed perfectly content with their marriage."

Bree gave Kent points for keeping his marital problems private. She slowly made a cup of coffee.

Hanover jotted down a few notes, then focused on the sister again. "When was the last time you saw your brother?"

"We had lunch a few weeks ago. He's been very busy with work. We talked on the phone a few days ago, though."

"Did he seem fine?"

"Perfectly. Just as always. He wanted to schedule a lunch date next week." Elizabeth broke down, sobbing.

Hanover waited. The crying subsided into jerky breaths a minute later.

Bree selected a cardboard sleeve and plastic lid, taking her time.

Hanover changed gears to a less emotional question. "Who might have a key or access to Kent's house?"

"He has a housecleaning service, but he's used them for years. He's always been happy with them. I don't know of anyone else who has a key." Elizabeth sniffed and pulled another tissue from her purse.

"Do you have a key?" Hanover asked.

"Yes."

"Are you positive you're still in possession of that key?"

Elizabeth opened her purse and unzipped a compartment. Seemingly alarmed, she began opening other compartments. "It should be in here."

"When did you last use the key?" Hanover asked.

Elizabeth moved to a nearby table and began emptying the contents of her bag. It was a smallish purse, and it didn't take her long to remove her wallet, key fob, lipstick, a roll of antacids, and a travel pack of tissues. "It's not here." She froze, her brow furrowing. "I haven't used it for a few months. Kent went to a conference last September. He was gone for a week. I brought in his mail and watered the plants a few times. I *know* I put it back in the zipper part." Slowly, she began putting her items back into her purse. "It must be at my house. I'll check when I get home." But she was clearly upset by its absence.

"Does your brother leave his door unlocked?"

Elizabeth nodded vigorously. "I always tell him to lock up, and he laughs at me. He thinks he's safe living out in the country."

Hanover made a note. "That's all for now. I might have more questions tomorrow."

With a finger swipe under her eye, Elizabeth gave him her contact information. "I'm canceling all my appointments. I'll be here."

"Are you also a doctor?" Hanover asked.

"Dentist." She chewed her lip, her eyes on the corridor, likely watching for the doctor.

"Is there anyone I can call for you, Dr. McFadden?"

She shook her head. "I would normally call Kent." She stifled a sob with her fist. After a deep, shaky breath, she said, "Five years ago, my fiancé died in a car accident three months before our wedding. Kent and Jane were my rocks. I wouldn't have gotten through it without them. I can't lose him."

Bree made a few mental notes. This wasn't officially her case, but she preferred to have more info than less.

Hanover turned away from Elizabeth and walked straight to Bree. He made himself a cup of coffee. "You heard all that?"

"I did." There was no point in denying it.

Hanover tasted the coffee and grimaced. "What did you think?"

"Some interesting points, but I think you need more information to decide what's relevant. The handgun was on the floor?"

45

"Yes, and the biometric safe was open and empty." Hanover added sugar and fake creamer to his coffee, as if desperate to make it palatable.

"So he opened it himself. The shooter didn't find it and ambush him."

"Seems like."

"Do you know if any valuables are missing?" Bree asked.

"We'll have the sister walk through the house, but we found a money clip containing over four hundred bucks in cash and a Rolex watch in plain sight on the dresser."

"Unlikely it was a burglary gone wrong, then," Bree mused. "Signs of a struggle?"

"Yes." Hanover frowned. "But it was a short one."

"Ending in a gunshot."

Hanover nodded in agreement. "I have a bad feeling about this case."

"A home invasion and shooting are never good."

Hanover tasted the coffee again and made a face. "You'll let me know if you learn anything?"

Bree nodded. "If you'll do the same."

"Deal." Hanover tossed the still-full cup in the trash and walked away.

Bree returned to the triage area. Matt stood against the wall outside Dana's cubicle, watching everything. Bree handed him the coffee and snack packs, then peeked between the curtains. Dana appeared to be sleeping, so she ducked out again.

"Thanks." He gestured to the curtains and spoke in a low voice. "They're still waiting for a bed upstairs." Matt filled her in on Hanover's short interview with Dana.

Bree summed up the information provided by Kent's sister and the chief. "I don't know what to think of Hanover."

"Me either." Matt removed the lid from his cup and blew across the top of the steaming liquid. "I suspect he feels the same way about us."

"Makes sense. I haven't worked with him yet, and most of the chiefs are wary of me." Bree might have been born in Grey's Hollow, but her law enforcement experience had been in Philadelphia.

"Speak of the devil." Matt inclined his head down the hall.

Hanover was striding toward them, his face grim.

Bree squinted at the chief. She saw something in his eyes. "What happened?"

Hanover looked away.

And Bree knew. "Kent died, didn't he?"

Hanover's eye twitched. He was annoyed she'd seen past his crappy poker face. Seriously, the guy should stay away from casinos. Clearly, he hadn't wanted her to know, but he acknowledged her statement with a tight nod. "Dr. McFadden passed away a few minutes ago."

Kent was dead. It shouldn't have been a surprise. A bullet to the chest was always dicey, and Dana had been covered in so much of Kent's blood she hadn't even realized she'd also been injured.

"I need answers from your friend," Hanover said.

"She's sleeping." Bree fought a wave of protectiveness. Then she imagined Kent's sister's grief with a rush of her own.

"Tomorrow." His voice rang with determination.

She waited for Hanover to retreat. She stepped inside the curtain. In the dim light, she could see that Dana's eyes were open, her face tight.

"You heard?" Bree asked.

Dana nodded. She opened her mouth, then closed it as if unable to speak. She swallowed hard, then cleared her throat. "You won't be able to put off Hanover for long. This is now a murder investigation."

Chapter Six

Twenty minutes later, at eleven thirty, Bree eased out of the ER cubicle.

Matt crumpled up a snack wrapper and tossed it in a nearby trash can. "Is she OK?"

"She's sleeping." Bree crossed the tile and leaned on the wall next to him. She pressed her shoulder to his. "Maybe I should stay the night."

"You want me to go to your place and get the kids off to school in the morning?"

"Would you do that?" Bree asked.

"Of course."

"Thank you."

When had Bree gotten so lucky to have met this man? This kind, patient man who was willing to wait for her to catch up at every stage of their relationship. Many years ago, she'd resolved to never let down her guard, to never trust anyone, to never let herself be vulnerable. Yet here she was, giving her whole heart to Matt and trusting him with the kids as well.

Her exhaustion brought her back to the night her father had murdered her mother. Sweat broke out under her body armor as she relived the terror for the thousandth time. Eight years old, huddling under the back porch, freezing, heart hammering, trying to shush her crying baby brother, her little sister shivering beside her, certain that Daddy would hear them . . . find them . . .

Kill them.

Unable to locate his children, Daddy had taken his own life that night, but not before he'd killed their mother.

Plenty of people had known how he'd abused his family. Not one of them had been willing to stand up to him. Bree knew one of the reasons she'd gone on the offensive with Party Boy earlier was the spoiling-for-a-fight gleam in his eye. She knew that look well. Party Boy got mean when he drank, just like her father. Daddy had been mean sober, too, but drinking had taken him to a whole different level of nasty. Like most bullies, Party Boy had recognized her lack of fear. She could have kicked his ass, and he'd known it. Bullies fed on fear. It gave them a high like an addictive drug. Bree had not been able to stop herself. She couldn't let Party Boy's challenge go untested. Men like him needed to know there were people like her who would not tolerate their aggression.

Before Matt, memories of her childhood had made her more determined to remain independent. Now, her flashbacks simply made her appreciate him more and filled her with a sense of gratitude she hadn't thought possible just one year ago. After all the tragedies she'd suffered, she could still experience joy and love and wonder.

She lowered her voice. "I love you."

"Love you back."

Her phone buzzed on her hip. "It's Luke."

Matt tensed.

They both knew Luke would never call unless it was an emergency. Alarmed, Bree answered the call. "Luke?"

"There's someone outside," Luke said without any greeting.

"Where?" Bree put the phone on speaker so Matt could hear.

"In the pasture, leaning on the fence." Luke's words were rushed.

"You're sure it's a person?" Bree opened the app on her phone that controlled the security cameras and tapped "Live View." She saw nothing but darkness.

"I'm using the binoculars," Luke said. "I can't be a hundred percent sure, but it looks like a man. He's wearing dark clothes, and the light doesn't reach there. I only spotted him because he was moving and the snow makes him stand out."

"I'm sending a deputy to the farm, and I'm on my way home now." She used her radio to send a patrol car to her house. Deputy Collins responded and gave an ETA of fifteen minutes, no faster than Bree would arrive.

"OK." Luke's voice wavered.

"Deputy Collins is on the way." Bree pointed to Matt, then to Dana's cubicle, silently asking him to take care of her friend.

Matt shook his head and whispered, "I'm coming with you."

She covered her phone speaker. "I need you to stay here."

"No." Matt's tone did not welcome discussion.

Frustrated, Bree started toward the hallway. "Dana could be in danger. I need you here."

"No," Matt repeated, pushing off the wall. "I'm going with you."

"He's going with you," Dana called out. "I'm in the middle of a busy ER. I'll be fine."

Matt pulled out his own phone and pressed it to his ear.

Bree had no time to argue with either of them. On the way to the exit, she said into the phone, "Is the man still out there?"

"No. I don't see him anywhere." Luke's tone shifted to a higher pitch. "I have the shotgun out."

She wanted to tell him it would be all right, that he didn't need the gun. But she didn't. He wasn't a child, and he knew violence on a personal level. "The alarm is on. If he approaches the house, the motion lights will go on."

"I know."

Bree rushed through the sliding exit doors and ran across the asphalt to her vehicle.

Matt caught up to her as she opened the door. He jogged toward his Suburban parked a few rows away and yelled over his shoulder, "Nolan is coming to stay with Dana."

Nolan was Matt's older brother, a former MMA fighter with personal-protection experience.

With a wave, Bree screeched from the lot, lights flashing. The roads were empty, and she didn't need the siren.

She put the call with Luke on the vehicle's speaker. "I'm on the way, Luke. Be home soon. Just hang on."

Luke's sharp intake of breath echoed in her vehicle. "Aunt Bree? The outside motion lights just came on."

Bree's muscles went as tight as bridge cables. She pushed the gas pedal to the floor of her vehicle. "Stand back from the doors and windows." She glanced at her phone on the console. She'd left the live camera window open. The rear yard was lit up like a football stadium, but she saw no one. The brightness made the pasture beyond its reach seem darker in comparison.

"I don't see him," Luke said. "I turned off the kitchen light so he can't see inside."

"That was smart. The motion light could have scared him off." She hoped.

But he must have been close enough to the house to trigger the motion detector.

The minutes crawled by. Luke knew how to use a shotgun. Bree took him shooting regularly, but it was easy to shoot paper targets and clay pigeons. Aiming a gun at another human being and pulling the trigger was entirely different. Experienced cops froze when confronted with the same situation, and the decision had to be made in a split second.

For normal people, taking a life was a burden they carried to their own graves.

Bree had shot multiple people—and killed a few. Unlike many of her law enforcement colleagues, she didn't suffer from remorse. The ghosts of her dead did not keep her awake at night. Ironically, it was their absence that worried her. At times, she felt like it was too easy for her to kill. Her father had had no conscience. Was that an inherited trait? She shared that monster's DNA—and so did Luke.

She wasn't sure which option frightened her more: Luke not being able to pull the trigger or Luke firing at an intruder with no hesitation. Could he live with failing to protect his sister? Whatever split-second decision he made, he would carry the consequence for the rest of his life.

A glance in her rearview mirror told her Matt was right behind her. She took a bend in the country road at top speed, her vehicle careening, tires squealing.

"I'm almost there," she said to maintain the contact between her and Luke.

"OK." His voice quavered.

A few minutes later, she turned onto the road that led to her farm. Gravel sprayed from her tires as she took the turn into the driveway on two wheels. Her headlights swept over the house, barn, and meadow. She saw nothing but snow and darkness.

"I'm here." At eleven forty-five, Bree shoved the gearshift into park and leaped from the SUV, her weapon drawn.

"I see you." His voice rang with relief.

She looked at the house. The outside lights blazed, and the windows were dark.

Matt parked beside Bree and was at her side in an instant. They raced up the back porch steps. Luke disengaged the alarm and opened the door. The shotgun barrel was tipped toward the floor, the gun resting in the crook of his arm. Ladybug jumped against Bree's legs. Bree patted her with one hand, then pushed her down with a gentle shove. She was the sweetest animal ever but completely useless as a guard dog.

After greeting Bree and Matt, the dog returned to Luke, leaning against his knees. Emotional support was definitely her strength.

"Everything is all right," Bree murmured, enveloping her nephew in a hug.

"I know." Luke stepped back.

"Are you OK?" she asked, looking him over.

His shoulders were back, but his eyes looked misty, grateful, and a little embarrassed. "I'm fine."

"You did good," she said.

Luke nodded, but he made no move to put away the shotgun, and Bree didn't ask him to.

Matt gestured toward the driveway, where a set of headlights bounced down the driveway. A sheriff's department patrol vehicle parked alongside her own. "Collins is here."

"I'm going to check on Kayla, then we'll search the yard," Bree said. She was sure her niece was fine but needed to see with her own eyes.

"I'll take a quick look around the first floor." Matt moved past Luke into the living room.

Bree raced up the stairs. She cracked the little girl's bedroom door. The light fell across the child's sleeping face, and Bree felt like she could take her first full breath since Luke's phone call. Even though the alarm had not tripped, Bree checked the rest of the second floor, then returned to the kitchen.

"Downstairs is clear," Matt said.

"Upstairs too." Bree turned to Luke. "Where did you see the man?"

Luke gestured toward the wide windows behind the table. "Near the water trough."

"Lock the door and reset the alarm," she said. "We'll be back in a few."

Bree and Matt went outside. They waited for the dead bolt to slide home before meeting Collins in the backyard. Greta barked from the back of the K-9 unit.

"Do you want the dog out?" Collins asked.

"Not yet," Bree said. "We'll check for footprints first." The snow might make the dog unnecessary. Though hoofprints obliterated any tracks inside the pasture, much of the snow outside the pasture was pristine.

Moonlight glowed on the frozen pasture. The barn loomed on the horizon, casting a deep shadow on the ground.

"Should we check in the barn?" Collins asked in a low voice.

"No. We'll check that last. The barn has its own alarm. If he went in there, we'd know." Bree used her flashlight to scan the snowy ground as they walked toward the fence. Ice crystals crunched under her boots, and her breath fogged in the night air, but she barely felt the cold. Anger warmed her from the inside out. Someone had been out here, watching her house, frightening Luke, threatening her children. She might not have given birth to them, but they were *her* children now. She loved them with a fierceness that bordered on feral. Not for the first time, she understood deep in her soul that there wasn't anything she wouldn't do to protect them, including die—or kill.

The intensity of her rage alarmed her. The trespasser was likely long gone—probably scared off by the motion lights—but she wanted to find him. She wanted to make him pay for scaring Luke, for invading their privacy, for trespassing on their sense of security and violating the sanctity of their home.

For making Luke feel unsafe. After all he'd been through, he deserved a normal life.

At the rear of the yard, she came to an abrupt halt. Her flashlight illuminated a very clear set of footprints. She'd believed Luke, but seeing evidence that supported his story stoked her anger to new heights.

"Fuck," Matt said.

Collins moved her light on the ground in a wide arc. "He came from behind the barn."

"And stopped when the motion lights picked him up," Matt added.

Bree pointed to the rear of the house, where a security camera was mounted. "He must have stepped back into the shadow immediately or we would have gotten him on video."

An image would have been helpful, but their security measures had done their job—they'd deterred an intruder.

They walked in a line parallel to the footprints. The water trough sat just inside the pasture. The horses had trampled the snow around it. But on the outside of the pasture fence, she spotted boot prints.

She moved her light in a circle on the ground. "This is where he stood and watched the house for a while." Other than the trespasser's footprints, the snow was undisturbed. The horses had been in the pasture Friday, the day the snow fell. But icy spots had formed the next day, forcing her to keep the animals inside since then. Being a horse owner had taught Bree that if there was even a remote chance for a horse to injure itself, it would.

Following the footprints in the beam of her flashlight, they passed in and out of the shadow of the barn. The snow was flattened behind the barn as well, as if the trespasser had been pacing. Had he been weighing options? Making a decision of some kind?

The thought of what he could have been considering lifted goose bumps on Bree's arms.

He'd made his approach as covert as possible. The prints led from behind the barn and looped around the equipment shed. Bree headed for the rolling door, but Matt stepped in front of her. "You promised to stay out of the shed."

"Really?"

"Yes, really." Matt crossed his arms. He was working on some sort of surprise for the family and had declared the shed off-limits weeks ago.

"Fine." She turned around.

Behind her the doors rolled open. A minute later, they rolled closed.

"You can turn around. It's clear."

They continued following the footprints to the road. Matt stopped on the shoulder. "He parked on the road and walked around to approach the house from the back. Stayed in the shadows of the outbuildings the best he could."

Collins stooped to study the prints. "They look too big to belong to a female."

Matt lifted his foot and studied his own print. "The shoe prints are about two or three sizes smaller than mine."

Bree knew that Matt wore a size fourteen. "Let's photograph and cast the footprints." She had no other options. She had no neighbors within sight. The house was too far from the road for the security cameras to have captured the trespasser's vehicle. She asked Collins, "Do you have a camera and kit in the car?"

"Yes, ma'am."

"Have you recorded impressions in snow before?"

Collins's prior experience was with the LAPD, and she was unlikely to have worked with snow in Los Angeles. "Once."

"Do you feel confident in doing so now?"

"Yes, ma'am."

"Be sure to use a tripod with the camera," Bree instructed. "Getting good pictures in snow can be tricky. You have to get the angle and light just right. Snow crystals can reflect light like mirrors. You might need to experiment a bit with light placement."

"Yes, ma'am," Collins said. "I have some gray primer paint in my kit too."

Photographing a white-on-white impression was challenging. Gray spray paint increased contrast. The primer would also coat the snow and prepare the impression for the casting material so it didn't slip between the grains of snow. They didn't want to lose the details in the impression.

"Good," Bree approved. "Also, when doing the cast, you don't want to melt the print, though the primer will help with that as well. Use snow in your mixture. Get the temperature of the material down below freezing."

"Yes, ma'am." Collins turned and jogged toward her patrol vehicle.

"You want to trust her with this?" Matt asked.

Bree waved a hand. "There are at least a hundred clear footprints out here. I'm not concerned if she messes up one or two. This is a good opportunity for her to fine-tune her skills." Much of police work was learned on the job.

Matt nodded, then turned away to walk down the road toward the mailbox at the end of her driveway. "I'm going to check the front yard."

"I'll check the barn, just to be sure." Bree stayed well away from the intruder's footprints as she trudged back to the barn. Now that her adrenaline had ebbed, the cold seeped through the soles of her boots, leaving her toes painfully numb. The wind whipped across the open pasture, and the night air was cold enough to prick the inside of her lungs like tiny pins. She disengaged the alarm and rolled open the barn door.

A giant head poked over a half door. Matt's horse, Beast, nickered. She patted his nose as she quickly peered into his stall. Empty. She turned away. Doglike in personality, Beast tried to drag her closer with his nose.

"Chill, you goofball." She evaded capture and continued checking stalls. All horses were accounted for. No extra life-forms, except the two scraggly, nearly feral barn cats that watched from the feed room doorway.

She took a quick look into the tack and feed rooms as well, before locking up again and resetting the alarm. Before returning to the house, she took one last turn around the barn, sweeping her light back and forth on the snow. If the trespasser had dropped something, the wind could have carried it away from his tracks.

But she found nothing. As she turned, she lifted her flashlight and gasped. He hadn't been pacing behind the barn. He'd been leaving a message. In two-foot-tall white letters, he'd spray-painted DIRTY COPS SHOULD DIE.

"Bree, where are you?" Matt called.

"Behind the barn," she answered. She moved her light around. Something gleamed in the snow. Bree moved closer and spotted a rusty can of spray paint.

He joined her, standing at her side. "Fuck."

"You keep saying that."

"It keeps being the most appropriate response."

"I can't disagree," Bree said. "I'll have Collins get photos of this too, along with a sample of the paint. Bag and tag the can."

"Has anyone threatened you lately?" Matt asked.

Bree paused at the edge of the yard. She was cold, but this was a discussion she didn't want to have in front of Luke. He was scared enough. She stamped her feet. Her toes felt like blocks of ice. She told him what Mrs. Ekin had said. "One of Travis's brothers was at the scene. I've no idea where the other was."

"The Ekin family goes on the list of potential stalkers." Matt nodded. "Anyone else?"

"You know I get hate mail all the time."

"Anything stand out recently?" Matt shoved his hands into his pockets.

"I don't know." She searched her memory. "I'll have to go through my hate mail folder." She looked back at the message on the barn. "*Dirty cops* seems inconsistent with Mrs. Ekin and her son's comments. They're more focused on payback."

"Maybe they want to believe Travis is innocent."

"His mother did make that claim." Bree turned away from the spray paint, toward the house, where she could see Luke's silhouette—and that of the shotgun he held—through the kitchen window. Once again she wondered if her job was worth putting her family in danger.

CHAPTER SEVEN

Dana opened her eyes. Daylight stabbed her in the brain. She firmly squeezed her lids shut, but not before she saw that Nolan Flynn was still reading in the uncomfortable hospital visitor chair in her private room.

Closing her eyes helped with the pain, but another vision of Kent bleeding under her hands appeared in her mind. The flashback felt real, complete with the warmth of blood seeping between her fingers.

She heard a book close, chair feet scrape on the floor, then footsteps. Plastic rattled. Behind her eyelids, the light dimmed.

"That should be a little better, but take your time. Concussions are the worst," Nolan said like a man who'd had a few of them.

She risked cracking her lids again. He'd closed the blinds, and the room was dark enough that her vision alone didn't make her head feel like it was going to split in two. Nolan stood at the bedside, just far enough away that he didn't loom over her. He hadn't left her room for a second all night. Every time she'd woken, he'd been there.

"Water?" he asked.

"Yes, please." She shifted up the pillow a few inches. Aches and weakness rattled every inch of her body.

He moved the wheeled tray until the plastic cup on it was within reach. Dana picked it up, fumbled the cup, and spilled water on the front of her hospital gown.

She felt the burn of impending tears in the corners of her eyes. She hadn't slept much during the night. Exhaustion and pain were taking a toll on her self-control.

"Hey." Nolan took the cup and lowered it, holding the straw near her lips. His gaze lingered on her throat, which hurt and must be bruised. "Give yourself a break. You look like you went three rounds with the heavyweight champ."

To avoid another dousing, she pushed the button to raise the head of the bed halfway before she drank more water. "I just want to go home."

Nolan set the cup on the tray. "Maybe you should ease into it. Take it slow."

Hell no. She was getting out of there. Dana punched the bed button again until she was sitting all the way up. Her head swam, and she gritted her teeth.

He shook his head and lifted an eyebrow. "Did that hurt?"

"I'm fine." If *fine* was defined as "shaky and weak as a newborn puppy."

"Bullshit," he said without malice. "Just sit there and let your brain level itself."

It did feel as if she were off balance. Like her head was a cruise ship pool, the water sloshing back and forth in high seas. But on her second attempt, she managed to lift her own cup and drink without dumping water on herself. She counted that as a win.

"What time is it?" She scanned the tray for her phone but didn't see it.

Nolan checked his. "Seven thirty." Obviously reading her mind, he reached for her nightstand, unplugged her phone, and handed it to her. "I charged it for you."

"Thanks." She glanced at the screen. Bree had messaged an hour before. Dana replied with I'm awake, then settled her head back against the stiff pillow. "And thanks for staying here last night. I know it eased Bree's mind. She was worried."

"With good reason," he said, those blue eyes focused intently on her again. They'd met at joint Taggert-Flynn family functions and holidays, and they'd spent time together a few months back. Nolan had helped her protect the kids while Bree worked a particularly worrisome case. Behind that rock-hard body, easy smile, and quick sense of humor was a very perceptive man, the kind who could see through an act. She supposed he'd had plenty of practice sizing people up during his fighting career. She hadn't minded when his superpower had been turned on other people, but his ability to read her now made her acutely uncomfortable.

Not only was she off her game—way off—today, she also preferred being the one doing all the judging. Even as she thought it, she recognized that the former-cop control freak was still alive and well inside her, nearly a year post-retirement. May as well accept it. At this stage of her life, she wasn't going to change.

"Bree is going to take Kayla to school, then swing by here," Nolan said.

"If you can drive me home, she doesn't need to do that. I'm planning to be out of here ASAP, except I don't have clothes. The Redhaven cops took mine." The jeans, white sweater, and boots she'd purchased specifically for her hot date were now evidence. A quick wave of sickness passed through her. She didn't want them back, not after they'd been soaked in Kent's blood.

She couldn't wrap her mind around the fact that he was dead.

"I can drive you home, and I have some gym clothes in my truck." He scanned her. "They'll be a little big but better than what you're wearing now." He gestured toward her hospital gown.

"That'll work." Dana texted Bree, who responded with I'll stop home later if I can.

Someone rapped on the door and it opened.

"Knock, knock." A young man in scrubs carried a tray into the room. "Good morning." He set the tray down and lifted the molded plastic lids one at a time, giving her a guided tour of her breakfast. "Scrambled eggs, toast, milk, coffee, and orange juice."

She thanked him and he bowed out with the fanfare of a Broadway star. His cheerfulness grated on her with Kent's death so fresh.

Nolan peered at the food. "You should eat the eggs. Protein is good for healing."

Dana poked at the yellow blobs on the plate. "But are they actually eggs?"

He handed her a paper packet. "Add some salt. The OJ is good for you too. Vitamin C."

She tasted the eggs and set the fork down. "Hard pass. I'll make myself breakfast when I get home."

Nolan laughed, his head shaking. "Not everyone is a gourmet cook. Food is fuel."

"I'm not that hungry anyway." Dana pushed back the rolling tray and eased her legs over the side of the bed, letting them dangle, allowing her brain to adjust before going fully vertical.

"Where are you going?" Nolan asked.

"To the bathroom." She put her feet on the floor and clutched the back of her gown together. The room spun only once before settling.

"Take it slow. A face-plant will not help. Been there. Done that." He came around the bed and hovered—one hand near her elbow—until her legs steadied. She shuffled to the bathroom and back without incident. Moving her body hurt but also eased the stiffness. She returned to bed, both exhausted and restless, and saw the book Nolan had been reading closed on the chair. The face on the cover was unmistakable. "Is that the new biography of Abraham Lincoln?"

"It is."

"I didn't know you were a history nerd."

Before he could respond, the resident doctor came in, and Nolan went out to his truck. The doc ran through Dana's chart and vital signs, and she downplayed her symptoms. Anything to get out. By the time Nolan returned carrying a small duffel bag, Dana had been proclaimed fit enough for discharge. Paperwork arrived in record time.

Dana sat on the edge of the bed. "That's some unexpected efficiency."

"The ER is busy. I'm sure they need the bed for someone who isn't *fine*." Nolan set the gym bag on the bed, unzipped it, and lifted out a short stack of folded clothes.

Dana was average size for a woman, but the Flynn brothers were giants. Matt carried a Hollywood Viking vibe. Battered and scarred with a shaved head, one cauliflower ear, and a nose that had clearly been broken more than once, Nolan looked more like a gladiator.

She took the clothes and went into the bathroom. His sweats were ridiculously large on her. She rolled the waistband down and the cuffs up and still nearly tripped coming out. An orderly brought a wheelchair. Easing into the seat, Dana looked down at the grippy gray hospital socks. "I guess I'm going home in these." She didn't have a coat either, but she wasn't staying in the hospital another minute. She'd willingly suffer.

Nolan wrapped his jacket around her shoulders. Straightening it, he tugged the lapels together. "You don't have to walk anywhere. I'll meet you at the door with my truck." He left the room in two long strides.

By the time the orderly pushed her to the main entrance, Nolan's black F-150 was waiting at the curb.

Dana took a gulp of cold morning air, appreciating the lack of hospital smell. Nolan opened the door of his truck and helped her into the cab. He slid behind the wheel. As they drove away from the protective overhang and into the sunlight, he handed her a pair of sunglasses just as she realized she needed them.

She put them on. "Thanks."

The passing landscape gave her a flash of vertigo. She pressed a hand to her forehead.

"You might want to look straight ahead or close your eyes."

Did he have ESP? She chose to stare out the windshield. The steadier horizon did help. "How many concussions have you had?"

"A few."

"But you haven't had one in a long time."

"Not since retirement. There's only so much damage a body can take."

She'd seen pictures of him bloody and battered after fights. Did she look that bad? She'd been in a rush to get out of the hospital. She hadn't looked in the mirror. She folded down the visor, intending to check.

Nolan folded it back up. "You might want to clean up a little first."

"It's that bad?"

He winced. "It isn't good."

At the farm, he parked. Thankfully, it seemed no one was home. She didn't want the kids to see her all blood-crusty and gross. Dana opened the door. Before she could step out, Nolan was there. To her horror, he scooped her up in his arms.

"Hey," she protested. She squirmed for about a second, then realized that was pointless. Nolan was one giant muscle from head to toe. Even his neck was ripped. Plus, he had a black belt in Jiu Jitsu, which made him a master of leverage and body manipulation. She wasn't getting down until he put her there.

"Just hold still," he huffed. "You're not wearing shoes, and it's icy." He carried her up the walkway, set her down on the back porch, and used his key to open the back door. Inside, he turned off the alarm and greeted the dog. Ladybug loved hard. "Easy, girl." He contained the dog until she calmed enough for Dana to pet her.

Vader the black cat jumped down from his countertop perch, stalked across the floor, and sniffed her as if she smelled of manure. Dana stroked both animals.

"Do you want food or a shower first?" Nolan asked.

"Can you cook?" She'd never seen him eat anything but chicken breast and broccoli.

"Yes. I'm no chef, but following a strict training diet means you cook or you don't eat."

She waved at the fridge. "Eggs and toast would be great. I can shower while you cook." She walked out of the kitchen.

But Nolan was right behind her. "Just going to make sure you don't get dizzy on the steps."

"I'm fine." But she kept a firm grip on the banister all the way up.

"Liar."

She ignored his response. When she reached the upstairs hallway, Nolan sat on the top step and pulled out his phone.

"What are you doing?" she asked.

"Waiting," he said without looking up. "You could fall in the shower."

Whatever.

She went into the hall bathroom. Her image in the mirror stopped her cold. "Oh, my God."

"I told you not to look," he said from the hallway.

Luckily, her face had been spared a direct hit, but her complexion was the grayish white of unflavored yogurt. Purple fingerprints ringed her throat, and the circles under her eyes looked like Halloween zombie makeup. Dried blood still matted her hair and was crusted on the skin of her neck. She turned on the shower.

"You're not supposed to get the stitches wet!"

"I know! Geez, you need to relax." Dana took a hand mirror from the drawer to examine the railroad track of black stitches in the back of her head. "These stitches are very Frankensteinish."

"I hate to say it, but you'll probably look worse tomorrow, when all those bruises reach full color."

"Fan-fucking-tastic." She put the mirror away. What was the point? She used a washcloth to clean the remaining dried blood from her hair and neck, then went to her room for yoga pants and an oversize hoodie.

As she walked past him with her clothes, he asked, "Are you sure you're steady enough to shower?"

"I'll keep it short."

"I'll be right here if you need help."

Dana choked back an unexpected rush of emotion at his concern. Hot tears pressed against the corners of her eyes. The Flynn brothers weren't just badasses—they were nice and thoughtful and all that sensitive bullshit. She turned to the bathroom so he wouldn't see and closed the door.

Trauma was a sneaky bitch. You pushed it out of your mind, and it crept back in when you least expected it.

Donning a shower cap to keep the water off her stitches, she undressed. In the bright bathroom light, developing bruises made the skin on her back look like camouflage print. Her hip was the color of a ripe eggplant.

She stepped into the shower, letting the hot water soothe all the sore spots. Too exhausted to remain upright for long, she barely lasted in the shower five minutes before she needed to sit down on the closed toilet to dry herself. *Fine* was definitely an overstatement. When she emerged, Nolan stuffed his phone in the back pocket of his jeans and stuck close all the way down the steps.

In the kitchen, she made it to the table before her legs folded, and she collapsed into a chair.

Nolan made quick work of scrambling a half dozen eggs. He slid whole-grain bread into the toaster and peeled two oranges. The plate he set in front of her was loaded. "Just eat what you can. I'll finish whatever you don't."

Dana forced down some eggs and half an orange. "Am I keeping you from work? Don't you have classes to teach?"

Nolan owned his own MMA gym. "Nope. I have someone covering for me. I can stay all day."

"I don't need a bodyguard. I need a gun."

"Which you don't have at the moment."

"You could lend me yours," she suggested.

"You are in no condition to be on your own today, even if we weren't worried about your safety."

She gave him a Look.

It didn't faze him. He ate an orange segment. "I know you're the kind of person who prefers to be on the other end of this protection situation, but that isn't the hand you've been dealt. We just don't know what we're working with yet. Between your situation and what happened out there last night, an extra adult on hand won't hurt." He pointed to the back window with the wooden spoon.

Excellent points, all of which annoyed Dana. She kept thinking about Luke and Kayla being here alone while some weirdo stalked around outside. She would be useless to protect them today. So Nolan should definitely stay. Not for her, but for the kids.

The motives for threatening the sheriff were both obvious and endless. Bree arrested bad people who didn't want to be arrested. Also, she was a public figure, and people liked to complain. There were plenty of wackos out there.

Dana's mind went back to Kent. "Why would someone kill a cosmetic surgeon?"

"Robbery?" Nolan suggested. "He had money and expensive toys?"

"He did, and robbery is a possible motive." Dana pictured Kent's bedroom, the effort of concentrating making her head pound. "There were some valuables lying in plain sight, but it's possible I interrupted the shooter before he had a chance to take what he wanted."

"You don't like that theory." Nolan popped another piece of orange into his mouth.

"Your average robber doesn't usually walk into a house when someone is clearly home. The lights were on. Music was playing."

Romantic music.

Her throat clogged.

"You OK?"

"Yeah." She shoved back the plate. It wasn't like she'd been in love with Kent. She'd liked him, and she definitely felt his loss, but her emotions also felt oddly out of control. "I give up. I can't think."

"Kent's case belongs to the Redhaven PD anyway," Nolan pointed out.

"You're right." She stood. "I'm going to take a nap." Her brain was screaming for rest. She chose the living room couch to avoid having him follow her upstairs again. Stretching out, she closed her eyes. She tried to ease into a nap slowly, but exhaustion dragged her into the darkness like hands around her ankles.

But even in sleep, she couldn't put Kent's shooting out of her mind. She was mired in those moments, reliving them over and over, like a video loop. Racing to the steps, being knocked flat, hands around her throat, fighting for her life.

Finally, kneeling at Kent's side, up to her elbows in his blood.

CHAPTER EIGHT

Matt drove to the county forensics lab and went in search of forensic tech Rory MacIniss. Rory specialized in computer forensics but was also proficient in general forensics as well. Rural departments were routinely short-staffed. Employees needed to wear multiple hats.

He spotted Rory in the lab and knocked on the open door.

With his phone pressed to his ear, Rory motioned for him to enter. His tall, thin frame was bent over a keyboard. "Yes, that particular compound is commonly known as light rosin. It's primarily used on the bows of violins and violas." He squinted at his monitor screen. "We found traces of it on Kent McFadden's sleeve and on the lapel of Dana Romano's jacket." Rory paused. "Yes. We also found a few horsehairs in Dr. McFadden's house and on Romano's boots and jacket."

Matt pretended not to be interested, pulling out his phone and scrolling through his email. But he made a mental note about the rosin. The horsehairs didn't mean much. Dana likely had tracked those into the scene.

"Hey, Matt." Rory ended his call. "Sorry about that."

"No worries." Matt waved a careless hand. "Murder cases take precedence, and that's a nasty one."

Rory set down his phone. "I assume you're here about Sheriff Taggert's trespasser?"

"You know it." Matt nodded.

Rory walked over to a stainless-steel table. Two 3D casts of shoe treads lay side by side. The casting material needed up to forty-eight hours to fully dry. "These casts are the footprints found at Sheriff Taggert's farm. We can see the tread pattern very clearly. These impressions were made by a men's size eleven Timberland work boot."

"Did you run the print through SoleMate?" Matt asked. SoleMate was a comprehensive footwear database.

"Didn't need to. I recognized it. It's a common boot." Rory shook his head. "Also, the tread is a bit worn, but if you look closely, you can read the first few letters of *Timberland PRO* here on the sole." He positioned a gooseneck lamp over one of the casts and pointed to the gap between the heel and toe tread in the center of the print.

Matt leaned closer. The impressions of the actual knobby tread were clearer, but in the bright light, he could see part of a rectangular box with the faint letters TIMB inside it.

Rory moved to the computer, woke the screen, and clicked on a window showing a photo of the sole of a Timberland PRO work boot. "This is the sole of their standard waterproof work boot. As you can see, it's a match."

Matt straightened. "They must sell a million of those." There would be little point in trying to trace purchases of Timberland PRO boots.

"True," said Rory. "We identified over a dozen retailers just in this area, including sporting goods stores, the military surplus store, and that big outlet on Route 9."

"And that wouldn't include online retailers." Matt had been hoping for a less common shoe tread.

"But this pair is worn enough to have distinct characteristics." Rory pointed to a divot in one tread, then a small channel in another. "If you find *this* pair of boots, we can match them to these impressions."

Matt asked, "What else can you tell me?"

"A men's size eleven is the equivalent to a woman's size twelve and a half. While it's possible that this was a woman, it's not a common size."

"So, it's most likely a man." Matt wasn't surprised.

"Yes." Rory clicked his mouse. A photograph of a half dozen boot prints in the snow appeared. "A size eleven shoe and a stride of this length indicates an average-size man. The rest of this information comes from studying the suspect's strides." Rory's descriptions wouldn't be useful to prove guilt, but they might help narrow down a pool of suspects. "Based on his stride length and foot size, I estimate his height to be five eight to six feet. His stride is long and steady. No shuffling or foot dragging."

"A young man?"

"Not necessarily young, but he's unlikely to be elderly or have a major injury." Rory sighed. "I wish I could give you more."

"Every bit of information helps," Matt said.

Rory brightened. "We did get lucky with the can of spray paint."

"Did you trace the paint?"

"No." Rory shook his head. "The can is rusty. You can't even read the barcode."

"Then he probably didn't purchase it for this purpose but already had it lying around."

"Yes." Rory waggled his brows. "Go see Darcy."

"She got prints?"

Rory grinned. "She did."

Darcy Stevens, latent fingerprint examiner extraordinaire, worked on the second floor. Matt took the steps two at a time. As always, Darcy wore her hair in a tight bun and dressed in all black in deference to the dark powders used in her job. Though she must be somewhere around fifty—she'd worked in the department forever—she looked ten years younger. Maybe because she was always in her office and her skin rarely saw sunlight.

"Do you have anything for me?" Matt asked.

She beamed. "Oh, yeah. A partial, slightly smudged fingerprint and a whole palm."

"I'm shocked he left prints, and also that you could develop them with the can being wet from the snow."

"Ninhydrin doesn't work well on wet surfaces because it acts with the amino acids, and water dissolves amino acids," she explained. "But cyanoacrylate—or superglue—fuming works just fine for nonporous surfaces that have been in contact with water. In fact, I've developed prints from a knife that had been submerged for weeks."

In simple terms, the technique required Darcy to place the can in a clear fuming chamber with superglue that was heated until it produced vapor. The sweat and oils in the fingerprint attracted the gas, and a white fingerprint was produced.

"I'm impressed," Matt said.

"Don't get too excited." Her chair squeaked as she leaned back. "I got prints but no match."

"Nothing?"

"Nope," Darcy said.

Both Benjamin and Ford Ekin had criminal records. If the prints belonged to one of them, Darcy's search should have returned a match. But mistakes happened when prints were submitted to AFIS, the Automated Fingerprint Identification System. Sometimes prints were kicked back.

"If I send you two names, can you compare their prints directly?" Matt asked.

"Sure."

Matt gave her Benjamin's and Ford's information.

"Give me a couple of hours. I'll call you later."

Matt headed out to his vehicle. If the prints didn't belong to either Benjamin or Ford, then several things were possible. One, the prints belonged to Benjamin or Ford, and the submission of their prints in AFIS got screwed up. Two, the prints could belong to someone else who handled the can, and Benjamin or Ford could have spray-painted Bree's barn wearing gloves. Three, the stalker wasn't either Benjamin or Ford.

Matt wasn't sure which scenario was better. Benjamin and Ford were violent criminals, but they were known entities.

The idea of an unknown person stalking Bree raised the hairs on the back of Matt's neck.

He left the lab and drove to the sheriff's station, stopping to pick up a coffee for himself and a cappuccino for Bree. A deputy sat at a computer in the squad room, a phone pressed to his ear while he typed a report. Through the walls, Matt could hear the faint whine of power tools and other sounds of construction. Ground had been broken on the addition to the sheriff's department the previous week. By spring, the sheriff's station would have brand-new locker rooms, including a dedicated one for female deputies. Before Bree had taken over as sheriff, the force hadn't had a single female deputy. When the new building addition was complete, the department would move into it while the existing space was renovated. Either way, the next year was going to be noisy.

Bree had a budget meeting with the board of supervisors, so Matt settled in a cubicle and spent the next hour pulling background information and criminal records on Travis's family, starting with his parents and moving on to his two brothers.

Bree walked into the squad room from the back hall, peeling off her gloves as she crossed the room. She stopped at the corner of his desk. "My office in ten minutes? Todd will be here in a few. I'd like to review."

"OK," Matt said. "How did the meeting go?"

"We went through the budget—again. It was like having my molars ground with a power sander. Can't wait to do it again next month."

Matt chuckled. "I got you a cappuccino." He handed it over.

She took it and sipped, then whispered, "I love you."

"Are you saying that to the coffee or to me?"

"Yes." She grinned, took another long sip, and sighed. "Have you heard from Nolan? I texted Dana a while ago, but I haven't heard back from her."

"He's been keeping me updated. She's sleeping."

"Good." Bree exhaled in relief.

"I'll be right in." Matt began collecting his notes.

She nodded and ducked into her office. Todd came through the back door, his face red from the cold. He hung his jacket on the back of a chair.

"The sheriff wants to review," Matt said.

"OK. Give me ten minutes."

"Can I ask you a favor?" Matt asked.

"Sure."

Matt grinned. "It's about Cady's birthday."

Cady was Matt's sister. She and Todd were dating, another romance that made Matt happy. It was almost as if, now that Matt was happily involved in a great relationship, he wanted the same for everyone else.

"Sure. What's up?" Todd asked.

"I thought we could do a birthday party at the farm, but I wanted to make sure I wasn't interfering with any special plans you made."

Todd shook his head. "I'm taking her to Aruba as a present. She can't go until next month, so her birthday is open."

"Great."

"Can I help?" Todd asked.

"I got this." Matt hoped.

CHAPTER NINE

Matt went into Bree's office, his folder and notepad tucked under one arm. He eased into a chair facing her desk. "I picked up an extra tidbit on Kent's murder." Matt described the rosin trace evidence found on Kent's and Dana's clothes.

"Maybe our shooter plays the violin," Bree said. "Rosin creates the friction that produces the sound when the bow is drawn across the strings."

"That's a random piece of knowledge. Have you had it turn up in a previous case?"

"No." Bree set her cup on her blotter. "I played the violin when I was younger."

"You never told me that," Matt said. He slept at her house half of the time. Yet there was so much they didn't know about each other.

"I haven't touched my violin in years." She lifted a palm. "Kayla used to take lessons too. She lost interest. We now have two violins collecting dust in the backs of closets. Sometimes I feel bad for letting her quit, but she had enough on her plate keeping up with school after losing her mom."

"You prioritized, and you did a great job. Both kids are doing so well."

"They still struggle sometimes. I'm sure they always will. You never really recover from the death of a parent—especially a violent one—but

I'm proud of how far they've come." Bree knew all about living with the aftermath of violence. Matt wished she didn't.

He spotted a sheet of paper on her desk. "Is that a criminal background check on Kent McFadden?"

Bree placed a hand over the page. "Maybe."

"I thought it wasn't our case."

She crossed her arms. "I'm the sheriff. I can do a little digging if I want. It's in my jurisdiction. I'm not interfering or handling evidence."

Matt lifted a hand. "I'm not judging. I think we should do a lot of digging."

"Don't trust Hanover?"

Matt sighed. "His reputation is clean. He's known as a by-the-book, fair cop. His men respect him."

"But?"

"But I don't *know* him, and I don't like being shut out of the case." Matt crossed his arms, mirroring her. "You promised not to take over the case. You didn't say you would completely stay out of it."

"This is true. He did say he would keep us informed." But she didn't sound convinced.

"But how will we know if he does?" Matt didn't trust anyone, law enforcement or not. He'd been shot in a friendly-fire incident that he'd always suspected had not been an accident.

"I can't push myself into the active investigation," Bree said. "I decided in the very beginning that's not the kind of sheriff I want to be. I can't change my approach just because the case is personal. In fact, the personal nature of this case forces me to step back. I can't compromise my integrity." She rubbed a temple. "But I can't leave Dana out to dry either. She's my partner." Bree was nothing if not loyal.

"No one who knows you would ever doubt your integrity."

"But it's not about people who know me. I serve every citizen of Randolph County. The county has dealt with corruption for decades.

All those backroom deals cost the public. I won't—can't—be that sheriff. I won't abuse my office."

"Dana wouldn't want you to."

"I know." But Bree looked miserable.

"You like to be in control."

"I do," she admitted. "So we're going to have to hope Hanover is honest and keeps his word."

"Seems like." But Matt—who admittedly also preferred to be in control—didn't like it one bit. "So, what did the background check show?"

"Absolutely nothing. Kent has nothing on his record more serious than a couple of speeding tickets."

"Have you checked out his family and business partner?"

"No." Bree's voice suggested she meant *not yet*. "I'm hoping Hanover shares and I don't have to."

Her phone buzzed. She glanced at it. "Hanover."

"Speak of the devil."

She answered the call. "Sheriff Taggert."

"This is Chief Hanover."

"Can I put you on speaker?" Bree asked. "My investigator, Matt Flynn, is here."

"Yes," Hanover said, though he didn't sound happy about it. No one liked being on speaker. You never knew who was actually in the room. Matt always assumed he was on speaker when on professional calls.

Bree pressed the button, and Matt greeted Hanover.

"I promised to keep you updated," Hanover began. "We recovered two bullet casings and one slug that was buried in the ceiling, all 9mm. The bullet the surgeons extracted from Kent's chest is 9mm. Ammunition in Kent's gun safe was also 9mm. A Sig Sauer P229 was found on the floor. We've spoken to Dr. Veer Bhatt, Kent's partner, who says Kent's handgun is a Sig Sauer P229."

"9mm," said Matt.

"Yes."

"So it's possible Kent was shot with his own gun," Bree added. "A bullet in the ceiling might suggest McFadden and the shooter struggled over the gun. If the shooter had the gun, fired at McFadden, and missed, what are the chances the bullet would end up in the ceiling?" She leaned back.

"That would be a terrible shot." Hanover sounded doubtful. Was he thinking about the theory or just being tactful?

Bree continued. "Picture this. The shooter walks into the house through the unlocked front door. He surprised Kent, who was expecting Dana. Kent ran upstairs for his gun, but the shooter was right behind him. They wrestle. The gun goes off. The bullet hits the ceiling. Then the assailant overpowered Kent and shot him in the chest."

"That's a lot of conjecture," Hanover said. "Who would know Kent routinely left his door unlocked?"

Matt thought of Bree's stalker, pictured him staring at the back of her house. "Someone who was watching him, knew him, and/or planned to shoot him."

"Why didn't he finish him off right there and then?" Hanover asked. "He left while Kent was still alive."

"Because Dana pulled into the driveway," Bree said. "Kent was bleeding heavily. The wound was clearly dire. If the shooter had fired again, Dana might have heard and called 911 immediately."

Matt imagined Dana walking in, and the shooter gauging his best escape route. Had he come down the back steps hoping to sneak out the back door unseen?

"It's an interesting theory." Hanover emphasized the last word. "Let's stick with evidence for the time being."

Matt didn't roll his eyes, but he wanted to. Kent McFadden was dead. The only other person who knew what had happened was the killer.

"We'd appreciate copies of the crime scene photos," Bree said. Her tone indicated she was more than asking.

Hanover hesitated, then said, "Of course," in a reluctant tone. Matt thought the chief wasn't going to rush to fulfill that promise. "The ME finished the autopsy a short time ago. She officially declared the case a homicide."

This wasn't news. A gunshot to the chest couldn't be anything but a homicide. *Murder* and *homicide* were not synonymous terms. *Murder* was the unlawful, intentional killing of another human. Technically, the term *homicide* simply meant one human caused the death of another. There were many types of homicide, including murder, manslaughter, and justified—as in self-defense.

"Any interesting findings?" Bree asked.

"He was in good health before taking a bullet to the chest," Hanover said. "The shooter was standing level with Dr. McFadden. The gun was approximately three to four feet away when the shot was fired."

The official autopsy wouldn't be available for at least six weeks—maybe longer—because toxicology tests took time, but Hanover would have received a preliminary report. Neither Bree nor Matt requested a copy.

"I'll be giving a press conference tomorrow morning," Hanover said. "And I'll update you again in a couple of days."

"Thanks for the heads-up," Bree said.

Hanover ended the call. Bree and Matt both stared at the phone.

Bree tapped a fingertip on her chin. "He didn't mention the traces of rosin found on both Kent's clothes and Dana's. In fact, he didn't share anything interesting. We would have heard all of this in his press conference."

"Do you think he's holding more information back?" Matt asked.

She lifted a shoulder. "We have to assume he is."

CHAPTER TEN

Bree swallowed a huge gulp of cappuccino and hoped the hit of caffeine would ease her frustration. There was no point beating herself up over something she couldn't control. Chief Hanover was in charge of Kent's murder investigation, and she would have to live with that.

After a quick knock, Todd carried in a mug of coffee. His laptop was tucked under one arm. After closing the door, he took the seat next to Matt, facing Bree's desk.

While Todd settled in, Bree asked Matt, "How was your trip to forensics?"

Matt summarized his meeting with Rory. "Man between five eight and six feet tall, not old."

"That's it?" Bree raised a brow.

"Sadly."

She turned to Todd. "Did you recover any Timberland boots from the search of the Ekin house last night?"

Todd scrolled on his laptop. "No. We bagged three pairs of Air Jordan athletic shoes because the muddy footprint left at the murder scene was left by a pair of those. The sole is distinctive."

"As we know, every member of the Ekin family has a criminal record." Matt consulted his notes. "Mr. Ekin is currently serving a two-year sentence on a drug trafficking conviction." He flipped a page in his notepad. "Mrs. Ekin served six months on a drug possession charge and another for assault. She attacked another woman in her neighborhood for reporting the family's drug activity to the police. She dragged her out into the middle of the street by her hair, punched her in the face, and broke her nose."

"Making an example of her for the neighborhood," Bree said.

"And discouraging anyone else from sticking their nose into the family's business," Todd added. "Very true to family form. But the search of the house took a few hours, and Mrs. Ekin was outside the whole time."

"One of her sons was with her when I left. Did he stay as well?" Bree asked.

Todd closed his eyes. "No. He didn't stick around. It was just her. She called her lawyer, who came and made herself a nuisance. I saw them both frequently throughout the night."

Bree said, "I could see Mrs. Ekin ordering one of her boys to do the dirty work."

"As we know, Travis has two brothers, Benjamin and Ford." Matt turned his phone so Bree and Todd could see the screen. "Benjamin and Ford are both average-size guys. Either one of them could have left the footprints on your farm."

"What size were the Air Jordans at the Ekin house?" Bree asked.

"Ten and a half," Todd said. "But Travis was in custody, and neither of his brothers lives at that address."

"That's the one who threatened me outside the house." Bree pointed to Benjamin. "Criminal history?"

Matt answered, "Benjamin was recently released after serving eighteen months for selling Oxy. He was eligible for parole in six months, but he couldn't resist fighting in prison and ended up serving his entire sentence. That's the only time he's served despite a rap sheet that also includes arrests for possession of narcotics, assault, animal cruelty, and stalking."

"Stalking?"

"A girl refused to go out with him, so he followed her and tried to set her dog on fire. She stopped him. He broke her nose instead."

"Let me guess. She didn't file a complaint."

"She did not."

"Ford Ekin is currently out on parole from an assault conviction. He beat up his girlfriend's brother for trying to get her away from Ford. The brother did not file a complaint, even though Ford put out a cigarette on the guy's forehead." Matt paused. "Ford has also been arrested for narcotics possession and animal cruelty." He looked up from his phone.

"Are some people just evil?"

"Yes." Matt scanned his notepad. "Ford rents a unit at the trailer park off the interstate. The conditions of his parole prohibit him from living with known criminals. In his case, that's his whole family. Benjamin lives out near the train station at E & E Salvage Yard and Auto Parts, which his family owns."

The Grey's Hollow "train station" was just a platform with a parking lot.

"We should pay them a visit." Bree drained her cappuccino.

"I'll call Ford's parole officer and get his feedback." Matt made a note. "Then we can have a talk with both of them. I'd like to know where they were last night."

"Also, I received a nasty bit of email this morning." She pulled out her phone and opened her email. "I almost wrote it off as same old, same old. I ignore most of my hate mail. But RedBloodedMale03 wants to know who I fucked to get the job as sheriff, and that he won't forget what I've done."

"Isn't that what Mrs. Ekin said to you?" Matt asked.

"Yes. I'll forward the email to you." Bree had been appointed to the position of sheriff between elections after solving her own sister's murder the previous year. She hadn't been elected.

"The position had been vacant for a year," Matt pointed out. "Corruption mandated they bring in someone from the outside. The department was tainted. No one wanted the job."

"Maybe they were the smart ones." Bree sighed. Much of her first year had been spent dealing with leftover boys' club deputies who had been loyal to the previous sheriff. They'd wanted to scare her off the job, but she'd held firm. Instead, they'd all quit. Most had found jobs with other law enforcement agencies. She still had to deal with the contentious county board of supervisors, whose members didn't appreciate her attempts to modernize and diversify the department. But Bree was stubborn to the core. Luckily, most of the citizens of Randolph County seemed to appreciate her refusal to play politics.

"You're a great sheriff, and the residents know it. You care. You don't abuse your power or steal tax dollars. You make the public safer."

"But at what cost to my family?" Bree asked. She loved her job, but was it selfish of her to continue doing it when Luke and Kayla paid the price?

"What else does RedBloodedMale03 have to say?" Matt asked. "There has to be more for his email to stand out to you."

Bree cleared her throat and read aloud: "'Someone should teach you a lesson and put you in your place you dirty fucking bitch.' No punctuation, and that last part is in all caps."

"Of course it is." Matt rolled his eyes.

"I get all the best hate mail." Bree's joke felt inappropriate, but humor was how they coped. It kept the darkness from seeming overwhelming. "In light of all the other threats I've received, this one is pretty mild. If I hadn't been personally threatened with similar language and my barn hadn't been painted with *dirty cop* last night, I probably would have sent this to the folder and gone on with my day." Over the past months, she'd been threatened with hand-drawn pictures of her being gang-raped and been the target of deepfake pornography. Words seemed mild in comparison. "Threatening me is one thing. I'm a public figure. I can take it, but I won't let anyone frighten my family."

"The word choice of *dirty* definitely stands out, as does them not forgetting what you did." Despite the quips, Matt's jaw was set. "What are you going to do about it?"

"I already forwarded it to Rory to see if he can trace it," Bree said.

She thought about Luke's fear the previous night and queasiness gripped her belly. She checked the time on her phone. "I'd like to run by the house before we question Benjamin and Ford Ekin." She turned to Todd. "You work on wrapping up Travis's reports. Let's get his case file in perfect order and over to the DA. I won't let any intimidation from Travis's family jeopardize his conviction. I want that bastard to go to prison forever for what he did."

"I'm on it." Todd got up and left her office.

She turned to Matt. "We'll talk to Benjamin and Ford. Maybe by the time we're done, Rory will have traced the email from RedBloodedMale03."

"Maybe straight to the Ekin family," Matt said.

"It crossed my mind." She tilted her head. "I want to pick up Kayla from school, then stop home and check on Dana, and . . . things." The personal threats worried her.

Matt frowned. "The Ekin family is used to being able to bully their way out of trouble. We need to turn that around and send a solid message to them that any retaliation against the sheriff's department will bite them in the ass."

Bree's intercom beeped, and she pressed the button. "Yes."

Marge, her administrative assistant, said over the line, "We received a call to report a missing elderly man. Apparently, he wandered away from his house, which is in the middle of nowhere." Marge gave a location out in the countryside.

"I'll head over. Call Collins. I want the K-9 unit to respond. We need to find him before the temperature drops." Bree stood. The only predictable thing about a job in law enforcement was that everything could change in an instant. The day was cold and getting colder. An elderly man lost in the countryside wouldn't survive for long. She turned to Matt. "Would you follow up with Rory?"

"Yes," Matt said. "Make sure you eat something before you go hiking in this cold."

"I will." Bree wasn't hungry, but he was right. As usual.

"Also, trust the dog. She'll be great."

Bree nodded, but she didn't share his confidence. "Last night I was worried she wouldn't bite. Today, I'm worried she will."

"It takes time and experience for a new K-9 handler to know how their dog will react in different situations. Give Collins a chance," Matt said. "I'll pick up Kayla and check on things at the farm."

"Thank you," she said, grateful that Matt and his brother would keep her family safe while it felt as if she were continually putting them in danger.

CHAPTER ELEVEN

Matt called Rory as soon as Bree was out of the building. "Hey, Rory. Have you had a chance to trace the threatening email Sheriff Taggert received?"

"I did," Rory answered. "I also went back through the sheriff's hate mail folder but didn't find any more emails from RedBloodedMale03."

"I wish she didn't need an entire folder to store hate mail."

"Most of them are just people venting. Any that seem violent or concern her, she forwards for us to look into."

Still . . .

Rory continued. "Anyway. RedBloodedMale03 used an anonymous email account, but he didn't attempt to hide his location. I geolocated the IP address to a coffee shop in Grey's Hollow. He used the café's Wi-Fi to send the email at 11:06 this morning."

"I know the place." Matt made a note. He'd swing by on the way to the farm. "What else can you tell me?"

"This particular anonymous email service is inexpensive and not very robust. There's a chance we can trace him if the service required his personal information to set up an account." He hesitated. "I already contacted the service. They won't cooperate, so I'll need a warrant. I'll get back to you when I have more information. Could be a day or a few weeks before I hear anything."

"Why would someone not use a VPN or other means to conceal his whereabouts?"

"Who knows?" Rory asked. "He might not be very tech literate. Maybe he thinks the anonymous email account and public Wi-Fi are good enough to hide his identity."

"A cybercrime amateur." Matt wasn't sure if that was good or bad news.

"He definitely isn't experienced. A sophisticated hacker would have spoofed his IP address."

Matt thought about Benjamin and Ford Ekin. They were experienced criminals, drug dealers. How much did *they* use and understand technology? He texted Todd, asking about technology seized from the Ekin house. They would have Travis's phone and computers, but he didn't send the email. He was in jail at the time. They didn't have probable cause to obtain a warrant for either Benjamin's or Ford's phone.

"Thanks, Rory." Matt left the station. On the way to Bree's farm, he stopped at Lily's Internet Café, the place RedBloodedMale03 had used to send his email. Matt parked his SUV at the curb down the street and walked a block to the café. He didn't spot any security cameras on the outside of the building. He went into the café, which was busy with the end of the lunch rush. The email had been sent just a few hours before. Was the sender still here? Or had he left?

The shop seemed larger on the inside. Patrons occupied all but one of its twenty bistro tables. Matt scanned the patrons. Several groups of women clustered together. But thirteen people—predominantly males—worked alone on laptops. The clientele varied from early twenties to senior citizens. Assuming RedBloodedMale03 was actually male, Matt discounted the groups and the lone females. Eleven men remained.

A female barista worked behind the counter. A second young woman ran the register, and a third bused tables. All three women hustled to fill orders. The air smelled like freshly ground coffee and baked goods. The lunch menu included smoothies, salads, and a dozen varieties of panini. He texted his brother, asking if he or Dana wanted lunch. Nolan answered immediately. He didn't want anything, and Dana was still asleep.

Matt scanned the inside of the café for security cameras and spotted two: one trained on the register and a second aimed at the entrance. The barista had a unicorn tattoo on her inner arm and a name tag proclaiming her to be Lily. Matt ordered one black coffee, a half dozen blueberry scones, and a ham-and-cheese panini to go. He noted the daily Wi-Fi password written on the menu blackboard. "Are you the owner or manager?"

"I'm Lily." She pointed to her name tag. "I own the shop."

Matt flashed his county ID and introduced himself.

"Are you investigating a crime?" Her eyes gleamed. "Like on TV."

"I am," he said, not commenting on the TV comparison. "I'd like to see some of your security camera footage."

Lily barked out his panini order over her shoulder. Her employee closed the register drawer and began making Matt's sandwich.

"For what dates?" Lily filled a cup with black coffee and set it on the counter in front of him. She leaned over the counter. Her display of impressive cleavage felt intentional.

"This morning," Matt said. "How many cameras do you have?"

"Three. Front door. Back door. Register."

"Is the back door open to anyone except employees?"

"Never." She straightened, then twisted at the waist and pointed to each of the cameras. "The system is old and only stores footage for a week, but I should be able to pull this morning's footage no problem."

"Great. Thanks."

"Always happy to help the police." She propped one hand on a hip. Was she posing? She gestured to the table area with one hand. "I'm short-staffed today, but I can probably do it later today or tonight. Do you have an email address I can send the video to?"

Matt handed her a business card printed with his sheriff's department email address. "Thank you."

"You're welcome," she said in a suggestive tone. "Is this your phone number?"

"Yes," Matt said.

The barista pocketed the card with a smile.

Matt gestured toward the menu board. "How often do you change the Wi-Fi password?"

"Every morning." Lily batted her eyelashes. "I can't keep people from accessing the Wi-Fi without making a purchase, but I can make it more difficult."

The second employee brought Matt a bakery box filled with the scones and his panini. He paid and left the café with his food.

On the sidewalk, he tested the Wi-Fi with his phone. Unfortunately, he could tap into the signal from the sidewalk and street. He didn't lose connection until he was thirty feet from the door. He climbed into his vehicle and ate the panini in a few bites before pulling away from the curb.

He stopped at his own house. He'd bought the place after receiving his settlement following his shooting. His acreage included a large house, the kennels he'd built to house K-9s he'd planned to train, and plenty of land. His intention had been to build a business training K-9s. His sister had filled the kennels with rescue dogs before Matt could even get his business started. Now, with Greta successfully transitioning to a K-9 unit, he'd changed his goal to looking for rescues that would make good working K-9s. Sometimes, the most annoying, difficult-to-place, destructive dogs wanted jobs. There were dogs that just didn't make great house pets. The need to work was hardwired into their DNA.

Matt entered his kitchen. His retired K-9, Brody, greeted him with a nose bump and tail wag. "Good boy. Want to go see the kids?" When Matt first moved into the house, he'd loved the isolation. But then, he'd been mad at the world and had wanted to sulk in solitude. Now that he spent half his time at Bree's, with all its crowded chaos, his house felt lonely.

As if he agreed, Brody trotted to the hook by the door where his leash hung. Matt grabbed the leash, clipped it on his collar, and went back outside. He opened the rear door and lifted Brody into the seat. The dog tolerated the indignity with a humanlike expression of disdain. "Sorry, buddy. Vet's orders. We don't want another shoulder injury. Don't worry. Everyone knows you were a big bad police dog."

Brody sighed. He'd been Matt's best friend for the dark years, and Matt would do whatever he could to give his former partner the longest and best life possible.

Matt drove to Kayla's school. He waited his turn in the pickup line. When he pulled up to the curb, Kayla spotted him and raced over in her blue snow boots and matching jacket and a Philadelphia Flyers knit hat. She yanked open the door, tossed her backpack on the floor, and bounced into the seat. "Yay! Brody!" She half crawled over the seat to greet him. Brody did the same.

"Don't I get a hello?" Matt teased.

"Hello," Kayla called, her face buried in Brody's ruff. The dog's tail thumped with joy.

The woman in charge of the line gave Matt a *move it along* hand signal.

He nodded and waved, then called over the seat to Kayla, "Seat belt!"

Kayla flopped down. Ignoring the impatient glare of the line boss, Matt waited to hear the latch click before pulling away from the curb.

"Where's Aunt Bree? Is Dana OK? Why is Brody here?" Kayla fired questions like a three-shot burst from an AR-15.

"Work. Yes. He missed you," Matt answered without missing a beat.

Kayla grinned at him in the rearview mirror.

"Did you lose another tooth?"

"Yeah!" She poked her tongue in the gap. "The tooth fairy gave me five dollars."

"Nice." He narrowed his eyes with mock drama. "Now—where did you get that hat?"

She pulled it off and waved it at him, giggling. "Dana got it for me. She said to tell you Flyers rule and Rangers drool."

Matt couldn't stop the belly laugh. He and Dana had an ongoing rivalry with their favorite teams.

"How was school?" he asked.

"Mrs. Stewart wore blue boots. They were really pretty. Dixie Jennings didn't finish her math homework." Kayla chattered nonstop all the way back to the farm, and Matt learned everything that had happened at school that day.

Every. Single. Thing.

Matt was thrilled to hear it. A year ago, this little girl had been so sad, so traumatized. Listening to her happily recount her day felt like a privilege.

At the head of the driveway, he stopped, rolled down the window, and collected the mail. A delivery driver had wedged two plastic envelope packages and a small box into the space. Matt wiggled them free and stacked them and the mail on the passenger seat. As he coasted to the house, he was surprised to see his dad's car parked next to Nolan's pickup.

"Who's here?" Kayla peered from the back seat.

"My dad," Matt said.

"Why?"

"I don't know."

After helping Brody out of the SUV, he let the dog loose to race Kayla to the back door. The door opened, and Nolan let them inside. Carrying the mail, packages, and bakery box, Matt retrieved Kayla's backpack from the back seat and walked up the shoveled and salted path to the back porch. He felt like a pack mule. No one opened the door for him, and he'd brought scones. He juggled items, then used an elbow and his hip to open the door. Inside, the warmth heated his face.

Ladybug and Brody were happily sniffing each other. Nolan stood at the counter, drinking a green smoothie. Matt's dad had Kayla in a bear hug, her skinny jean–clad legs wrapped around his waist.

"Why are you here?" she repeated, her hands smooshing his white-whiskered cheeks.

"I came to cook," Matt's dad said. "Want to help?"

"Yes!" Kayla looped her arms around his neck.

He set her down. "Go wash your hands."

The little girl hesitated, then said in a serious tone, "I have to check on Dana first."

"Of course." Matt's dad pressed his finger to his lips in a *shhh* gesture. "She's in the living room. Tiptoe, OK? She's sleeping."

"OK." The little girl gave a solemn nod. She kicked off her shoes on the way across the room.

Matt dropped the mail on the sideboard, set the bakery box on the counter, and propped Kayla's backpack against the wall. He shed his own jacket, then picked up Kayla's from the floor and hung them both by the door. Finally, he hugged his dad. "Why are you here, really?"

"To cook, really." His dad turned back to the bag of potatoes he was emptying into a colander. He placed a kitchen chair in front of the sink and rummaged through three drawers for a vegetable brush. "You all can't live on pizza."

"We could," Matt said. "Or we could cook something."

His dad snorted. "I thought I'd check in on Dana too." He might have been retired, but once a family doctor, always a family doctor.

"Well, thanks. We appreciate it."

"Of course," his dad said. "She's family now."

The speed at which Matt's family had absorbed Bree's still astounded and pleased him.

Matt turned to his brother. "How's things?"

Nolan closed his laptop. "It's been very quiet here."

"Good." Matt crossed the kitchen and picked up Kayla's shoes.

She padded back into the room. "She's still sleeping." She looked to Matt's dad for reassurance. "Is that OK? You're a doctor, right?"

"I am, and that's exactly what she needs to get better." His dad waved her over to the chair and handed her the brush. "Can you scrub the potatoes?"

"I can!" The little girl went to work with amusing enthusiasm.

Matt's dad set an onion on the wood chopping block next to the sink and began slicing it. They worked in companionable silence, shoulder to shoulder, for a minute.

Kayla stopped and turned off the water. "Mr. Flynn?"

"Yes?" Matt's dad paused.

Kayla turned off the water. "Rylee Brockman has two grandpas, and I don't even have one. Would it be OK if I called *you* Grandpa?"

His dad coughed, and his voice sounded strained when he answered. "Of course you can! Nothing would make me happier."

"Can I call Mrs. Flynn Grandma?" Kayla asked.

"I'm sure she'd like that." Matt's dad wiped his eye on his sleeve. "This darned onion."

Matt knew the onion had nothing to do with it. Matt choked up a little too, and he was way too far away from the onion to blame those fumes.

Bree and her brother, Adam, were the kids' only living relatives. They'd lost their mother to violence, and their biological father—who'd never been involved with their lives—was in prison on a fraud charge. But they kept moving forward, making efforts every day to be happy despite their losses. Over the past year, Matt's parents had slowly brought Bree and her family into Flynn functions until it seemed odd if they weren't all together.

The back door opened again. Adam walked in and set a reusable grocery bag on the counter. "Hey. I just stopped over to see my horse and Dana. Brought her some of the stuff she likes from the Italian deli."

"Stay for dinner!" Matt's dad loved a crowd. "Kayla, better wash all those potatoes."

"OK, Grandpa!" She jumped down, raced over to hug Adam around the legs, then rushed back to washing potatoes.

Adam didn't even raise a brow at her use of *grandpa*. "I'll be out in the barn grooming Bullseye."

"Pet Pumpkin for me!" Kayla said.

"Will do." Adam left by the back door.

"You're going to feed everyone?" Matt asked his dad after Kayla turned on the water again.

His dad grinned. Not much made him happier than having a crew to feed or kids to fuss over. "You bet. I'll call your mother and tell her to come over too. Once I tell her Kayla wants to call her Grandma, she'll be in the car in seconds."

"I'm going to check on Beast." Matt grabbed some carrots from the fridge, put on his coat, and followed Adam out to the barn. Adam went into Bullseye's stall and began checking his blanket straps. The Standardbred stood calmly, extending his neck as Adam scratched an itchy spot under his mane.

Matt's Percheron nickered like a big baby. Matt grabbed a lead rope and led him out of the stall. Once Beast was secured on the crossties, Matt fed him a carrot, checked his blanket, and picked his dinner plate–size feet. Once he'd been fussed over, Matt put him away. He checked the blankets on Bree's, Kayla's, and Luke's horses. Then he carried each water bucket outside, dumped the ice, and refilled the buckets with fresh water from the spigot inside the barn, a chore that needed to be repeated several times a day in winter. "I'm investing in heated buckets next year."

"Bree looked into that. You'll need to upgrade the barn's electrical panel." Adam changed his own horse's water, then forked hay to all the animals.

"Worth it." Matt dumped the last bucket outside. Looking up, he saw the graffiti that still adorned the barn. He called through the open barn door, "Hey, Adam. Would you help me with something?"

"Sure." Adam swore when he joined Matt behind the barn.

Matt went to the garage for a tarp, some nails, and a hammer. "I don't want the kids to see this."

"No." Adam held one side of the material taut. "Is there anything else I can do to help?"

Matt drove the nails into the wood. "Would you drive Kayla to school in the morning? Then Nolan can stay on the farm with Dana." And Matt and Bree would have more time to work on the stalker case.

"Sure. I'll be here first thing," Adam said.

Matt wanted to find this bastard fast. The tarp covered the graffiti, but he was well aware that the threat remained. He glanced at Bree's brother, who was always quiet but was now staring at the tarp. "Are you OK, Adam?"

Adam shook himself. "Yeah." Bree's brother had nearly been killed during their last big case.

"You're sure?"

"Not gonna lie. I still have some tough moments, but overall, I'm doing OK."

"I'm always available to talk. I've been through some of my own shit."

"Thanks." Adam turned toward the barn door. "Honestly, focusing on the new horse has been great therapy." He jerked a thumb over his shoulder toward the tarp. "But things like this bring it back, you know?"

"Yeah, I do, and I'm impressed you can jump right in to help protect the kids after everything that happened."

Adam stopped and faced Matt. "I know I haven't always been the best uncle, but I'm not that person anymore. There's nothing I wouldn't do for those kids. They're what's important. I don't know why I didn't always see that. I was too focused on myself. I couldn't see beyond my own problems."

Adam was being hard on himself. He'd supported the kids financially for years. He'd paid the farm's bills when their mother hadn't been able to. But his relationship with Bree and the kids—and Matt—had grown over the past year. They'd all become family. Matt saw Adam as a younger brother.

"You and me both." Matt tossed an arm over Adam's shoulder. "We grow wise with age."

Matt glanced back at the ugly black tarp covering even uglier words, vowing silently to get the bastard who threatened his new family.

CHAPTER TWELVE

"How long has he been missing?" Standing on the patio, Bree stamped her feet. The pavers had been shoveled clear of snow, but the stone still felt like ice beneath her boots.

"About an hour." The nurse, Gavin Nielsen, ran a hand through his dark hair. The nurse was somewhere under thirty, athletic, with a poofy beard and short, gelled-up hair. Black-framed glasses completed the hipster look. "I've only been working for Mr. Pomar for a couple of days. I didn't think he was mobile enough to get out of the house, let alone go very far. Yesterday, he slept almost all day."

"Mr. Pomar has dementia?" Bree scanned the expansive rear yard covered in several inches of snow. The fifty-acre estate was located in Grey's Hollow, far outside of town, in the middle of nowhere. There were no close neighbors to canvass. Nothing in sight but yard, woods, and windswept fields.

"Yes." Nielsen pointed to the end of the patio. "His footprints lead away from the house. I tracked him across the backyard. But that line of trees is the end of the property. Beyond that, the ground rises and it's all empty meadow. The snow's been blown off the ground. I walked all the way around and couldn't find another footprint." He looked bewildered. "It's like he just disappeared."

"What was he wearing?" Bree asked.

"Jeans, a brown sweater, and orthopedic sneakers."

"Coat?"

Nielsen shook his head. "His coat is still hanging by the back door."

"Does he have another he might wear?"

"Maybe, but I doubt he'd think to put it on. Dementia patients live in the moment. They don't plan. They just do," Nielsen explained. "He was wearing heavy wool socks and a thermal base layer, at least, and a wool sweater. He gets cold around the house."

Bree's gaze went to the fields beyond. "Why would someone who gets cold run out into the snow?"

Nielsen shook his head. "You can't think about whys. They don't make sense."

"How incapacitated is Mr. Pomar?"

"He's only seventy-two years old. Before the dementia, I'm told he was very active when he was younger. I clearly overestimated his physical decline. Mentally, he's in worse shape. He can't form coherent thoughts. When he talks, it's gibberish."

"Does he respond to his name?"

"Not really. He's a little paranoid too, so there's no guarantee he won't hide."

Bree nodded. "We don't have time to waste. There's only about four hours of daylight left. It's already below freezing, and the temperature will drop fast as soon as the sun starts to go down." She used her radio to call for more deputies and reported a Missing Vulnerable Adult Alert. She also called for the ETA of the K-9 team.

Deputy Juarez arrived, and Bree filled him in. "We're going to search the whole house while we wait for the dog."

Juarez jerked a thumb toward the nurse, who was pacing the kitchen in front of the french doors. "Didn't he already check the house?"

Bree nodded, moving toward the stairway. "We had a dead dad and a missing kid in one of the first homicide cases I ever worked. She was autistic. Like Mr. Pomar, she was nonverbal and likely to hide from searchers. The dog found her under a neighbor's porch. She'd been within sight of her own house all along."

Bree and Juarez searched every closet and cabinet big enough to hold a human but found no sign of Mr. Pomar. She paused in what looked like it had been Mr. Pomar's study. On the huge mahogany desk was a framed photo of a middle-age Mr. Pomar. He had a rifle tucked in the crook of one elbow, and two black Labrador retrievers sat at his feet. He wasn't afraid of dogs, at least.

She found Nielsen in the huge country kitchen. Bree opened the map app on her phone. Using the satellite view, she studied the empty fields and patches of woods on the side of the estate where Mr. Pomar's tracks disappeared. The lake worried her, though it should be frozen. But how thick was the ice? If Mr. Pomar wandered onto it, would it hold?

Bree used her fingers to move the map on her phone. She scanned the rest of the surrounding area in case Mr. Pomar somehow got turned around. The Pomar estate sat on Rural Route 18. A horse farm was to the south. Surely, if he'd gone there, someone would have spotted him. Less than a mile to the north lay E & E Salvage Yard and Auto Parts. Bree hoped he hadn't roamed in that direction. A salvage yard was inherently dangerous, and that property was owned by the Ekin family. Bree hated to think of a vulnerable old man wandering onto their property.

Nielsen supplied a recent photo of a thin, older man staring into the distance with a vacant expression. His blue eyes simply looked lost in a way that broke Bree's heart.

The K-9 unit rolled up, and Deputy Collins stepped out. She wore gloves and thick boots. Her blonde hair was tucked under a knit hat. She slung a small backpack over her shoulder as she approached. Bree could see the black dog in the back of the SUV, watching.

Bree nodded toward the house and summed up the situation. "I don't know if he'll even respond to his name. We don't know if you or the dog will frighten him, but we have to find him ASAP." Hypothermia and frostbite would set in quickly in this weather. "Greta's good at this too?"

Collins nodded toward her vehicle. "She's an all-round rock star."

"She won't attack like she did with Travis?" Bree asked.

Collins didn't look so sure. "This is our first search for an elderly man. We know she's good with kids." She tilted her head, thinking. "I'll keep her leashed."

While Matt had fostered Greta, the dog had spent time at Bree's farm to acclimate her to kids and large animals. But K-9s were taught to hunt suspects. Bree could understand how dogs differentiated kids from adults. But how could they determine the difference between a good adult who was lost and a bad one who was dangerous? If Mr. Pomar ran from the search team, would Greta see an elderly man or a fleeing suspect?

"I'll let you work." Bree stepped back. She had to trust Collins to handle her dog.

Collins opened the rear door of her unit. The dog leaped out with the grace of an athlete. Bree saw a flash of Greta biting Travis's leg, then another of her standing over him, blood dripping from her mouth. The sun gleamed on her jet-black coat. The dog was gorgeous, but there was a tension in her lithe body, an underlying lethalness that couldn't be denied. But she could mean the difference between life and death for a sick, old man.

The black dog paced at Collins's side, her tail waving, like it had when she'd arrived at Travis's house.

"She's wearing boots." The sight of the dog trying to shake off a bright red bootie made Bree smile.

"She doesn't love them." Collins adjusted one of the straps. "But her feet need to be protected from the ice and snow. We don't know how long we'll be out there. Once she starts working, she'll forget she's wearing them." Collins straightened. Greta shook a paw and gave her handler a comical side-eye.

"Do you need something that smells like the missing man?" Bree asked.

Collins shook her head. "No. Greta will pick up the scent from his tracks."

Nielsen met them at the edge of the patio. He'd donned a coat, hat, gloves, and heavy boots. He also carried a backpack. "I'm going with you. I can treat Mr. Pomar wherever you find him."

"Do you have a coat in that bag for him?" Bree asked.

He nodded. "Along with dry socks and boots, gloves, a hat, two thermal blankets, electrolyte solution, energy bars, a basic first aid kit—"

Bree held up a hand to stop him. "I believe you."

Unfortunately, having a nurse on hand might be important.

More deputies arrived, along with a few uniforms borrowed from neighboring Scarlet Falls. Bree dispatched men to check outbuildings. The estate included a four-bay detached garage, an old barn currently used for garage overflow, and several storage sheds. Even though the nurse had said he'd looked, they'd look again. Other uniforms drove their cars on the surrounding country roads, in case Mr. Pomar took the easiest path—paved streets. Bree was still hoping Mr. Pomar, like the child in Philly, had stuck close to home.

"Juarez, you're with me," Bree said.

The four humans and one dog went to the back of the house and crossed the patio. Collins let out Greta's lead, giving the dog about twenty feet of range. As Collins had promised, once Greta was given a command, she went to work with impressive focus. The dog picked up the footprints immediately and started across the backyard. There were two sets of tracks leaving and one set returning.

"Are these extra tracks yours?" she asked Nielsen.

"Yes. I thought he couldn't have gone far." Nielsen adjusted his hat to cover his earlobes.

Bree stooped to examine the single prints until she found one that was very clear. The tread had swirls and bore the brand name Orthofeet.

"Does Mr. Pomar have family?" Bree asked.

"He has two kids. They moved to California and have families of their own."

"Did you call them?" she asked.

Nielsen focused on the ground. "Not yet. They're too far away to help, and I didn't want to panic them if we found Mr. Pomar right away."

Or he didn't want to get fired for losing his patient his first week on the job.

"They're not close to their father?" Bree asked.

Nielsen shrugged. "They hired me through an agency. I spoke to his son on the phone yesterday, to let him know how Mr. Pomar and I were getting along. The conversation was all business. He didn't get personal, so neither did I."

To Bree, that seemed pretty cold, but then, she knew nothing of the family's dynamics. As she well knew, not everyone's life was an episode of *Full House*.

The dog led the team across the backyard. The ground rose. As Nielsen had stated, wind had swept the ground mostly clear. What snow remained was dry and powdery. The footprints stopped but Greta continued on, nose to the ground, following an invisible trail.

They passed through a patch of winter-bare oaks, where the ground dipped. Bree spotted a few clear footprints beneath the trees. She noted the swirls and brand name in the tread, then took a photo. Her phone would automatically geotag the photo with the GPS location should they need to backtrack for any reason.

The visible trail disappeared again when the terrain rose and opened up. They crested a rise. The wind hit her smack in the face like an icy slap. The cold burned her cheeks. She turned up her collar. Despite her base layer, body armor, uniform, and jacket, she felt the chill through to her bones. How could Mr. Pomar still be on his feet, wearing only a sweater and sneakers? Wool socks were a good choice, but jeans would stay wet. The fabric might even freeze.

Bree scanned the landscape. A large lake stretched out in front of them, its muddy gray surface frozen and windswept.

The dog hesitated, circling and sniffing.

"Did she lose the scent?" Nielsen hunched his shoulders and braced against the wind. He hadn't complained once during the trek, but he was shivering.

"The wind messes with the scent cone," Collins explained. "She'll pick it up again. Give her a minute."

Bree scanned the frozen lake, looking for anything denim blue. Unfortunately, a brown sweater would blend with much of the winter landscape.

The wind ebbed. The dog's head lifted. She shifted from sniffing the ground to sniffing the air. Then she surged forward, straight across the frozen lake. Collins paused at the shore.

"Hold on. Make sure the ice is thick enough." Bree walked out onto the ice and bounced. Nothing gave. Nothing cracked.

"The temperature has been below freezing for weeks," Collins said.

"The kids have been playing hockey on the lake near my place since Christmas," Juarez added.

Nielsen's voice quavered. "We have to keep going."

"We're not giving up yet." Bree's teeth were chattering and her body shook in an involuntary shudder. How was Mr. Pomar still moving?

She checked her watch. It was nearly four o'clock. The sun would set around four thirty, leaving them another thirty minutes of twilight. Without the sun, the temperature would continue to drop, and darkness would make the search difficult and dangerous. Nielsen was right.

Going around the lake would take at least an hour. They didn't have the time.

"OK," Bree said. "But spread out to avoid putting too much weight in one place."

They spaced out every dozen feet and started across. The ice held strong, but the slippery surface forced them to slow. Fifteen minutes later, they reached the other side. Suddenly, Greta's head snapped up and she lunged toward a patch of woods. As they reached the tree line, the snow underfoot thickened again, and footprints appeared.

Greta and Collins broke into a jog, with Bree and Juarez right behind them. The nurse kept pace. He was clearly fit, but then, nurses often had to lift patients, so strength must help.

They entered the trees. Greta lunged, whining, toward a clump of evergreens. Collins held her back, and Bree moved forward. On the other side of a scotch pine, she spotted a dark-blue leg and pointed. "There he is! Keep the dog back."

Mr. Pomar sat curled in an upright fetal position at the base of the tree, his back to the trunk. To Bree's surprise, he was conscious. He turned toward her with questioning but grateful eyes. Snow dotted his eyebrows. He wore gloves and a thick fleece pullover on top of his sweater.

"Who? House in yard truck." His words trembled as he shivered.

Bree yelled, "Nielsen! Get over here."

The nurse jogged to her side and dropped to his knees beside the old man. Nielsen tugged off his gloves, opened his backpack, and started taking out items. "Somebody change his socks and shoes."

Twenty feet away, Collins was praising the dog. Greta whined, clearly wanting to get close to the man she'd found. She didn't look vicious like she had with Travis, but Collins obviously wasn't taking any chances. Bree now knew that the wagging tail didn't convey happiness.

Juarez planted himself next to the nurse and started removing the old man's wet sneakers. Mr. Pomar didn't object. He watched with detached curiosity.

Bree opened the map on her phone. There was a road just on the other side of the trees. They wouldn't have to carry Mr. Pomar all the way back to the house. She called in their position and requested an ambulance, then arranged a ride for the rest of them.

"We need to move him to the road." She gestured. "It's less than a quarter mile in that direction."

Mr. Pomar now wore dry boots, a hat, and thick gloves. He was wrapped up in a coat and Mylar blankets. Only his pale face showed. He blinked, his eyes locked on the sheriff patch on Bree's jacket.

"You," he said. "Bright noise or red. Boom."

Bree had no idea what he meant.

Mr. Pomar jabbed a glove at her. "You."

"I'm sorry," she said. "I don't understand. We're going to get you somewhere warm and dry, Mr. Pomar. You're going to be fine."

Mr. Pomar shook his fists, visibly frustrated by his inability to communicate. His eyes met hers, and goose bumps that had nothing to do with the cold rose on her arms. There was something in his expression she couldn't identify, but it chilled her to the core. And just like that it was gone.

Nielsen stuffed Mr. Pomar's wet shoes and sneakers into the backpack. "I don't think he's injured. Just hypothermic. I can carry him."

But when he tried to pick up his patient, Mr. Pomar thrashed his arms, swatting at the nurse. "Gone. Red and run." His speech might be garbled, but he was getting his meaning across.

"I think he can walk." Bree was impressed with his physical strength. She reminded herself that the dementia made him seem older than he was.

Juarez stood. Bree's youngest deputy wasn't particularly big, but he was solid. He and Nielsen lifted Mr. Pomar to his feet. Draping one of his arms over each of their shoulders, they half carried him to the road.

Fifteen minutes later, Mr. Pomar and his nurse were on their way to the hospital. Patrol cars transferred Bree, Juarez, and the K-9 team back to the estate, where their vehicles waited. The extra uniforms had cleared out after searching the outbuildings.

Freezing, Bree slid into her SUV, started the engine, and turned her heater to max. She saw Juarez doing the same in the vehicle next to her. In the K-9 unit, Collins rubbed her hands in front of the dashboard vents. The only one who wasn't cold was Greta, whose double coat was made for the cold weather.

A quick burst of anxiety flooded her. Bree checked her sprinting pulse with a deep breath. She should be happy. They'd found Mr. Pomar. He was going to be all right. But she couldn't shake a sense of foreboding. Adrenaline was surging through her veins as if she'd walked into a convenience store robbery. She glanced around. The K-9 unit was pulling away. Juarez was still in his vehicle, no doubt making notes for his report before he forgot the details. He'd drive to the hospital and get a statement from Nielsen—and Mr. Pomar, if possible.

While her vehicle warmed up, Bree checked her messages. Nothing from Matt or Nolan or Dana. Another punch of nerves hit her.

Relax.

They knew she was tied up. In an emergency, they would have called. No news was good news.

But she texted Matt anyway. He responded immediately and asked when she would be home. She exhaled. She replied: NOW.

Adrenaline letdown didn't help. Many times, after a situation was resolved, Bree experienced delayed anxiety, as if her body were allowed to react now that she didn't need to be useful. She should go back to the station and fill out a report. But she wasn't going to do that. She was going home to have dinner with her family. Though Matt had said they were fine, she needed to see them with her own eyes.

CHAPTER THIRTEEN

Dana saw Kent's shooter—running at her—running away from the house. A woman flashed. Pale flesh. No, she was blue—dead? Her eyes were open and looking straight at Dana. Not dead yet. Maybe she was dying.

Blood, the source not clear, spread in an expanding puddle. Then the man was on top of the woman, his hands around her throat. The woman morphed into Dana. She gasped and struggled to breathe until her lungs ached and burned. Pain burst through her head. Tiny pinpricks of light dotted her vision.

In the dream, she—they—became one, paralyzed, unable to fight back as he choked the life out of her. His weight pinned her, crushing her throat as he leaned on his hands. Even as she lay there, helpless, she knew the sequence was all wrong. It wasn't a replay but a rewrite. Yet she was locked into it, forced to experience this alternate, fatal, fucked-up version as it played out. Gunshots sounded, splattering more blood on the walls, on the floor.

On her.

She startled awake.

The woman . . . In the dream, she'd looked like a cartoon—not an actual woman.

What the actual fuck?

Flashbacks. No, dreams. Weird-ass, disturbing dreams worthy of an M. Night Shyamalan movie. Her recent trauma had merged with crime scenes she'd walked over her lengthy career, with her imagination doing its damnedest to create a terrifying mishmash of violence.

She lay still, breath rasping, orienting herself. Pain thumped through her head. Sleep threatened to drag her back under like a pair of hands, but she fought it. The dream had been exhausting, and she didn't want to experience another. It felt as if she'd barely blinked, but the dimness in the room told her the sun had set.

She heard the crunch of tires on snow outside. Someone was here. They didn't drive around to the side door, so it wasn't family.

Package delivery maybe?

Dana reached for the coffee table and tapped her phone. It was after six in the evening. She'd slept all day? Her brain needed more. She felt like she could sleep for a week and it wouldn't be enough.

Sitting up, she swung her legs off the couch and nearly stepped on Ladybug. The dog sat between the coffee table and the couch. Dana gave her a rub behind the ears. The pain crescendoed like an orchestra. With her elbows on her knees, Dana rested her head in her hands.

Rushing to answer the door wasn't an option. That telltale spot between her shoulder blades itched, like she was being watched. Dana raised her head, slowly.

Kayla and Brody stood in the doorway. How long had they been there?

Watching her . . .

She hadn't known what it would be like when she'd offered to help Bree raise the kids, but learning that kids could be kind of creepy hadn't been on her list of expectations. She tugged the top of her sweatshirt higher to cover the bruises around her neck.

Kayla turned around and yelled, "She's awake!" The little shout bounced around inside Dana's skull like a hockey puck. The little girl tiptoed over, which was comical considering how loudly she'd shouted. "Are you better now?"

Brody followed the child, sticking close, as if he were babysitting.

Dana gritted her teeth and smiled, afraid she wasn't going to pull it off. "I'm a little better," she lied.

George Flynn walked into the room. Matt's seventy-year-old father was still a big man. With his thick white hair and beard, he looked like a fit Santa. What was Santa's name in Scandinavia?

Dana eyed him suspiciously. "Why are you here?"

"He's cooking," Kayla said.

Dana gave George a look, which he ignored. They both knew he was being a busybody. He touched the top of Kayla's head, his fingertips gently turning her around. "You'd better get back to that cookie dough. It's not going to mix itself."

She skipped off. "OK, Grandpa." Brody followed at the child's heels.

"Grandpa?" Dana asked.

He grinned. "Her idea. Isn't it great?"

Dana felt her annoyance fade into mush. "Yeah. It is."

He crouched in front of Dana and stared into her eyes for a few seconds. "I'll get you something for that headache." He went back to the kitchen, returning in a minute with a glass of water, a bottle of over-the-counter pain relievers, and a sleeve of crackers. "How's the throat?"

Dana tugged at the neck of her hoodie. "A little sore. Not bad, though."

Ladybug eyed the crackers and licked her lips.

"Not for you," George admonished.

The dog sighed and slid to the floor. But Dana kept the crackers close. The pudgy pointer mix could move faster than one would suspect given her lack of obvious athleticism. But then John Belushi hadn't looked like he could do cartwheels, and yet . . .

Dana swallowed the pills with water and nibbled on a cracker. The scent of something roasting drifted from the kitchen. She hadn't eaten all day. The smell should have been appealing, and yet it wasn't. "What are you making?"

"Scalloped potato casserole, roast chicken, green beans, cookies." He ticked the items off on his fingers. "Matt brought scones. Adam brought burrata and that prosciutto you like from the Italian deli. I used your leftover french bread to make crostini. Hope you don't mind. It's a shame to let fresh bread go to waste. Are you hungry?"

"I wish." As much as her heart warmed that the family had brought her all her favorite foods, the thought of eating made her nauseated.

"Let those painkillers work, then you'll eat something," George said, as if it were decided.

She heard a car door close. Heavy footfalls thumped up the front steps. A minute later, someone knocked on the front door.

Nolan came through the doorway. "I've got it." His sleeves were pushed up, revealing muscled, tattooed forearms. Dana fixated on the blue ink. Something flashed in her mind. A blindfolded woman. It was gone before she could tell what it was. She tried to bring the image back, but concentrating amplified the pain in her head. Frustrated, she let it go.

Nolan opened the front door. Ladybug rushed forward. Nolan held her off with a leg across her chest.

Chief Hanover stood on the front porch. He looked beyond Nolan to Dana. "I have some follow-up questions for Ms. Romano."

Nolan shook his head. "Ms. Romano is—"

Dana held up a hand. "It's OK, Nolan." She shifted her gaze to Hanover. "You'll have to give me a minute. I need coffee."

George frowned. "You shouldn't be drinking coffee." He glared laser beams at Hanover. "Or being questioned. You need to rest."

"Just a little coffee?" Dana begged. "A very small Americano."

George sighed. "*One* shot of espresso." He held up a finger. "One. Just to ward off a caffeine-withdrawal headache."

Dana smiled. "Thank you."

George huffed and returned to the kitchen.

Hopefully, caffeine, crackers, and the pain relievers would ease the ache in her head and enable her to think more clearly. Because nothing about Kent's shooting made sense.

Nolan was still blocking the doorway. He moved back slightly, grabbing Ladybug by the collar and looking over his shoulder at Dana. "You're sure you're up for this? You look terrible."

Like a vampire, Hanover waited to be invited inside.

She felt terrible, but avoiding Hanover wouldn't help find the man who had killed Kent and given her this concussion. She nodded.

Nolan opened the door. "Come in."

Hanover stepped across the threshold. The door banged shut, and Nolan released the dog with a deceptive smile. Clearly, he didn't like Hanover bothering Dana. "She's very friendly."

Ladybug slammed into Hanover's knees, buckling them. To give him credit, he handled the exuberant dog with grace, crouching to pet her. Excited, she nearly knocked him flat.

"Ladybug, sit." Nolan's command was a few seconds too late, which seemed intentional.

The dog complied, pawing at Hanover's ankles, her chubby butt bouncing on the floor.

Dana got up and headed to Bree's office, leaving Hanover to follow her. She carried the glass of water and sleeve of crackers with her. In the office, she turned and pressed the backs of her legs against Bree's desk. Her bruised back was aching too much to sit. Besides, she didn't want Hanover to get too comfortable. She wasn't up for a long interview.

George appeared at the door with a demitasse cup. He didn't offer Hanover anything. Dana sipped the coffee and willed the caffeine into her bloodstream. What she needed was an IV infusion of espresso.

The chief didn't sit. He shifted his weight back and forth. "How's the head?"

"Not great," Dana admitted.

He frowned and touched his own throat. "That looks painful."

"Yeah."

Hanover winced. "I'll get right to it, then. No reason to drag this out. You know the drill."

"I appreciate that." Instead of easing her heartache, the espresso was souring her stomach. She switched back to water and ate a cracker.

Like a magician, Hanover produced a spiral notebook that looked too large for his pocket. "Did Dr. McFadden ever talk about his ex-wife?"

Dana sipped more water. Her gut churned as she tried to remember. "A little. The divorce hadn't been final for long, but they'd been separated for a while before that."

"What was the nature of his relationship with his ex?" Hanover asked. "Was he angry or sad?"

"He didn't seem angry." That would have been a red flag for Dana. She didn't date men with unresolved relationships or anger issues. "He said he was ready to move forward with his life."

"No jealousy? No cheating? No resentment?" Hanover continued to push.

"Not that he mentioned. He said he and his wife had both been dedicated to their careers and had grown apart over the years." His explanation had resonated with Dana after her demanding career and two failed marriages. She did not add this personal information, however. Experience told her to keep her answers on point. Hanover didn't need to know anything that wasn't directly related to Kent's murder.

"Did you ever meet Kent's sister?"

"No."

"What about his business partner?"

"No."

Hanover made notes. "Have you thought about the shooter? Can you add any more details about him?"

"I've been asleep. I haven't thought about anything."

A shadow appeared in the doorway. Matt, and he did not look pleased. "Everything OK in here?"

Hanover's eyes flickered to Matt for a nanosecond. Matt looked ready to toss him out on his ass.

"Fine," Dana assured him. "We won't be long." She wasn't going to last more than another five minutes.

Matt backed away. Hanover frowned at the still-open door, then turned back to her. "I understand you have a concussion, but I need some way to track this shooter. We have nothing. No footprints in the snow. No sign of forced entry. No one saw his vehicle. The neighbors are too far away for their security cameras to be useful. Dr. McFadden didn't have cameras." His tone seemed incredulous at this. "It's like this guy was a ghost."

Or he'd planned the murder.

A professional?

She said nothing. Hanover was looking for evidence. He didn't need her conjectures.

Dana had been leaning on the desk. Now she walked around it and lowered her body into the desk chair. She rested her elbows on the desk and stared at the giant calendar. "I don't know how much more I can tell you. I didn't date Kent long enough to know his personal history."

"OK. Tell me again about your assailant." Hanover grabbed the back of a chair, spun it to face the desk, and sat.

She dropped her head into her hands for a few seconds, then lifted it and repeated the description she'd given him in the hospital.

"You don't remember anything else?" Hanover asked.

Dana was afraid her memories were fuzzier instead of clearer. "No. I'm sorry. If anything comes to me, I'll call you."

Hanover sighed, the sound full of frustration. "OK. Thank you for your time," he said, looking as tired as Dana felt.

Matt must have been lingering by the door, because the second Hanover stepped out of the office, Matt said, "I'll see you out."

Dana left the room and carried her coffee cup into the kitchen. She stopped at the entrance. George was pulling a roasting pan out of the oven. His wife, Anna, helped Kayla transfer cookies from a baking sheet. Adam was crowding extra chairs around the table, while Luke set out plates and utensils. With the oven and stove running, the room was hot, even stifling. Dana felt a sweat break out at the base of her spine.

Adam and Luke both greeted her with the sort of gentle hugs reserved for frail ninety-year-olds, as if they were afraid she might break.

"Oh, Dana." Anna Flynn's voice rang with pity. "You poor thing." She was a robust woman with kind blue eyes that missed nothing.

"I'll be OK in a few days," Dana said without much confidence.

She wasn't fooling Anna, who had raised three children and been married to a physician for most of her adult life. "Why don't you sit down? I could make you some tea," Anna offered.

"We're holding dinner for Bree, but I could feed you now if you're hungry," George said.

"I'm fine waiting for Bree." Dana wasn't very hungry anyway. Through the kitchen window, she spotted Nolan and Matt on the back porch. "Actually, I really want a little fresh air." She headed for the back door. She slipped into her boots and down parka.

"Fresh air always helps," George encouraged.

She stepped onto the back porch. The crisp evening air felt refreshing, and her headache eased a little. Brody stood between Matt and Nolan.

Despite the cold, neither of the brothers wore a jacket, nor did they seem cold. They glanced at her as she approached.

"Feeling any better?" Nolan asked.

Not really. But she nodded. "I'll live."

"Good to hear," Matt said. "We were discussing improvements to the security system."

"I think we should add a camera to the rear of the barn," Nolan said. "Last night's visitor pointed out it's a blind spot."

Dana asked, "What happened last night?"

Matt described the graffiti left on the back of the barn.

"No one told me about the graffiti," Dana protested. She'd only known Luke had spotted a trespasser. Though what would she have done from the hospital?

"I should have mentioned it this morning," Nolan said. "But you were indisposed."

"I was," she admitted. "Has Bree gotten any particular threats lately?"

"A couple," Matt said. "She busted a very bad person yesterday."

Something thumped from the kitchen. Matt started for the door. "I'll meet you inside. Go ahead and order that camera."

"The graffiti explains why you're here." Dana glanced at Nolan. "Bree's worried about the kids."

"She's worried about you too," Nolan said. "There's a lot going on right now."

"That's the truth." Her gaze dropped to his arm. To his full-sleeve tattoo of a hawk. The hawk dived for prey, talons and beak pointing down Nolan's corded forearm. The rest of the ink was hidden by his shirt, but she'd seen it before. There were pictures of him shirtless pre- and post-fights all over the internet and on the walls of his MMA studio. The outstretched wings extended up and around his arm and shoulder. It was a work of art.

But Dana wasn't seeing the hawk at that moment. The image of the blindfolded woman flashed in her mind, clearer this time. She carried a sword in one hand and a set of weighing scales in the other. Dana grabbed Nolan's arm and pushed his sleeve past his elbow.

He raised an amused brow. "You want me to take off my shirt?"

She almost said yes, then heat flooded her cheeks. She dropped his arm. "No. Sorry. I've been seeing an image on and off. I couldn't figure out what it was. Now I know. Kent's shooter had a tattoo. Can you draw?"

"Not really."

"Adam." Dana headed for the door, and they went inside.

"Adam, can we borrow you for a minute?" Nolan asked.

Adam set a glass of water on the table. "Sure." He followed them into the office.

Dana shoved a notepad and pencil at him. "I need you to draw a tattoo."

"OK." Adam sat at the desk, pencil in hand like an obedient grade-schooler.

Matt walked in. "What's going on?"

Nolan explained.

Dana gestured toward Nolan's forearm. "The woman was oriented the same way as Nolan's hawk." She described the tattoo in as much detail as she could see, rushing to get out the words before the image vanished from her mind again.

Adam sketched and showed her the pad.

"The size is right, but her face wasn't that realistic." Frustrated, Dana rubbed her temples. "I don't know how to describe it. More like a cartoon, but not one for little kids. Does that make any sense?"

Nolan turned on the computer and hit a few keys. He turned the screen to face her. "Here are a whole bunch of tattoos that fit that description."

Dana pointed to one in the middle of the page. "The face was more like this one."

"Like comic book or graphic novel style?" Adam asked.

"I think so." Dana had never read a graphic novel, and her comic book experience leaned toward an occasional superhero movie. "Her sword wasn't this prominent. Just the tip showed over her shoulder."

Adam sketched. "How's this?"

Dana made a few more comments, and Adam changed the drawing.

"That's close. Really close." She stared at the new image. "It's Themis. I should have recognized her right away."

"Themis?" Matt asked.

"The Greek goddess of law and order," Nolan said.

Dana nodded. "She and the Roman goddess, Justicia, are the basis for Lady Justice. You can see her depicted on the Supreme Court Building. The scales represent balance. The sword gives her power. The blindfold represents impartiality so she can render justice regardless of identity, wealth, or power." Dana dropped into a chair, her headache roaring back like a subway train. "I have to call Hanover. He'll want this drawing ASAP."

"I'll do it." Matt nodded. "And I'll make copies."

Dana shivered, despite the warmth of the office. She'd noticed more about the shooter than she'd first thought. How much more would she remember?

And if he found out, would he try to silence her?

Chapter Fourteen

Bree had cranked the heat in her SUV all the way back to the farm, but she couldn't get warm. She wanted a huge plate of steaming-hot food. She didn't even care much what was on the plate. While she drove, she left a message for the hospital social worker about Mr. Pomar. His home situation needed to be assessed by a professional to make sure he was safe in the future. At the house, she slowed near the mailbox, preparing for the turn, when she spotted a Redhaven police vehicle in the driveway.

Annoyance and apprehension filled her. She knew Hanover would have follow-up questions for Dana, but she didn't like him at her house. What was the alternative, though? Haul Dana into the station with her concussion? That would be worse.

Bree squeezed her SUV between Nolan's truck and Matt's Suburban. Adam was here, and both of Matt's parents' cars. Hanover was coming down the front porch steps as Bree got out of her vehicle. They met at the edge of the parking area. He held a folder tucked under his arm.

"What's happening with the case?" Bree asked.

"Ms. Romano remembered a tattoo on the shooter's forearm," Hanover answered. "Your brother drew it." He opened the folder and drew out a paper.

Bree shined her cell phone flashlight on the page. "Is that a comic book hero?"

Hanover shrugged. "Ms. Romano said it's Lady Justice. I didn't recognize it."

"Any other developments?"

"Not really, but Ms. Romano didn't remember this tattoo until after she talked to me this afternoon," Hanover said. "Fortunately I was still in the area when Flynn called about it and could just double back." He tucked the paper into the folder and, looking doubtful, added, "Maybe she'll remember something else."

Bree gestured toward the sketch. "Hopefully that helps."

He lifted the folder. "I need a suspect to match the tattoo. So far, we have none."

"None?"

"Everyone we talk to loved Dr. McFadden. He even had a good relationship with his ex-wife, who is currently out of the country with a medical nonprofit organization. His business partner is clean and also has a solid alibi. He's skiing in Utah this week."

"Did forensics come up with anything?"

"Trace evidence is still being processed," Hanover said evasively, then continued walking toward his vehicle. "Have a good night."

"You too." Bree noted that he still hadn't mentioned the light rosin found on Kent's and Dana's clothes. She wasn't sure what to think of that. Would she have withheld information from another jurisdiction? Only one she didn't trust. She put it aside for the night. She couldn't change his mind, and her family deserved her full attention.

The wind shifted, burrowing inside the neck of her jacket. She hurried up the walk and into the house. Heat enveloped her. Bodies crowded the kitchen. Ladybug greeted her with a full-body ram. Bree braced herself with one hand on the wall and gave the dog an ear rub. Brody was more polite. The cat watched, disgusted, from the top of the refrigerator. After toeing off her boots, Bree spotted Dana sitting at the table. Her face was pale and tight with pain, but she was vertical. Her eyes were clearer too.

Relieved, Bree asked, "You OK?"

Dana nodded.

"Everything go OK with Hanover?" Bree washed her hands.

"I guess." Dana made a *meh* gesture. "I have to go into the station tomorrow to sign my formal statement. I wish I remembered more. My statement is going to be short."

"The tattoo is a start," Bree said. "Maybe more details will come."

Dana shrugged. "You find the missing old guy?"

"Yeah. It reminded me of the Tyson case, remember that one?"

Dana nodded. "Dead dad, missing kid."

"I was hoping he'd be close to home like the little girl was." Bree dried her hands on a kitchen towel.

"No such luck?" Dana asked.

Bree shivered. "I can't believe how far he walked. No coat. Wearing sneakers. He was in amazingly good shape when we found him." She lowered her voice. "I can't imagine being that confused and helpless. I don't mind getting old, but dementia is a monster."

"It's fucking terrifying," Dana said.

Matt greeted Bree with a kiss. "You're freezing. Go grab a shower. Dinner is almost ready."

Bree jogged upstairs. She peeled off her damp socks and rubbed her toes. She could barely feel them. She took a three-minute shower, dressed in a pair of sweatpants and a thick hoodie, and returned to the kitchen.

Everyone squeezed around the table, but no one minded the tight fit. Bree filled her plate and ate every bite while the kids chatted. Dana was quiet and didn't eat much, but she seemed pleased to have the family around her.

Kayla sat between Matt's parents. She pushed back her plate. "Can we have dessert?"

"As soon as the table is cleared." George stood and began stacking dirty plates.

Bree started to rise, but Matt lifted a hand. "You relax. We've got this."

Dana leaned back. "Thank you for dinner, George."

"You're very welcome," he said.

Luke cleared. Nolan loaded the dishwasher, and Matt scrubbed pots. Kayla raced for a plate of chocolate chip cookies on the counter. "Me and Grandpa made cookies!"

Grandpa?

Anna leaned close to Bree's ear and spoke in a low voice. "Kayla asked us if it was all right to call us Grandpa and Grandma, and we said of course it was. I realize now that we should have checked with you first. I apologize if we overstepped."

A barrage of emotions choked Bree. She didn't know what to say. She cleared her throat. "Of course it's fine. I was just surprised."

And blown away by their kindness.

What else could they have done? Rebuffed a nine-year-old orphan? Of course they wouldn't do that. They were wonderful people. Kayla was thriving these last few months, and Bree suspected Matt's family had helped. Matt's parents and siblings provided love, security, and stability. They had family traditions and included Bree's household like it was the most natural thing in the world. Like they belonged. Children needed to belong.

"I'm sorry if she put you on the spot," Bree said.

Anna waved off her concern. "I'm glad. It seemed important to her, and we're more than happy to oblige. She's such a sweet child. Luke can still call us Anna and George, of course. He's almost an adult. I want you to know we love those kids like our own." She smiled.

"That means a lot." Bree's heart swelled with gratitude. "You know I appreciate everything you do for them."

"It's our pleasure." Anna touched Bree's forearm, and Bree knew she meant it.

After the kitchen was tidied, they served dessert. Adam left with a container of cookies. George and Anna went home after many hugs from Kayla. Luke went upstairs to finish his homework, and Bree put Kayla to bed.

When Bree returned to the kitchen, Nolan and Matt faced a laptop. On the other side of the table, Dana nursed a cup of tea.

"What are you doing?" Bree turned on the teakettle and grabbed a cookie.

Nolan looked up. "Are you OK with adding an additional security camera behind the barn? I'd also like to add a motion sensor on the driveway."

Bree lowered the cookie without taking a bite. Thinking of the kids home alone with the trespasser outside turned her stomach. "Yes to both, and I'm open to any other ideas."

"Good," he said.

Carrying her tea to the table, she spotted the mail and a package on the sideboard. She opened a plastic shipping envelope and shook out the new cell phone case she'd ordered for Luke. A cardboard box sat under a small pile of letters. She grabbed the letters, shuffled through the junk mail, and set aside the single item of actual mail. Most of her bills were paid electronically.

Matt opened his phone. "The barista sent me the surveillance video from her café."

"That'll be fun to review. Not." Bree stared at a package the size of a shoebox.

"Going to take some time," Matt agreed. "That's for sure. I'll tackle it tonight."

"What's this?" She turned the box over, looking for the shipping label.

Matt set down his phone and turned toward her. "It was in the mailbox."

Bree scanned the plain brown box. A chill swept through her. "It didn't go through the post or a package delivery service."

"Could it be from a neighbor?" Nolan asked, his tone suspicious.

Bree shook her head. "We don't have anyone close."

"A friend?" he suggested.

Dana shrugged. "I can't think of anyone who would shove a package in our mailbox. Friends would knock on the door. If we weren't home, they'd leave the box on the porch."

Matt walked over to stand beside her. "Let's take it outside."

"Good idea." She'd already handled the package but fished a pair of gloves out of her uniform jacket that hung by the back door. They went out onto the back porch. She set the box on the railing, then used a box cutter to slit the tape. She opened the lid, slowly, with her arm fully extended. "Toys?"

They *had been* toys, but no longer. The chill burrowed into the neck of Bree's sweatshirt.

"What the hell?" Matt turned on his phone flashlight and shined it into the box.

The insides of the box had been painted with black vertical stripes. A doll-size sink and toilet were glued down, and a tiny bunk had been fashioned from Popsicle sticks. A Polly Pocket hung from her neck from the bars. On the bottom of the box—the floor of the cell—red block letters spelled out a message.

Bree read it aloud. *"Dirty cops should die in prison instead of the innocent."* She went cold to her bones. She rubbed her arms. Another threat.

Matt gestured to the kitchen door, and they went back inside. The box was disturbing, but it wasn't going to explode. He set the box on the table.

Nolan glanced inside. "That's creepy. Dolls freak me out."

Bree shrugged. "As far as scare tactics go, this isn't even that original. I was once threatened with a blow-up sex doll."

"People are sick." Nolan turned to Matt. "Are you staying here tonight?"

Matt didn't hesitate. "I am, and so is Brody."

"Then I'm going home to get some sleep." Nolan nodded toward the box. "I'll be back in the morning, and I'll plan to stay here all day."

"I'll leave Brody with you tomorrow," Matt added.

"Good," Nolan said.

"Thank you." Bree gave him a quick hug.

"Yes, thank you," Dana said. "I know it's inconvenient. You have a studio to run."

He shook his head. "This is more important. I'll see you all first thing."

After he left, Matt continued to frown at the weird box. "What did Mrs. Ekin say to you when you arrested Travis?"

"She said she would never forget what I did to her son," Bree said. "We'll track down Benjamin and Ford Ekin tomorrow." They were her primary suspects. "This feels crude, like them."

"And we know they like revenge." Matt closed the lid of the box. "You'll want this preserved as evidence. I'll get a box."

"We'll lock it in my vehicle. I don't want the kids to see it." Bree stepped back. "I'll drive it over to forensics in the morning. I want the fingerprint tech to have a go at it."

Though Bree doubted forensics would find prints. Thanks to TV crime shows, everyone knew to wear gloves.

Frowning, Dana peered into the box. "That reminds me of a case from my Philly years, before you were my partner. I was working with Stuart Hoffman back then. Anyway, this dude—Anthony—stalked a woman for weeks. I can still see the photos of her lined up on her parents' mantel. Her name was Rachel Brown. She was petite, with long brown hair. He sent her creepy gifts, stuffed weird shit in her mailbox, and left nasty messages on her car." Dana sat down and grabbed a cookie from the plate. Ladybug rested her head on Dana's thigh and watched the cookie.

Matt straightened. "You worked homicide, so I assume he killed her?"

"He broke into her house and strangled her," Dana said.

"Did you catch him?" Matt asked.

"Oh, yeah." Dana bit into the cookie. "He went to prison. We wrapped that case up like a Christmas present. But here's the thing." She met Bree's eyes. "This stalker came here twice, and left two nasty messages. Yet he wasn't caught on camera. He's not stupid."

"He didn't come close enough to the house," Matt said. "Nolan is adding additional cameras to cover more of the property."

"The question is, will he come here again, or will he try to get to you somewhere else?" Dana finished her cookie. "You've been focused on keeping the family safe. Make sure you're taking as much care with yourself."

"That's why I'm armed," Bree said.

Dana frowned. "That stalker? He turned out to be someone she'd only interacted with once, at a party at a mutual friend's house. He asked for her number, and she turned him down. That was all it took to enrage him."

"Now you have me thinking." Matt drummed his fingers on the table. "We should be looking at other people who have a grudge against Bree. The Ekin family is first on the list, but we don't *know* it's them." He turned to Bree. "Has anyone you put away for a serious crime been released from prison lately?"

Bree turned over both palms. "I've been responsible for a number of criminals going to prison during the last year, but no particular cases stand out where someone was released. Most of them are serving terms longer than a year. I'll be notified of any parole hearings."

"What about cases from when you were in Philly?" Matt glanced between Bree and Dana.

Bree shrugged. "We've been here a year. I worked homicide for four years before that. I can't think of anyone who would have been released already."

"Me either." Dana shook her head. "But then, I haven't kept track since we moved up here."

"What about before you joined Philly homicide?" Matt asked Bree.

"I'll have to think about it," she said. "But nothing comes to mind."

Matt snagged a cookie. "You ever work organized crime or narcotics?"

Bree shook her head. "No. Mostly burglaries, property crimes, et cetera. Not the sort of cases that inspire revenge years later."

"Anyone you put in prison can hold a grudge," Dana said. "A couple of years in a cage gives a person plenty of time to think—and plan. I'll make some calls about homicide cases we worked together those last four years. There were a couple of cases that pleaded down to manslaughter. It's possible they could be out on early release."

"Don't push it if you aren't up to it." Bree resisted another cookie. The plate was almost empty.

Dana gave her a Look. Bree knew it well. Dana would do as she pleased.

Bree lifted her hands in surrender. "OK. Thank you."

"Don't go anywhere alone for a while." Dana held eye contact. "It's great that I caught that stalker/killer in Philly, but sending him to prison didn't bring the victim back. She was still very dead."

Chapter Fifteen

After the horses were tucked in for the night and the house was quiet, Matt took his laptop and a cup of coffee into the home office. Reviewing surveillance videos was one of the most mind-numbingly boring duties. He was going to need another cup or two. He settled behind the desk and pulled a second chair around next to it. Bree brought in a cup of tea and her own laptop. They set up their computers side by side.

She opened her computer. "What an exciting date night, watching surveillance feeds from Lily's Internet Café."

"What can I say? Another wild night."

"You and me both." Bree laughed.

Matt waved a hand over their computers. "If you have insomnia, this will cure it." He opened the email from Lily. She'd sent three files, one from each security camera. Each video was four hours long. "She sent the feeds from eight in the morning to noon. We'll start with the front door and cash register. I also have the feed from the back door, but that's only used by employees."

"We want customers." Bree sipped her tea, wrapping both hands around her mug.

He forwarded the register video to Bree. "The Wi-Fi is accessible from outside the café, but the password is changed daily. They write it on the menu board. So, either customers have to come in or send someone in to get the password in order to use the Wi-Fi."

Matt began the tedious process of rewinding and fast-forwarding the surveillance videos.

Bree squinted at her computer. "I can't see the tables from this angle, so I have no idea who is working on a computer or smart device at 11:06 a.m."

"Let me begin with identifying male customers."

"While you do that, I'll work on reports." Police work was an endless sea of forms, and Bree began typing.

Matt set aside his laptop and retrieved a legal pad and pen from the desk drawer. Time for slo-mo. He paused the feed on every customer who entered the café during the morning hours. With constant back-and-forthing, he determined at least eighteen customers were inside the café at 11:06 a.m. Seven of these were men who entered and left alone. "I'm taking screenshots of all the male customers who were in the café during the hour before 11:06, but the camera is mounted on the side wall. I can't see their faces, just a profile, and even that is grainy."

Bree switched windows on the computer. "The register camera faces the customer, so we can compare images. We can also see how each one paid. If we're lucky, they used credit cards, there will be records of the transactions, and we can ID them."

Matt nodded. "Starting with the earliest one to arrive." He pulled up the screenshot and read the time stamp in the corner of the image. "Red parka, black skull cap."

Bree glanced at his screen, then fast-forwarded through the register video. "I've got him." She advanced through the clip frame by frame until he paid for his coffee and egg sandwich. "He paid cash. I can't see his shoes on this video. Can you?"

Matt went back to the clip with the same man entering the café. "He's wearing running shoes, not boots."

"I'll print this image." The printer whirred, and Bree retrieved the photo from the printer on the shelf behind her. She wrote *Number 1* on the back.

They repeated the process over and over for the next hour.

"How many is that?" Bree returned with another printed image.

"Five." Matt started the video once again. "Number six is wearing a black jacket."

He stopped the feed and turned to Bree's computer. They watched the sixth man step up to the register to pay for a single coffee.

"He looks familiar," Bree said.

Matt recognized the face from a mug shot, but he double-checked. "That's because he's Ford Ekin."

"There is definitely a family resemblance." Bree leaned closer. Her eyes narrowed. "The fact that he bought a cup of coffee at the café this morning doesn't prove anything." She squinted at the screen. "Dozens of other people also bought coffee there. It could be a coincidence."

"We don't need evidence to ask him some questions," Matt said. "Did he pay with cash or a credit card?"

Bree played another few seconds of video. "Cash."

"It's still him." Matt stared at the screen.

"Definitely. Let me see the last man." Bree was always thorough.

Matt showed her the seventh man's image.

Bree stiffened. "I know him. His name is"—she paused, snapping her fingers—"Toland. Louis Toland." She stabbed at the screen. "Six years ago, I put him in prison for a string of burglaries. He must be out."

"He paid with cash."

Bree frowned.

"Is there something about his case that stands out?" Matt asked.

"He was young, just eighteen, and he cried a lot during the trial." She sighed. "He did the crimes. There was no question, but I still felt sorry for him. He was trying to help his mother pay the rent. They were being evicted."

"How did you catch him?"

"I didn't really catch him." Bree shook her head. "He fell breaking into a warehouse, broke his femur, and knocked himself out. Once we had him in custody, we linked him to five recent burglaries through footprints. He would go into homes and businesses barefoot to be quiet. He didn't know toe and sole prints had ridge patterns that can be matched just like fingerprints. We should be able to find him." She sat back. "What about the other five men?"

Matt dealt out the screenshots on her desk like playing cards. He tapped on the pictures. "Maybe the café will share the sales records for these four." He indicated the men who used either credit or their smartphones to pay. "We identified two of the men who paid cash. Not sure if we'll be able to ID the third one."

"If the customer is a regular, the employees might recognize him. It's worth a try." Bree tapped her fingers on her desk. "Without the trespasser and threat on the barn, I'd say let it go. But he was physically too close to my family."

"That *was* ballsy," Matt agreed.

The image made Matt ragey, and he was glad Nolan was staying at the farm when he and Bree couldn't be there.

Bree gave him a grim nod. "I'll send a deputy to the café in the morning to ask for the receipts."

"I might get a better response from the owner." Matt remembered the flirting. It felt cringy to use that to get information, but they were desperate. "I already talked to her once. She gave me the surveillance feeds without balking."

"We'll stop first thing. Then we'll talk to both of the Ekin brothers, and we'll find Louis Toland."

"I'll check in with Rory about the anonymous email server." Matt sent a quick email. Then he slid the seven photos into a manila file folder.

"The entire Ekin family hates me, so they're still my primary suspects for the threats against me. But putting them away for murder and/or drug dealing would be even better. A defense attorney would call their shenanigans at the farm *pranks*. I want them in prison. I'll take whatever crime I can prove to get them out of the community."

"Definitely." Matt locked up their files in the desk. He never wanted the kids to stumble across anything disturbing.

Before they went to bed, they took the dogs out one final time. Ladybug peed and raced back to the house as if she were freezing. Bree hunched against the night wind.

Matt and Brody took a tour around the house and barn. Alarms were great but not as good as Brody. Matt watched his dog. With his double coat, he didn't seem to feel the cold at all.

Snow grated under Matt's boots. When they approached the barn, Brody froze. His tail and nose went up. He rushed for the back of the barn. Matt broke into a run to keep up. He turned the corner. The dog had his paws on the side of the barn, just under the nailed tarp. He dropped to the ground and sniffed every inch of snow.

Matt waited, but a few minutes later, Brody stopped and stared into the darkness. Had he smelled the person from the other night? Nolan hadn't set up the camera yet. There was no way to know if someone had been here, watching.

Chapter Sixteen

Matt woke long before dawn in his favorite place: beside Bree. He attempted to roll over, but his legs were pinned by a still-snoring Brody. Matt nudged the dog. Brody's entire body heaved with an irritated sigh. He'd learned to enjoy sleeping late during his retirement.

"I have room." Bree laughed. Ladybug slept on her side of the bed. The big dog could curl up into an unbelievably small ball. When Bree moved, Ladybug rose to stand over her face. Bree wiggled up the bed to lean on the headboard. Ladybug didn't budge. "If you would move, I could get up and feed you."

"You should make her wait." Matt swung his legs off the bed. "Serve breakfast later, and she'll learn not to associate you getting out of bed with her meal."

Bree tossed off the covers and stepped into her slippers. "If you can teach her that, I'll give you a hundred dollars. I can't decide if she's stubborn or stupid."

The dog jumped off the bed and barked. The cat sat on the nightstand, glaring at the dog with disdain.

"Shh." Bree hushed her. "I'm up already. Don't wake the kids."

She took a three-minute shower and dressed in her uniform. Then she led the dog out of the bedroom. Matt heard them go down the stairs. Brody groaned again.

"Ladybug got exactly what she wanted, right?" Matt patted him. "She's definitely not stupid."

Brody closed his eyes. He wouldn't get out of bed until he heard the kids rise. Unlike Ladybug, he didn't live for food.

Matt took a quick turn in the bathroom, dressed, and went downstairs. Normally, he and Bree went for a run several days a week, but they wouldn't leave the kids alone today.

Bree had fed the dog and taken her out already. Matt made coffee, and they drank it together at the table, watching the sun rise, its golden rays gleaming on the snowy pasture. These were the moments he'd grown to appreciate. Just him and Bree, not talking, just being together. The peace didn't last more than twenty minutes, but some days, they were the best moments of his day.

Then Bree's phone pinged with her wake-the-kids alarm, and the following hour evolved into the morning frenzy, which ironically, Matt also enjoyed. Without Dana to cook and organize, they scavenged breakfast and barely managed to get everyone ready on time. Luke left for school. Adam collected Kayla. The dogs stretched out on the floor, ready for their morning naps.

Nolan arrived and helped himself to coffee. "Is Dana up?"

"Not yet." Matt put on his jacket. "Bree checked on her. She's fine, just sleeping in. Thanks for helping out again today."

"You're welcome, but no worries." Nolan opened his laptop, but his eyes kept straying to the doorway. "I don't mind."

Something in his brother's face caught Matt's attention. "Don't mind helping me out or don't mind hanging with Dana?"

Nolan answered without hesitation. "Both."

"Interesting," Matt said.

Nolan lifted a shoulder. "It isn't yet, but I think there's potential."

"Does she know how you feel?"

Nolan cocked his head. "I doubt it, but now isn't the time."

"Good thing you're a patient man."

"Definitely." Nolan sipped his coffee, nonplussed.

Matt went outside and took an ice scraper to the frost-covered windshield of the sheriff's vehicle. His breath fogged in front of him like a small cloud. Despite the bright sunshine and crystal-clear sky, the air held a frigid bite.

Bree exited the house and strode toward him, jamming a pair of sunglasses on her face. "From inside the house, it looked like it was going to be warmer out here, but it seems colder. Why is the sky bluest in winter?"

"I assume the answer is science science something science."

She laughed, pulled gloves from her pocket, and tugged them on. Then she slid behind the wheel and started the engine.

Matt rounded the front of the vehicle and scraped the passenger side of the windshield. After he finished, he climbed into the passenger seat. The windshield fogged on the inside. "Did you know that Nolan has a thing for Dana?"

Her brows shot up. "I did not."

He gave her a look. "Do you think she feels the same?"

She considered the question with a pursed mouth. "I wouldn't rule it out, but her latest date was just murdered, and she has a concussion. I doubt she'll be thinking about dating again for a while."

"True." But the more Matt thought about it, the more he liked the idea. Mentally, he rolled his eyes at himself. What was he, a matchmaker? He needed to work. He clearly had too much free time.

She jerked a thumb at the back of her vehicle. "Let's drop the creepy diorama at forensics and stop at the café before we start interviews."

The windshield cleared. Bree adjusted the defroster and turned the heat on full blast. Warm air began to blow from the dashboard vents. Matt turned them all toward Bree.

She backed out of the space. "I called Ford's probation officer. Ford is working maintenance at the warehouse on Robins Road. Graveyard shift. He might not be home yet."

Common requirements for parole include being employed, not associating with known criminals, agreeing to warrantless searches and regular drug testing, a curfew, and check-ins with a probation officer.

"Does he wear an ankle bracelet?" Matt asked. If he did, they could take him off their list.

Bree steered the SUV onto the driveway. "Unfortunately, the terms of his parole do not include electronic monitoring."

"Do we want to question him at work or home?"

At the road, Bree stopped and tapped a finger on the steering wheel. "Home. I don't want to be accused of harassment. If he's innocent, I also don't want to jeopardize his employment." She turned onto the road and accelerated.

"Drug dealers don't deserve your consideration. Remember what drugs did to Justin."

"I do." Bree's voice turned sad. Justin had been her sister's husband, and Matt's best friend. Bree and Matt had met at their wedding.

"Addiction destroyed their marriage and his life."

"How is he?" she asked.

Matt shrugged. "Back in rehab. I doubt he'll ever be OK. He still blames himself for her death."

"I'm sorry."

Matt cleared his throat. "Ford agreed to warrantless searches. We can and should look around his place."

"We still have to follow the law. We can't harass him. He did his time. He's lawfully out on parole."

Matt grunted. He could never be sheriff.

She drove to the forensics lab. While Bree logged the box as evidence, Matt detoured to Darcy's office, where he learned the fingerprints on the spray can did not belong to either Benjamin or Ford Ekin. Back in the SUV, he relayed this information to Bree.

"Doesn't rule either of them out." But she sounded disappointed. "They probably wore gloves. The print could belong to someone else who handled the can recently."

They stopped at the internet café, which was very busy. Lily was cooperative, but didn't recognize the cash customers. She would pull the transaction records for the remaining four purchases, but using the time stamp and not having the actual transaction number would make the process more laborious. She would work on it and try to have the information for them in a day or so.

Back in the vehicle, Bree sipped her cappuccino. "This is excellent. Not quite as good as Dana's, but excellent."

Matt drank his black coffee while he used the dashboard computer to pull up driver's license information for Louis Toland. "Toland lives in Redhaven. He moved close to you."

"Coincidence?" she asked. "Or not?"

"Let's stop by his house and find out." Matt reverse searched the address. "Stanley Toland has owned the property for twenty-seven years. Could that be his father?"

"His father is dead." Bree tapped the wheel. "Louis was born and raised in Philly."

"Must be some other relative," Matt said. Who else could he go to when he was released from prison? Many employers didn't hire felons. Landlords often shut them out too. Louis had been eighteen when he'd been arrested. Did he even have a high school diploma?

Bree drove to the address, a well-maintained farmhouse on a mul-tiacre lot. The driveway ended in a spacious asphalt square between the house and barn. A large white truck and enclosed utility trailer sat side by side. Both vehicles bore matching logos for Stan's Landscaping & Snow Removal. Matt paused. The logo looked familiar, but he could have seen it around town. The barn doors stood open, and equipment filled the wide-open space. Just inside the doorway, a man worked on a snowblower.

As Matt stepped out of the SUV, the man straightened, wiped his hands on a rag, and shoved it into the pocket of his winter coveralls. In his midfifties, he stood a few inches taller than Matt's six three. The man's ruddy face had seen the worst weather. He didn't leave the barn but waited for Matt and Bree to approach him. As Matt stepped inside, he learned why. An outdoor space heater took the bite out of the temperature in the barn.

Matt scanned the space. Animals hadn't been housed here for a long time. Landscaping equipment formed neat rows. Smaller tools occupied shelves or wall hooks. The entire place was ruthlessly organized, almost militant. A closed door was marked Office.

"I'd shake but my hands are greasy." The man held up both hands apologetically. "Can I help you?"

Bree introduced herself and Matt. "We're looking for Louis Toland. I assume you're related."

"I'm his uncle, Stan Toland." Stan's posture went stiff. "Why do you want to see him?"

"I'd like to ask him a question," Bree said.

Stan crossed both arms over his lean chest. "About what?"

"Is he here?" Matt asked.

Stan turned, cupped his hands around his mouth, and shouted into the barn. "Louis."

A younger man walked out of the office. He saw Bree's uniform, flinched, and stumbled. Then lifted his chin and continued walking. His eyes darted back and forth between Bree, Matt, and Stan. In them, Matt saw pure terror.

"Hey, Louis," Bree said. "Haven't seen you in years."

He nodded, his face tight. He shoved his hands into the pockets of his coveralls, but not before Matt saw them shaking. He opened his mouth and closed it twice before getting the words out in a quiet voice that sounded almost rusty. "Um. Yeah."

"Wait." Stan's eyes narrowed in suspicion. "You two know each other?"

"She arrested me back in Philly." Louis swallowed.

"Where were you Monday night?" Bree asked.

Stan held up a hand. "He was with me."

Matt propped a hand on his hip. "You don't need to check your calendar?"

Stan didn't hesitate. "No, and you don't get to interrogate him. Do you have some grudge against him?"

Bree ignored the question, but Matt saw the small flinch in her eyes.

Louis licked his lips. "Why do you want to know where I was?"

"You don't have to answer their questions." Stan took a protective step toward Louis. "They're just trying to intimidate you."

Bree stared Louis down. "Someone trespassed and vandalized my property. This person also sent me threatening email, using the Wi-Fi at Lily's Internet Café, on Tuesday morning. I saw you on the security camera feed. You were there."

Louis took a step backward. "I didn't do any of that."

"Now hold on a minute." Stan stepped up beside him. "He was with me Tuesday morning as well. We stopped for coffee on the way back from a rock salt run. I couldn't find a parking spot, so I sent him inside for our order. Last time I checked, buying coffee wasn't a crime, and he was only in the shop for a few minutes."

"It doesn't take long to send an email," Matt said.

"Fuck you." Stan fumed. "You don't come to my property and accuse my nephew of"—he waved a hand back and forth—"whatever it is you're accusing him of."

Louis studied his feet, which were clad in heavy-duty boots.

Not Timberlands, Matt noted. "What size shoe do you wear?"

"Don't answer that." His uncle put a hand on his shoulder, then turned a hard glare on Bree and Matt. "He won't answer any more questions without a lawyer. He served his sentence. He should be able to get on with his life. He has rights. I never thought he was guilty back then. Did you railroad him into prison? Are you trying to do it again? If I had hired him a decent lawyer last time, he wouldn't have spent all that time in prison."

Bree protested, "He had a public—"

"Who didn't give a shit about him," Stan yelled. "Now, you get off my property." The red of his face deepened as he swept a commanding hand toward the driveway.

Matt kept his mouth firmly closed. He didn't trust himself not to yell back. The threats to the kids made him less than rational. But the man was right. They couldn't make Louis answer any questions.

"Yes, sir." Bree stepped back.

Matt turned to follow her. He felt the heat of Stan's stare all the way back to their vehicle. They climbed into the SUV.

"Well, Stan's angry." Bree exhaled. "But I didn't catch any anger from Louis, just fear."

"The uncle definitely has a temper." He drummed his fingertips on the armrest.

Bree drove out onto the road. "I'll assign a deputy to do a background check on his uncle. See if there's any violence in his past. Now, do we have Benjamin's address?"

"Yes. It's near the train station." Matt entered the address into the GPS on his phone.

Bree used the radio to check in with dispatch. She followed the directions. "We're going to pass the Pomar estate. I should call the hospital and check on Mr. Pomar."

"Maybe you could get a photo with Mr. Pomar and Greta when he's better." Matt formed air quotes with his fingers. "Elderly man and the K-9 that saved his life."

Bree frowned. "It feels exploitative to put a man with dementia on the news to further my own political agenda. He's entitled to his privacy."

"He'd have to agree," Matt said.

"He's not in any state of mind to agree or disagree," Bree said. "And his family lives on the West Coast."

"OK. You're right." Matt appreciated her integrity.

"But?"

"But you need to move your political agenda higher on your priority list. If you don't get reelected, you can't continue to do your job."

"I know."

"You don't seem bothered by that possibility."

"Sometimes I think it would be better for the family if I wasn't sheriff."

"It would be worse for the citizens of Randolph County."

She shrugged. "Maybe."

"You've cleaned house in your department."

"Yes. Whoever is the next sheriff will be able to start with a clean slate."

Matt looked at her. "Have you decided not to run?" He wasn't sure how he wanted her to answer.

"Honestly, I don't know. I don't have to decide right now." She paused at a stop sign, then moved through the intersection. "But I'm tired of my family being targeted." She held up a hand. "I know the threats mean I'm doing my job. Criminals are going to jail, and they don't like that. But at the end of the day, my most important job is to keep those kids happy and safe. They deserve a chance to thrive."

"They are thriving."

She didn't respond.

"What would you do if you weren't sheriff?"

"I have no idea." Her brow creased. "Thanks to Adam, his art, and his generosity, I don't have to worry about the kids' college funds, and he's set aside enough to keep the farm running for the next few decades. As much as I prefer to be independent, I won't let my pride get in the way of the kids' futures."

"You're enormously popular with most people in this county." But he also knew there was a minority that hated her with equal enthusiasm.

"I have time to make up my mind, but the idea of losing my office doesn't upset me like it once did." She reached across the console and took his hand. "Don't get me wrong. I still love the job. There's something about hunting down criminals that gets my blood humming. But my life used to be empty except for work. Now it's not. I have family and friends, more animals than I can count."

"You make an excellent point." He gave her fingers a squeeze through their thick gloves. He realized with sudden clarity that he felt the same. "I like investigating, following the evidence, putting the pieces together, taking scumbags off the streets, et cetera. But I don't love it enough to continue if you aren't the sheriff."

He'd struggled after losing his career. He'd been lost, aimless, bitter at the circumstances of his shooting and seeing no purpose in his life. But now when he thought about alternative careers, it wasn't with a sense of dread. He no longer felt adrift. Unlike Bree, he'd always been close with his family. They'd given him plenty of support, but it was Bree who gave him purpose. They were building a life together.

They passed the train station and continued for another half mile.

"Is there anything on his record besides the drug conviction?" Bree asked.

Matt checked his notes. "No. He's been arrested twice for assault and once for burglary, but he's always managed to slide out from under the charges. A cousin gave him an alibi for the burglary, and the evidence wasn't strong. On both assault charges, witnesses mysteriously recanted their statements."

"That seems to happen often for members of the Ekin family."

"They're bullies. Slow down." Matt scanned the roadside and read the numbers on the next mailbox. "There's the salvage yard."

Bree turned at the rusty mailbox. The driveway was long, unpaved, and not plowed, but dozens of vehicle tracks snaked through the snow, packing it down. Ice grated under the tires as they drove to the house, a run-down ranch-style with a sagging roofline. A two-story building sat behind the house, and the field beyond was covered with vehicles in rows and piles, crushed and whole, with no obvious organization. The property backed to winter-brown woods. A six-foot-tall chain-link fence surrounded the yard.

Bree parked in front of the house and rested her hands on the steering wheel. She could hear barking but couldn't see any dogs. "Is that concertina wire on top of the fence?"

"Yep."

"Seems excessive for a junkyard."

"Definitely." Matt squinted. Tension curled in his chest as he scanned the property. "Hard to get in and hard to get out. It's like a prison."

CHAPTER SEVENTEEN

Bree focused beyond the fence on the acres of rusty vehicles. So many places to hide. "Searching this place would be a nightmare."

Matt shrugged. "A few K-9s could handle it."

"We only have one."

"We need another." Matt grinned.

Bree agreed. She'd love to have two patrol K-9s and one dedicated drug-detection dog, but the answer wasn't that simple. "It took us months to raise the money for the training and equipment for one unit. I've pushed the budget as far as it can go for the next few years with the station overhaul. There isn't any money left."

For many departments, K-9s were funded by private donation.

"We need to get Greta and Collins in the news, mostly Greta," Matt said.

Bree sighed. "People loved her at the fundraiser. The money poured in that night."

"Dogs are awesome."

"I'm not sure I truly understood the value of having our own K-9 unit until this week. We used to be dependent on the availability of dogs from other jurisdictions." Bree replayed Greta's successes in her head. "Travis had a knife. Without the dog alerting us to his location, he could have ambushed one of my deputies. And who knows if we would have found Mr. Pomar before he froze to death?"

"Dogs are awesome," Matt repeated. "I know you don't love media attention, but the public should be informed of Greta's accomplishments."

"You're right." Thinking, Bree tipped her head. She did owe the citizens a glimpse into Greta's performance. "People came through for us with the funds. They should see they're getting their money's worth."

"What about Travis's apprehension? The public would love the details on that one."

Bree shook her head. "The board of supervisors is concerned about a lawsuit."

Matt sighed. "He was adequately warned before the dog was turned loose?"

"Two audibles, both recorded by multiple body cameras."

"Then I wouldn't worry."

"I'm not worried about the legal aspects." Bree didn't want to deal with any negative PR. "But I won't put the dog, the county, or my department at risk by broadcasting the apprehension. I won't take the chance that Ekin's attorney will claim we sicced the dog on his client as part of a publicity stunt. As far as Travis's case goes, the search was by the book and completely routine. All in a day's work. We won't make a big deal about it."

"I get it, but keep publicity in mind whenever the dog performs successfully. PR isn't a crime, and every callout carries the risk of a lawsuit. You can't let that hamstring you."

"I won't," she said.

But her unwillingness to fully utilize media outreach could be the end of her career. Sheriff was an elected position. The public couldn't vote for something they didn't see. Most people would have publicized the hell out of Travis's case. They would have praised Greta and Collins for bringing down a violent criminal with minimal risk. But then, Matt was willing to play the PR game hard. Bree was not. Ironically, her integrity could hurt her in the long run.

Bree reported the stop to dispatch, and they climbed out of the SUV. She turned in a circle, surveying their surroundings. The wind whipped across the field, stirring up small clouds of snow dust. A path the width of a single shovel led to the front door. Another continued to the hulking building behind the house. A sign reading E & E Salvage Yard and Auto Parts pointed the way.

"I assume *E & E* stands for *Ekin and Ekin*," Matt noted.

They continued to the front door of the house, stood aside, and knocked. No one answered. They tried again, but no one came to the door. The faint sound of music drifted through the air.

"Maybe he's in the shop." Matt started around back. They walked single file in the narrow path. A kennel enclosure the size of a volleyball court had been built adjacent to the yard with the same high fence topped with spirals of barbed wire. Inside, two Rottweilers barked at them. One of the dogs leaped onto the fencing, rattling it—and Bree.

She jumped, then flushed, one hand at her throat. "I know they're behind a fence." She breathed. She'd worked hard to overcome her fear of dogs, but every once in a while, her old terror revisited.

"They're large, agitated dogs," Matt said. "You'd be stupid not to be wary."

She nodded but didn't comment as they continued to the shop. Three overhead doors lined the east side of the building. Rust was eating its way up the closest exterior corner.

White block print over the door read E & E Salvage Yard and Auto Parts. A black-and-white sign on a string was turned to Open, and a second sign listed the store hours as nine to five, Tuesday through Saturday. Country music played inside, and under the twangs, Bree could hear the hum of voices.

He scanned the entrance. "I don't see any cameras."

Bree jerked a thumb toward the dogs. "Seems Benjamin prefers low tech."

The door wasn't locked, and Bree opened it. After the brightness of the sunlight, she couldn't see a thing in the dim lobby area. Goose bumps rose on her arms. A clang sounded in the back of the building, as if someone had dropped a metal tool on the concrete floor, a completely normal sound for a used auto parts store. But Bree's instincts went on alert. Her hearing and focus sharpened. Known criminals and blind spots were a bad combination.

Bree crossed the threshold. Matt stuck close as they entered a dusty lobby. Inside, the metal and concrete building felt colder than outside. The interior was all hard surface. The music echoed. Beneath it, she heard the buzz of conversation but couldn't make out any specific words. The door shut behind them, dampening the barking of the dogs outside.

"Hello?" Bree called out.

The voices ceased abruptly, lifting the hairs on the back of her neck. Metal scraped on concrete. They definitely weren't alone.

A long counter divided the space. Behind it rows of metal shelves were lined with labeled bins and small vehicle parts. A wide, open doorway led into the depths of the building. As Bree's eyes adjusted, she could see a large workshop, several vehicles, an engine, and a long workbench. Four men surrounded the workbench. Bree recognized Benjamin Ekin. He was average height and a little heavyset. He wore heavy winter coveralls, and—Timberland boots! A pair of safety goggles was pushed up onto his head. He stepped in front of the bench to block the view of its contents, but not before Bree saw a stack of cash and a large cluster of prescription bottles. Every hair on her body stood straight up.

Fuuuuuck.

They'd walked into a major drug deal.

The fingers of her right hand twitched, reaching for her gun—and ice formed in the pit of her belly.

Matt seemed to comprehend the situation at the same instant. For a long breath, they all stared at one another. Then the four men sprang into action. Benjamin raised his hands in surrender. A stocky man in an open black parka shoved him aside. The man's thick black eyebrows dropped into a deep vee as he pulled a shotgun out from behind his oversize coat.

Matt and Bree both yelled at the same time, "Gun!"

Chapter Eighteen

Bree pulled her weapon, dived behind a partition, and took aim over it. She saw Matt duck behind an engine block. Scanning the workshop, Bree used her lapel mic to call for assistance. "Shots fired. Request backup and an ambulance." Without waiting for a response, she gave her location.

Parka Man leveled his shotgun at her and fired, the boom deafening. The shot hit the wall somewhere behind her. Bits of debris went flying. Bree pulled her own trigger. The bullet hit him in the thigh. His body jerked, but he didn't go down.

He pumped the shotgun's lever, preparing to shoot again. Bree fired a second shot. He stumbled backward. A red stain bloomed on the front of the pale-gray sweatshirt he wore under the parka. Shock widened his eyes, and he dropped to one knee. The shotgun fell from his grip and clattered to the concrete.

"Push it away," Bree commanded.

But the man collapsed, clutching his side.

Bree made no move toward the weapon. In order to seize the shotgun, they would have to go through the doorway. They had seen four men, and one was down, but they had no idea if there were more suspects hiding or if they were armed.

Matt's mouth was moving, but Bree couldn't hear anything but ringing in her ears and her own slamming heartbeat. He pointed to the exit behind them, and Bree saw one of the men running for the door, clutching a wad of cash in one hand and stuffing prescription bottles in his jacket pocket with the other. They'd have to go after him once the immediate danger had been eliminated. Benjamin had taken cover behind the workbench. Was he armed?

"I'm shot!" the wounded man on the ground yelled.

"Push the shotgun away with your foot!" Bree commanded.

He lay on the concrete, moaning. Blood leaked from his leg and stained the floor dark red. But Bree couldn't assist him just yet. Moving into the open would make her a target.

One of the four men was still missing.

A movement to her left caught her attention. The fourth man charged out from behind a truck, running toward Matt. He was as tall as Matt but thinner. Most of his visible skin was covered with tattoos. Bree caught the gleam of metal in his hand.

A knife!

He raised the knife over his head. Bree shifted her aim, but not before Matt stood, jumped out from behind the engine, and assumed a ready stance. Bree had no clear shot. The knife arced down toward Matt's head as if the man were swinging an ice pick. Matt shifted sideways and caught his attacker's wrist in both of his hands. In a fluid motion, he stepped out of the path of the knife. As the man's momentum carried him forward, Matt twisted the man's arm. The knife went flying, and the man stumbled past Matt. Catching his balance, the man spun and jabbed a fist at Matt's face.

Matt ducked and weaved, delivering an uppercut with the power of his legs. His attacker moved at the last moment, and the blow glanced off his jaw. His head snapped back. He staggered and braced himself with a hand on a metal support column. With a quick shake of his head, he dived at Matt, trying to wrap both arms around Matt's thigh in a crude takedown attempt. But Matt pulled his leg backward out of reach.

Before the man could straighten or adjust his posture, Matt placed both of his hands back between his shoulder blades and used his weight to force him face-first into the concrete. Once the man was prone on his belly, Matt put him in an arm bar, yanked both hands behind his back, and handcuffed him.

Bree moved forward, her gun still aimed at the downed man when she saw Benjamin slinking out from his hiding spot. Seeming to move in slow motion, he went for the shotgun on the floor, his steps furtive, his eyes on Bree.

But Bree already had her Glock up and aimed. "Don't do it, Benjamin."

He hesitated, his focus still on the shotgun. "You're going to send me back to prison."

"If you pick up that gun, I will shoot you." Bree inclined her head toward the man she'd already shot as evidence. "And if you don't die, you'll still go to prison." Benjamin didn't strike her as the suicide-by-cop type. He would do whatever it took to survive.

Benjamin's gaze shifted to the bleeding man on the floor. "Fuck me." He stopped and raised his empty hands, but pure hatred shone from his eyes, and Bree knew he would also do whatever he could to hurt her. He was the kind of man who would frighten children to get even with his enemy.

And without a doubt, Bree was his enemy.

Bree gestured for him to turn around. "Hands on your head."

He complied. She stepped forward to handcuff him.

Matt dragged his prisoner to a sitting position. "Don't move."

Bree looked back and forth from Matt's suspect to Benjamin. Both had dark hair and hawkish features that were similar enough to Travis's to suggest a family relationship. He wasn't Ford. "Who are you?"

"Steve Ekin." He spit blood on the floor. His lip was swollen and bleeding, maybe from the face-plant on concrete. His sleeves were pushed up past his wrists. Steve Ekin had no known connection to

Kent, but Bree scanned his tattoos anyway. Steve's tats were a random hodgepodge of poorly drawn symbols and images. None resembled Lady Justice.

"A relative?" she asked Benjamin.

"My cousin," he said.

"Who is the man who ran away?" Bree patted down Benjamin for weapons while Matt handled Steve.

Benjamin lifted a shoulder.

"Sit." Bree guided him to the floor. He sat with his legs stretched out in front of him, hands behind his back.

"No weapons." Matt opened Steve's wallet. "His ID confirms his name is Steve."

Bree moved to the bleeding man and handcuffed him.

He cried, "Seriously? Do you think I'm going to attack you with two bullet wounds?"

Bree ignored his faux outrage—she had no doubt he would try if he could—and searched his pockets. "Are you carrying anything sharp or dangerous? Am I going to stick myself?" Besides weapons, he could be carrying needles. He was, after all, a drug addict and/or dealer.

"Bitch," was his only answer.

She found a switchblade and a wallet. She pocketed both. Once she was sure he wasn't a threat, she checked his wounds. The first bullet had gone clean through his outer thigh. The second shot had grazed the fleshy part of his flank. He'd been lucky. The wounds were messy but not life-threatening.

Matt brought the first aid kit from the SUV and applied pressure bandages.

Bree checked the wounded man's ID. Salvatore Orlando was from Albany. Bree rocked back on her heels. "Mr. Orlando, who was the man that ran away?"

"I don't know." He clamped his jaw closed. From the pain or because he was lying?

Probably both. Benjamin had his cousin with him for support. What kind of drug dealer went to a major buy alone? Orlando would have brought someone to watch his back.

"Hey, Benjamin," Bree called. "Who was the guy who ran?"

Benjamin glowered. "Fuck you."

Bree remember the razor wire that topped the fence. Now she understood why it was there, and it wasn't to protect a bunch of old cars. This was where the Ekin family conducted their major business enterprise, which was much larger than anyone had suspected. Drug dealers liked to keep their facilities secure. "Is there a back exit to the yard?"

Benjamin shook his head. "There's no gate, and there's two feet of buried mesh to keep the dogs from digging out. They get full run of the yard at night. Why don't you let them out now? They'll find the dude who ran. He won't get away." Clearly, he wanted the man punished for running away with the drugs and money.

"We'll use our own dogs, but thanks," Bree said.

Benjamin's eyes hardened with anger. He wanted to get even with Bree too. She'd ruined his operation—and his life.

"Do you have someone to look after the dogs?" Matt asked. "Otherwise, we have to call animal control."

"Yeah," Benjamin said.

Bree stood and pointed to Orlando. "We're going to find him."

Orlando glared back at her.

She stepped away and used her lapel mic to summon her K-9 unit and to request available K-9s from surrounding departments. Hopefully, they could borrow a dog or two. Leaving Matt to guard the handcuffed suspects, Bree went to the back door, where the missing suspect had exited. The snowy ground was too trampled to follow any tracks. They'd have to search the whole yard.

CHAPTER NINETEEN

Dana sat at the kitchen table and downed two shots of espresso. She'd already fielded a call from her old pal at the Philly PD. Two of the prisoners she'd inquired about had been released. One died six months ago. The other landed back in prison within a month of being let out. She sent Bree a quick text.

Nolan slid a plate of eggs and toast in front of her, picking up her empty espresso cup. "You did that like a frat boy tosses back tequila." He sat down across from her with his own plate.

"Practice." She forked eggs into her mouth methodically. Her head ached too much for her to be hungry, but if she took painkillers without food, Nolan would no doubt give her shit. When she'd lived alone, she would have washed the painkiller down *with* the espresso.

She chewed her toast and reached for the bottle of OTC tablets. "Who took Kayla to school?"

"Adam."

She pushed back her empty plate. "I need to go to the Redhaven Police Station first thing."

"OK. I'm ready whenever." Nolan took her dishes to the sink, navigating the two dogs sprawled on the floor and the cat weaving between his feet.

"I need five minutes to brush my teeth." Dana retreated to her bathroom and flinched at her reflection. She still looked like a corpse.

Melinda Leigh

She applied lipstick, her usual cure-all. The color made her skin look paler and brought out the dark circles under her eyes. Now she looked like a corpse wearing makeup—or maybe a clown. A dead clown. She wiped it off and applied lip balm instead.

"Ready." She strode through the kitchen to the back door and slipped into her parka and boots.

Nolan locked up and reset the alarm, and they went out to the truck. In the passenger seat, she leaned against the headrest, her eyes closed. They didn't talk on the short drive.

The Redhaven PD was next to the township offices. Nolan parked in the station's visitors' lot. He turned off the engine, rested his hands on the wheel, and looked at her. No. He didn't just look at her. He *saw* her. "There are no heroics in being here. It's paperwork."

She reached for the door handle. "I want this behind me."

Nolan shook his head. "One thing I learned when my brother was shot is that cops will run right into gunfire to protect someone else, but they are not as good at taking care of themselves."

She had to admit that was a pretty good assessment.

"Did you make the follow-up appointment with the neurologist?"

"Yes. It's tomorrow. You Flynns *are* persistent." Her voice held more animosity than she'd intended. She still couldn't get a good grip on her reactions. Her emotions were all over the place, like she was a toddler who'd missed her nap.

But he didn't seem insulted. He nodded. "Agreed. Flynns never give up. If we were dogs, we would be pit bulls." He locked his sidearm in the glove compartment, then got out of the truck.

She climbed out and closed the door. The parking lot smelled like food. She inhaled deeply. A spicy scent drew her attention to a large green vehicle parked down the street. "Is that a taco truck?"

He squinted down the street. "Yes. Seems early for tacos, but I could eat. Are you hungry?"

Her stomach growled, but she didn't fully trust it. "I don't know. Maybe. That sounds weird." She snorted.

"Not weird at all," he said. "Your body wants calories to heal, but you don't want to feel sick in there." He nodded toward the station.

She did not want to hurl tacos in the station. The fear of embarrassing herself in front of a bunch of cops was real.

Nolan took her elbow and started across the asphalt. "Why don't we get tacos when we're done?"

She noted his use of *we*, like they were a pair or a team. The thought didn't freak her out like it should have. "Good idea. I'm not even sure I'll be hungry afterward." Rock salt crunched under her boots as they stepped onto the sidewalk.

"Then we'll see." He opened the door for her.

The station was small and hadn't been renovated in a few decades. Dana presented herself at the lobby reception window. The uniformed officer manning reception looked like he was twelve years old. It didn't help that Dana felt like she was ninety.

"Can I help you?" he asked through the speaker in the bulletproof glass.

"Dana Romano for Chief Hanover."

"I'll need some ID," he said.

She slid her driver's license under the window. Before she could tell Nolan to wait there, he did the same.

The cop checked both IDs. "I'll buzz you through."

The door clicked. Nolan opened it for her. Another uniform met them in the hallway. They followed her to a small conference room with a table and four chairs.

"Chief Hanover will be right with you." She withdrew, closing the door behind her.

"You could have waited in the lobby," Dana said, though deep down, she was glad he was here.

"Nope. I promised Matt I'd stay with you."

"Definitely a pit bull." She shook her head.

He grinned. With his shaved head and lean face, the smile looked feral. He pulled out a chair and sat, folding his hands and displaying a patience she wished she could muster.

Dana took the chair next to him, but being on the victim side of the table was discomforting. She felt vulnerable and out of control in ways that former cops did not like.

The door opened, and Hanover stepped in. His gaze passed over Nolan with a small, irritated twitch before settling on Dana. "Thanks for stopping by."

He slid into the chair opposite her. Opening a folder, he slid a typed report in front of her. She read the statement twice, slowly. She signed one copy and kept the other.

"And you don't remember anything else about the shooter?" Hanover asked.

"No." Dana wished she did. Her memory was mostly static with the occasional burst of clarity, like she was trying to tune in to a radio station when she was just outside its range.

She felt like she was failing Kent. She'd wrestled with his killer and couldn't even help find him. Some cop she was. She'd never felt so useless in her life. But she didn't say any of that, nor did she let any of it show on her face.

Hanover leaned back. "Are you sure there *was* a shooter?"

Shock raced through her like a bolt of lightning, and everything shifted, like she was on a rotating platform and suddenly facing a completely different direction. Next to her, Nolan didn't move, but she sensed his muscles tense. She glanced at the ceiling, where a light on the camera told her they were being recorded. Shock quickly morphed into anger, and she chose her next words carefully. "I don't understand the question."

"You have a head injury," Hanover said. "Could you have imagined him?"

Nolan sat upright. "You're out of line."

Dana placed a hand on his forearm. "Thank you, but I've got this."

She didn't, but she had plenty of practice in faking confidence.

Nolan settled back. He crossed his arms over his chest and glared at Hanover.

Pain ricocheted through Dana's skull. She closed her eyes for a few seconds, but the image of her hands on Kent's blood-soaked chest made her open them immediately. Despite the white-hot agony blooming behind her eyes, she put on her own cop face and met Hanover's gaze without flinching. "No. Why would you even ask that question?"

Hanover twirled a pen around on its side.

Dana took the offensive. "Do you have the ballistics report yet? Was Kent shot with his own weapon?"

Hanover sent the pen spinning in the opposite direction. "Dr. Bhatt identified the Sig as Kent's gun, but it was not the weapon that killed him."

"No?" Dana was surprised.

"Also, the only fingerprints on the Sig were Kent's," Hanover said.

Which Dana had expected since the intruder had been wearing gloves.

The intruder brought his gun with him, which explained even more why Kent had run for his own. Dana pictured it. Kent was in the kitchen chopping garlic. He heard the front door open and expected to see her. He saw the masked and armed intruder instead. He ran for the back stairs and his own gun. The intruder chased him. Kent made it to the bedroom. Got his gun from the biometric safe, maybe knocked over the lamp doing that. How did the bullet get in the ceiling? Did the shooter fire and miss?

"Has my weapon been cleared yet?" she asked.

"Yes." That fact didn't seem to please Hanover.

Dana nodded. "Then I would like it back."

"You can pick it up on your way out." He propped his elbows on the table and steepled his fingers.

"Did the bullet in the ceiling come from Kent's gun?" Dana asked.

Hanover hesitated, as if deciding whether he should share. "It came from the same weapon as the bullet that killed him."

Cops trained constantly because the average citizen didn't understand how difficult it was to aim under duress. Firing shots at the range didn't compare to shooting while moving or while under attack or at a moving target, with adrenaline pumping through your veins, giving you tunnel vision and making your hands shake.

Hanover interlaced his fingers. "We found no physical evidence to confirm there was an intruder in Dr. McFadden's house."

Dana wanted to call bullshit, but she kept her expression as blank as if she had a face full of Botox. "Except for the bullets and the dead man."

"There was a few inches of snow on the ground, yet there were no footprints outside." Hanover watched her over clasped hands, his eyes intense as they scanned her face.

He was looking for her tells. She knew this because she'd done the same for more than two decades. But she'd been better at it. Except this morning she was using up all her energy to control her emotions. Her brain felt rusty.

"The paths were shoveled."

Hanover raised his eyebrows. "So the shooter ran out the back door and stuck to the shoveled pathways?"

"I don't know. I didn't see him leave. I only heard what I thought sounded like him leaving via the back door."

"We found no sign of forced entry."

"Right. The door was unlocked when I got there."

Hanover continued without a breath. "Both you and Dr. McFadden had minor injuries that indicate a physical altercation."

"We both fought with the shooter." Dread built in Dana's chest. The interview was sliding out of her control like a car cresting an icy hill.

Hanover's eyes brightened and his nostrils flared, putting her on alert.

He licked his lips. "Light rosin was found on your clothes and Kent's. How did it get on your clothes?"

"Wait. What?" This was new information to Dana. Hanover had been hoping to slide this question in with the other rapid-fire ones. But even with a headache and sluggish mind, Dana recognized the tactic. She'd employed it enough times in her past. Besides, Hanover had tells upon tells.

"Light rosin." Hanover enunciated each syllable precisely.

"What is that?" Dana asked.

"Something that's commonly used on stringed instruments. It was on your clothes and Dr. McFadden's."

"The obvious answer is that it either came from Kent or the shooter." Dana had no other explanation.

"Did Dr. McFadden play an instrument?" Hanover asked.

"Not that I know of," Dana said.

"His sister says no, and we didn't find one in the house."

Dana said nothing. The light rosin could have come from the shooter. If this were her case, she would have been thrilled to have a distinct piece of trace evidence. But Hanover was making an assumption about the origin of that evidence.

"There were horsehairs at the scene as well." Hanover raised a brow.

"I live on a farm, and I was there," Dana said.

Hanover pursed his lips, then his eyes gleamed again. "Did you and Kent struggle?"

"This isn't a scene from *The Fugitive*," Nolan interrupted.

Hanover ignored him, but raised an eyebrow at Dana as if implying *or is it?* "Did you and Kent have an argument?"

"No, I didn't even talk to him before I found him on the bedroom floor." Dana's instincts waved a red flag.

"Is Kent the one who put those bruises on your neck?" Hanover pointed at her throat.

It hit her like a SEPTA bus. She needed to shut the fuck up. Hanover was trying to confuse her, to get her to contradict herself or admit knowing a piece of information she couldn't have known. With her head injury, she wasn't as sharp as usual. She should have shut the fuck up ten minutes ago.

"Before I ask you any more questions." Hanover slid a Miranda warning acknowledgment in front of her and opened his mouth to recite her rights.

She pushed the paper back at him before he could start. Anxiety rolled around in her belly like a sick animal, but all she let him see was cool anger and indignation. "I'm not answering any more questions without a lawyer."

Pushing off the table with both palms, she pretended it was for effect instead of balance. She maintained eye contact with Hanover while she slowly stood. Then she turned and walked toward the door. Nolan was at her side. She felt his hand under her elbow again. She didn't lean on it, but she wanted to.

The walk out of the station was a blur. She stopped at the front desk and calmly requested her weapon and signed for it before tucking it into her purse and leaving. Staying on her feet and not throwing up took most of her focus. She marched to the truck, climbed into the passenger seat, and slammed the door.

Nolan slid behind the wheel. As he unlocked the glove box and retrieved his own weapon, he opened his mouth.

"Please drive." Dana could hold it together for only so long, and she didn't want to fall apart within sight of any Redhaven cops.

Nolan shoved his gun into the holster under his jacket, put the truck in gear, and drove away. Two miles down the road, they turned onto a rural road that led to Grey's Hollow.

Dana said, "Pull over."

He guided the pickup onto the shoulder immediately, then ran around to open her door, but Dana was already out of the vehicle. She took three steps, bent double, and vomited behind a bush. She heard Nolan behind her. Without looking, she held up a palm behind her to stop him. She didn't need an audience. Now empty, her stomach stopped heaving. When she'd caught her breath, she turned around. "I'm sorry."

Nolan was leaning on his truck, his arms crossed over his chest. "*You* have nothing to be sorry about." His word emphasis suggested that Hanover did. "Can I go back there and punch him?"

"Only if you want to get arrested and go to jail." But she took a second to imagine it. She'd seen him fight. Nolan hit like a charging buffalo.

His mouth twisted. "Might be worth it."

An unexpected laugh bubbled into her throat. "I'm really glad we didn't get tacos."

"I don't know. Maybe a conference room full of taco vomit would teach him a lesson." He reached into the truck for a water bottle and handed it over. "He deserves at least a broken nose."

"I don't disagree." Dana swished water in her mouth and spit. Then she took a very small, experimental sip.

"Stomach settled?"

"I think so."

He opened the passenger door and made a sweeping gesture. "Let's get you home."

She climbed back into the truck. "I'm going to need a lawyer." Dana, who'd been squeaky clean for her entire service with the Philly

PD, was on the defensive in her retirement. Un-fucking-believable. "I still can't believe it."

"Me either." He pulled out onto the road and headed for home. "Felt like a sucker punch."

A sudden attack of self-doubt flooded Dana. "I didn't look like a complete mess in there, did I?"

Nolan glanced over. "You were an ice queen. I'm surprised his eyebrows didn't frost."

"OK. Good."

He snorted. "Only you would take that as a compliment."

"I don't want him to think he rattled me."

"Did he?"

"Yes." Dana covered her mouth with her hand. She hadn't meant to say that out loud. Had she ever been this off her game?

Nolan didn't say anything else.

Dana did what she *never* did—she filled the silence. "Now I know what is worse than being a victim." She waited a single silent heartbeat. "Being the suspect."

He straightened his fingers, as if they had been clenching the steering wheel, but he still kept quiet. He should have been an interrogator. Suspects would confess and not even know why.

She continued. "And that isn't even the worst part."

He glanced at her. One brow lifted in question.

Dana turned toward the windshield. "If he's focused on me as his suspect, he's not even looking for the real shooter."

Which meant Kent's killer was free to find another victim.

CHAPTER TWENTY

While waiting for response teams, Bree called a judge and requested a search warrant for the property. The fleeing suspect could be chased without a warrant, but she needed to turn the property inside out to look for the drugs and cash he'd taken. Plus, she was certain Benjamin had additional drugs on the premises. The judge agreed to sign an electronic warrant, with the usual "this had better pan out" qualification. Bree didn't roll her eyes. She thanked him and returned to her vehicle to type up the request and probable cause affidavit. True to his word, the judge signed the warrant electronically.

Additional deputies and the ambulance arrived. EMTs loaded Orlando into the ambulance. A deputy went with him. Two additional deputies cleared the rest of the building and the house.

Bree crossed the floor and stood in front of Benjamin. He sneered at her. "You can't use anything you find as evidence. You didn't show me a warrant."

She smiled. "Actually, a judge signed off on a warrant."

His chin jutted. "You had no right to barge in here in the first place."

"The sign says the store is open." Bree jerked a thumb at the door. "There's no expectation of privacy in areas open to the public. That makes it plain sight." Evidence in plain sight was not protected.

"You didn't lock the door?" Steve yelled from across the room. "You're a fucking dumbass."

Silently, Bree agreed. "Don't you want to know why we came here this morning?" she asked Benjamin.

"You're the bitch who arrested my brother." He shifted his legs. "I figure this is about him."

Bree ignored the insult. Her lack of reaction seemed to irritate Benjamin.

His eyes narrowed and his mouth thinned into a nasty line. "I got nothing more to say."

"You don't even know what the questions are," Matt pointed out.

"Fuck off." He scowled. "I won't help you put my brother away."

"This isn't about Travis," Bree said.

Benjamin eyed them suspiciously. "Then what is it about?"

"Where were you the night before last about eleven thirty p.m.?" Bree asked.

"I don't have to answer that," Benjamin said, enunciating distinctly.

Legally, no one had to talk to the police, and Bree couldn't force him to, even under arrest. He had the right to remain silent and all that.

"You threatened me when my department arrested your brother," Bree said.

Benjamin rolled a shoulder. "Did not."

"I was wearing a body camera," Bree said. "I have it on video."

"I said I wouldn't forget." Benjamin smirked. "That's not a threat. That's a statement. Who would forget the day their brother got mauled by a vicious dog? One that *you* ordered to bite him."

Bree shuddered. She shook it off, lifting her chin, but she didn't verbally respond to his question. A lawyer would no doubt make the same argument. The *statement* had been carefully worded and veiled, but it had been intended as a threat. Didn't matter now, though. Bree had plenty of charges to choose from. "Someone trespassed on my property. Was it you?"

His face went smug. "I'm not answering any more questions without my lawyer. We're going to sue you, the township, and the dog bitch too."

And that was that. *Lawyer* was the magic word to end the interview. Benjamin was already going to prison, and this time he'd serve a longer sentence as a repeat offender. He knew he had nothing to gain by talking to Bree before his lawyer scrutinized every aspect of the arrest from a procedural standpoint. Benjamin would be hoping Bree or one of her deputies made a mistake that would invalidate all or some of the evidence.

On the bright side, there would be one fewer Ekin family member—two, including the cousin—free to terrorize the community. The Ekins evaded the law because people were afraid of their vengeance. They weren't particularly smart, just brutal and vicious.

Bree gave up. Maybe after he'd been booked and his lawyer explained how much time he might serve, Benjamin would be more talkative. But did Bree want the prosecutor to trade information for reduced charges or a lesser sentence? The longer Benjamin's sentence, the better for the community. On Bree's orders, deputies hauled Benjamin and his cousin to the jail to be processed. Bree issued instructions for their clothing—and boots—to be collected for forensics. She would be thrilled if Benjamin's Timberlands matched the boot prints at her farm.

She issued a BOLO alert for the suspect, called for more units, and coordinated patrol cars to search the surrounding roads. Just because Benjamin said the man couldn't get out of the yard didn't mean it was true.

Bree went outside. The Rottweilers had stopped barking, but the dogs were still agitated. They paced back and forth in the enclosure, occasionally stopping and growling. As soon as the K-9 units rolled up, the Rottweilers went ballistic again.

Greta ignored the salvage yard dogs, holding her head high as if she were too good for them. The state police brought a huge black-and-tan

German shepherd named Bruiser that barked and growled right back at them. Both dogs refocused when their working harnesses went on. The handlers outfitted their dogs with protective vests and boots. The ground was icy, and they had no idea what was buried under the snow and ice.

"Lots of sharp objects out there." Collins nodded toward the salvage yard.

Police K-9s weren't just shot and stabbed by suspects. Dogs fell from heights, cut themselves on jagged metal, encountered broken glass, and ran through barbed wire fences. Neither handler would let their animal loose unless absolutely necessary.

"Let's be as safe as possible out there," Bree called to the deputies gathered at the edge of the yard. "Unless he has bolt or wire cutters on his person, or there's a hole in the fence, the suspect is hiding somewhere in this yard. We don't know if he's armed, but we'll assume he is. He could also have drugs on his person. Be careful."

She sent Deputy Juarez to walk the exterior perimeter and check the fence for breaks, then she concentrated on the search for the suspect in the salvage yard. She divided the yard in half. The K-9s would lead the way. Collins and Greta took the east side. The state K-9 went west. Bree assigned a pair of deputies as backup to the state K-9. Bree and Matt followed Collins and Greta. Matt carried the AR-15 from Bree's SUV. Bree drew her sidearm. Collins had her hands full of excited German shepherd.

The dog walked back and forth along the wide track between rows of cars. She alternated between sniffing the ground and lifting her nose into the air. Collins gave her about six feet of leash, but the dog pulled for more.

They continued straight down the main track until Greta stopped at an intersection, her nose working. She turned right and put her head down again, leaning into her harness. She led them up and down several rows, then suddenly, her head snapped up. Her tail went rigid, and the thick fur around her neck puffed out.

"She's onto something," Collins said.

Greta pulled Collins across an oily puddle toward a wrecked, rusted van with no wheels, broken windows, and a missing rear door. The dog barked at the van, her tail waving, high and stiff. She wanted to go in.

"To the person in the van," Collins yelled. "The dog has found you. Surrender now or she will bite you."

Greta let out another string of high-pitched barks that sounded like canine profanity.

"Stop! Wait!" a man cried in a panicked voice. "Don't let it bite me! I'll come out. Please, keep it back."

"Show us your hands," Collins commanded.

"I'm opening the door now." The back door creaked, then popped open. Two hands emerged, then a head and shoulders. "I'm coming out." A wiry man stepped to the ground. Fear bugged out his eyes, which he didn't take off the barking dog. Without being commanded, he raised his hands high in the air, then dropped to his knees with his hands behind his head.

Greta barked again.

"Please don't let her near me," he begged.

He was a criminal, but Bree understood his terror. She knew Greta and still found her intimidating.

"Hang back a little with Greta," she said to Collins. "He's cooperating. We'll give him some space."

Collins moved Greta twenty feet.

"What's your name?" Matt patted him down and cuffed him.

The man licked his lips, still side-eyeing Greta. "Tony."

"Don't move, Tony." Matt stuck his head in the back of the van, then looked at Tony again. "Where did you stash the drugs and money?"

But Tony wasn't *that* dumb. He looked away without answering.

Shaking his head, Matt marched the prisoner toward the front of the yard. Collins rewarded Greta with her hedgehog, and the dog thrashed and chewed while the toy squealed like a small creature being disemboweled.

Once the dog was happy, Collins shoved the toy back in the cargo pocket of her trousers.

"Nice job," Bree said, truly impressed, as they started back. "I can't imagine how many man-hours it would have taken to find him without you and Greta."

Collins put the dog to heel. "Greta deserves all the credit. All I do is hold the leash."

The dog stopped suddenly. Whining, she pulled toward an aisle that led farther back into the yard.

"What's wrong?" Bree asked.

"I don't know." Collins watched the dog. "I'm still learning her body language."

The hairs on the back of Bree's neck stood up. The dog had Spidey-senses. She smelled or heard something that alarmed her. "Could there be another suspect hiding out here?"

Collins shook her head and gave the dog some leash. "I don't think so. She gets excited when we're chasing a live person. This alert is passive, but she's found something. Maybe the drugs."

Greta pulled toward a rusty old Buick near the fence. The vehicle had flat tires and a rear door hanging on one hinge. The snow around the vehicle was unmarked except for the dog's tracks. Sniffing, the dog went around to the trunk and abruptly sat in the snow and barked.

"What's she doing?" Bree asked.

"I don't know." Collins pulled the dog back a few feet. "I've never had her alert without giving her a command to search for something specific."

"There are no tracks in the snow, so whatever is in there has been there for a few days." Bree used her lapel mic to ask for a crowbar.

A few minutes later, Matt jogged over with one in hand. "Tony is in the back of a patrol vehicle."

Collins explained about the alert.

"It's possible she's catching the suspect's scent on an object," Matt said. "When I searched his pockets, I didn't find anything. But we saw him carrying money and drugs when he ran out of the building. He stashed them somewhere."

"He didn't fly up to the vehicle. Maybe he threw it under the car, hoping to come back for it at some point." Bree crouched to look underneath the Buick. "I don't see anything."

Matt wrinkled his nose. "Do you smell that?"

"What?" Bree sniffed and drew her handgun.

The wind shifted again, and she shivered. She was really tired of the cold, wet weather, and it was only January.

"Not sure. It's gone now." Matt inserted the crowbar under the lip of the trunk and pushed. The trunk popped open, and he flinched backward. "Not what I expected."

"What?" Bree moved closer, aiming her weapon into the trunk. "Not drugs, money, or a weapon?"

"Nope." Matt stepped aside, giving her a view of the trunk's interior.

And Bree stared down at a dead body.

CHAPTER TWENTY-ONE

Matt considered the body. "We don't have to imagine the cause of death."

The victim was a young adult male with dark hair. He'd been roughly wrapped in a blue tarp, but the fabric had twisted when he'd been dumped in the trunk. His face was turned away, revealing what appeared to be a gunshot wound in the back of his head. He wore athletic shoes, canvas work pants, and a gray sweatshirt but no coat, hat, or gloves. There was a blood splotch on the back of his shirt on the side of the torso.

The body was curled on its side, not in a natural way but as if he'd been folded to fit in the trunk. The skin on the back of his neck was waxy and grayish, but Matt saw no obvious signs of advanced decay. "He looks relatively fresh."

"He also looks like he's frozen, so looks can be deceiving." Bree returned her gun to its holster.

"It's been cold," Matt agreed. "He could have been in there for a while."

Bree sniffed. "I didn't smell anything before, but now that the trunk is open, I'm catching the faintest whiff. Not exactly decomp, but death."

Matt inhaled. "Smells like a meat locker."

"The temperature is about right." Bree glanced around. "This would be a pretty good dumping ground."

"Maybe the victim was Benjamin's business associate or a customer who got out of line," Matt suggested. "Drug dealing is dangerous. Check the pockets for ID or wait for the ME?"

"We'll wait. The body's position would require us to move him. I'll call her." She stepped aside and lifted her phone.

Greta whined. Collins backed up a few more feet and praised the dog. "Good girl."

Matt heard the hedgehog toy squeak, but it wasn't an enthusiastic sound. He turned his head. Greta was halfheartedly mouthing the toy, and she wasn't attempting to snap its fake furry neck at all. She spit out the toy and whined again.

She knew what she'd found. Brody had been disturbed by finding human remains too.

"She needs a break," Matt said. "Get her a drink of water."

Collins rubbed the sleek black head. "Permission to take her back to the vehicle, ma'am?"

Bree nodded. "Go. Let her decompress. If necessary, take her somewhere to play fetch for a while. We're going to regroup after this discovery, but we'll need the dogs to search the rest of this yard."

"Yes, ma'am." Collins led the dog away.

Bree turned in a circle. "Do you think Benjamin would be dumb enough to dump a dead body in his own backyard?"

"Tough question." Matt glanced around. "He's no genius, and we found it accidentally. But he'd have to think that it would start to stink as soon as we had a warm week or so. He could have simply stashed it in the trunk to wait for the ground to thaw. Hard to bury a corpse in the winter."

"True, but there are plenty of lakes nearby. Easy enough to slip him under the ice or just dispose of him in the woods for that matter, but then you take the risk that he's found, maybe more quickly than you'd like. Benjamin might have thought he could control access to his own salvage yard better." Bree frowned. "On the other hand, how could someone other than an Ekin get the body back here? The dogs are loose at night."

Matt skirted the Buick and several more junkers until he reached the fence. Tall dead weeds poked out from the snow. He peered around a stack of old tires and almost overlooked the opening. A neat rectangle had been snipped out, then zip-tied back in place. "Someone made an escape—or entry—hatch."

Bree trudged through the snow to his side. "But did Benjamin cut that hole to make sure he had a way to get out in an emergency? Or did someone else do it?"

Matt lifted a shoulder. "I could see either happening."

She pointed across the empty land and woods beyond. "Anyone with four-wheel drive could have pulled right up to the fence and dragged a body through."

"No one inside the yard would have seen unless they were really close, even in broad daylight," Matt said.

"Definitely a possibility."

There were no footprints on the other side of the fencing, so Juarez hadn't made it all the way around the property yet. Bree used her radio to contact him. A few minutes later, he came jogging toward them on the other side of the enclosure, his face red from the wind.

He squatted to examine the makeshift gate. "It's a neat job. They lined up the chain link really good, and it's hidden behind a lot of junk on that side."

"I couldn't see it until I got close," Matt agreed. "And I doubt many people approach the fence from that side."

"Do we know what it was for?" Juarez asked.

"Possibly to dispose of the dead body Greta just found." Bree pointed toward the Buick.

Juarez propped his hands on his hips. "A dead body on the property of a drug dealer isn't a surprise."

"Not really," Bree agreed. "Let's get some pictures."

"Yes, ma'am," Juarez answered.

Bree turned back to the car. "I'm going to call forensics, then round up the uniforms."

Matt and Bree walked back to their vehicle. Bree stepped aside with her phone. Matt called around for additional K-9 units. He got lucky and found an available dog in the sheriff's department of a neighboring county. An hour later, Todd had arrived to assist. Crime scene tape was strung up around the Buick, the property was crawling with uniforms, and the three K-9s had divvied up the area. Forensic techs assembled near their van.

The ME arrived in record time. Dr. Serena Jones was a tall African American woman with an athletic stride that ate up the ground. Today, she wore rubber boots and a knee-length down coat zipped to her chin. Her fake fur–trimmed hood was up. She looked like she was headed out on an Arctic expedition.

Bree and Matt escorted her to the Buick. As Dr. Jones approached the body, she hunched her shoulders against the freezing wind. She and her assistant carried plastic med kits.

She stopped fifteen feet shy of the car and set down her box. Looking into the trunk, she propped her hands on her hips and took in the scene for a minute. "Are all of these tracks yours?" She indicated the snow at their feet.

Bree nodded. "Yes. There were none before we approached the trunk."

Dr. Jones pulled out her phone and opened an app. "The snow fell last Friday. So, he's been here since before that." She shoved her phone back into her pocket, then sighed and tugged on exam gloves. She carefully touched the victim's arm, then prodded a few spots on the body. "He's frozen." She looked to her assistant. "I need some light."

The assistant shined a flashlight into the trunk. The ME contorted her spine to get a better look, then she carefully extracted herself from the trunk. "GSW to the back of the head. Looks like the bullet exited through the face, which will make ID'ing him more complicated. Second shot in the back of the torso." She pursed her lips. "The lack of blood and brain matter in the trunk indicate he was killed elsewhere. The body is at least partially frozen, so determining time of death will be challenging as well. The cold will have affected both rigor mortis and lividity." She straightened, her head tilting. "We're going to have to thaw him in the fridge before autopsy or we risk the outer skin decaying while the organs remain frozen." She pointed to the back of the neck. "You can see the skin has warmed from the sun on the trunk this morning. That's where the slight odor is coming from."

"Like a Thanksgiving turkey," Matt said. "It'll go bad if you thaw it on the counter."

"Exactly like that." Dr. Jones nodded.

"Any idea how long it will take to thaw him out?" Matt asked.

Dr. Jones turned up a palm. "Hard to say. A couple of days to a week. Depends how frozen solid he is."

"What about fingerprinting him?" Bree asked.

Dr. Jones leaned closer to the body. "We'll do that as soon as I'm sure his fingers won't snap off when handled."

Matt shivered. He'd visited plenty of death scenes, but unexpected details like that still had the power to make him cringe.

"We'll have to be careful getting him out of the trunk for the same reason. We'll lift him and the tarp out together so we don't lose any trace evidence." Dr. Jones stepped back. Her assistant moved in to photograph the scene from all angles, starting at a distance and gradually moving closer.

"We need to talk to Benjamin." Bree frowned.

"We needed leverage." Matt gestured toward the Buick.

A deputy rushed over. "Sheriff! The dogs found something."

Matt and Bree left the ME and forensic techs to do their jobs. They walked back to the workshop. Outside the building, Bruiser was playing a serious game of tug with a state trooper, thrashing his head back and forth. With his extra-thick coat, he looked like a grizzly bear. The trooper was no small man, but he was working hard to stay on his feet. The dog yanked the toy away, pranced backward, and went down in a play stance. Seemingly pleased with himself, he lay in the snow and chewed on his prize.

Todd motioned for them to enter the building. "We hit gold. Well, not gold exactly. But enough cash, drugs, and weapons to put all the participants away for a long time."

Matt's boots rang on the concrete as they strode across the workshop. "Where?"

Todd pointed to a stack of tires on a shelf. "The drugs are inside the tires."

They walked over. On the concrete, the sidewall of a tire had been sliced to reveal three plastic-wrapped bricks and a box of large pill bottles, the kind that looked like they came directly from the manufacturer.

"That's not particularly clever," Matt said.

"No." Todd shrugged. "These guys rarely are. So far, we've found heroin and a bunch of pills labeled as *Oxy*. There are more in a bottle marked *Vicodin*." Which didn't mean that's what the pills actually were.

Bree crouched to get closer to the pills. The first bottle was open, revealing tablets that looked legitimate, until she used her magnifying app on her phone to examine them in detail and then pulled up a photo of an actual pill. She did the same with the Vicodin bottle. "I think these are counterfeit," she said. "The print is just a little off." She stood. "Only the lab will be able to confirm what they are, but I doubt these are real Oxy or Vicodin."

"Probably fentanyl," Matt said.

"Probably," Bree agreed. The counterfeit pills weren't only dealt on the street as illegal. They were also being sold over the internet and through the mail to people thinking they were legitimate. Unfortunately, a lethal dose of fentanyl was a fraction of one of Oxy. People were overdosing and dying because of operations like the one the Ekin family was running.

"Didn't Prince die from counterfeit opioids laced with fentanyl?" Todd asked.

"Him and thousands of other people," Matt said.

"What about the cash?" Bree asked.

Todd jerked a gloved thumb at the rear of the shop. "There's a safe in the office. It was so easy to find, it was almost anticlimactic."

"How much money?" Matt asked.

Todd's lips curled into a satisfied grin. "We're counting it now, but definitely enough for felony charges."

Matt felt like dancing. This was what he'd missed when he'd been forced to retire—bringing violent and dangerous criminals to justice and getting them off the streets. These were the serve-and-protect moments that removed a threat from the community and made the job worth the sacrifice. He let himself enjoy the feeling for a few minutes. Because the flip side of the job was always that these moments didn't last. There was always more shit to hit the fan. You had to count your victories when they happened.

"In addition to the shotgun, we also found four handguns, one AR-15, and two switchblades, and we're not done."

"Good work!" Matt said.

A deputy was photographing the evidence. Another set a box next to the tires and wrote on a clipboard.

Matt scanned the confiscated haul. "There is enough here to put Benjamin away for a long time."

"And definitely enough to give us some leverage." Bree started toward the door. "Let's go talk to Benjamin and his lawyer. Maybe he'll feel more cooperative."

Chapter Twenty-Two

The Randolph County Correctional Facility was an old, decrepit building that smelled like mold and urine. As sheriff, Bree was in charge of the jail. It was chronically overcrowded and underfunded, and Bree had been unable to rectify the situation so far in her tenure as sheriff. She'd made attempts to improve the conditions—which were unsanitary and uncomfortable—but the problem boiled down to money. She didn't have enough of it. There were simply too many inmates and not enough places to put them. Thankfully, most of the inmates were housed here for only a week or so while they waited for their trials. Only a small percentage were serving actual sentences.

Bree entered the interview room with Matt at her side. Benjamin Ekin and his attorney already sat at the metal table. Benjamin wore the standard orange uniform similar to scrubs. His clothes—including his Timberland boots—had been sent to forensics.

The attorney was a thin blonde woman in her midthirties. Everything about her was pointy, from her facial features to her high-heeled pumps to the tips of her manicured fingernails. She laid a pen on the yellow legal pad in front of her and folded her hands.

Benjamin shifted in his seat. His hands were cuffed in front of his body and secured to a ring set in the table. The table and chairs were bolted to the floor. Despite his restraints, he managed to lean back a few inches, trying to look unaffected.

Bree sat across from Benjamin. Matt faced the attorney.

"I'm Mr. Ekin's lawyer, Veronica Wells." She handed Bree a business card that read SIMPSON, DOYLE & WELLS, ATTORNEYS-AT-LAW. The firm had a reputation as expensive and ruthless. The Ekins family invested in an effective legal team. Ms. Wells wore a silver-gray custom-tailored pantsuit that made Bree feel like a troll in her uniform, duty belt, and rubber-soled boots.

"This interview is being recorded." Bree listed the names of all present, read Benjamin his Miranda rights, then passed him the acknowledgment to sign. Once the procedural boxes had been checked, Bree began. "You're going to prison for a long time."

Benjamin's mouth flattened, but he said nothing.

"Get to the point, Sheriff." The attorney tapped a nail on the table. Her voice was as cold as her ice-blue eyes. She looked like the type of lawyer who would eat a kitten to win a case.

Bree went for shock next. Benjamin had been taken to jail before the body had been found. He didn't know. "Who's the guy in the trunk?"

He jolted upright, going from lazy and mad to attentive in a second. "What?"

"The dead guy in the trunk," Matt said slowly. "Who is he?"

Benjamin's face went pale. "There's no dead guy anywhere."

Matt and Bree exchanged a disbelieving look. Bree opened her phone.

"You can't just accuse my client of random crimes—" The attorney's mouth shut abruptly when Bree showed them a photo of the body.

Benjamin's eyebrows drew into a deep vee. When he looked up, genuine confusion replaced belligerence for a few seconds before hostility filled his eyes once again. "I ain't never seen that dude before. I'm being set up, just like my brother was set up. You cops have it out for my family."

"Stop talking, Benjamin," the lawyer crooned in a 1-900 voice. "Let me handle this. It's what you pay me to do."

Bree waggled the phone. "This dead man was found in the trunk of an old Buick at the back of your salvage yard."

"How was the man found?" the lawyer asked.

"By a K-9," Bree answered.

The lawyer scribbled a note on her legal pad. "Have you identified him yet?"

"No," Bree said.

The lawyer tapped her pen on the pad. "Cause of death? Has the medical examiner ruled out accident or suicide?"

"The ME hasn't officially issued a cause of death yet," Bree volunteered. "But there's a bullet wound in the back of the man's head, so suicide does not look likely."

The attorney shook her head and spoke in a condescending tone. "Why don't we wait for the medical examiner to determine that?"

Matt snorted. "It wasn't an accident either."

The attorney shot him a withering look. "And you're a medical examiner?"

"No, but I've seen plenty of shooting victims." The corner of his mouth turned up, mirroring the lawyer's condescending attitude. "People don't accidentally shoot themselves in the back of the head."

The lawyer wasn't impressed. The only body part that moved was the arch of one perfect eyebrow. She pointedly turned away from Matt and addressed Bree. "The body looks frozen. How long has he been there?"

"We don't know yet," Bree admitted.

"What *do* you know, Sheriff?" the lawyer asked coolly.

"The dead body was found on Mr. Ekin's property," Bree said. "The yard is fenced. The fence is topped with razor wire. The yard is patrolled by two guard dogs. Mr. Ekin assured me earlier today that his salvage yard is secure. So how did that dead body get there?"

The lawyer had no reaction. "Do you intend to charge my client with a crime? Do you even know for certain that a crime was committed?"

"Your client is definitely being brought up on drug charges," Bree said. "I have not had a chance to confer with the DA regarding the specifics of those charges at this time, but we all know they will be substantial. We recovered drugs, guns, and money from the property."

Benjamin's eyes narrowed to mean slits, and his glare felt almost like a physical touch. His hands curled into fists. The hairs on the back of Bree's neck quivered, and goose bumps rippled up her arms. Her instincts screamed that Benjamin was a killer. If Benjamin had a way to attack Bree right then and there, she had no doubt he would have, preferably with his bare hands. If he hadn't been handcuffed to the table, she wasn't sure he could have controlled himself.

Annoyed, the lawyer pursed her lips. "Do you intend to charge my client with a crime relating to this death?"

"Not at this time," Bree said.

The lawyer nodded. "Well then, my client has nothing to say about the body until we have specifics about the death—and the medical examiner has determined that a crime actually occurred."

"I don't know—" Benjamin protested.

"Benjamin." The attorney cut him off with a hand on his forearm. "Let me do my job. I won't allow them to railroad you on a crime you had nothing to do with."

Benjamin nodded, then rolled a shoulder, as if trying to get comfortable with letting the lawyer be in charge.

Bree held up the photo again. "We will find out what happened to him."

"Please let me know when you do." The lawyer didn't smile, but her lips curved a millimeter in satisfaction.

One thing Bree couldn't tolerate was smugness. "The DA will be in touch about those drug charges. We have a truckload of evidence on those." She looked at Benjamin. "You might want to rethink your uncooperative stance. She's not the one who will do the time." She tipped her head toward the attorney.

Ms. Wells's mouth froze, and it was Bree's turn to feel some satisfaction. It felt petty, but whatever. She was human, and her job could be incredibly frustrating. Today she would revel in the fact that the most expensive lawyer in the world wasn't getting Benjamin off without substantial prison time, and they all knew it. This was not his first strike. He had two previous drug convictions. The judge and DA would play hardball, especially if the pills Bree suspected were pharmaceutical fakes turned out to contain fentanyl. Overdoses involving synthetic opioids were increasing at a breakneck pace over the past few years. It was an epidemic.

Fifteen minutes later, Bree retrieved her sidearm from its lockbox. No one—not even law enforcement—was permitted to bring a weapon into the jail. Then she and Matt left the building. The fresh air was cold, but very welcome.

"As long as I've been a cop, I'll never get used to being inside the jail." Matt shoved his hands into his jacket pockets. "It gives me claustrophobia."

"You and me both."

"What did you think of Benjamin's reaction?" Matt asked.

"To the news that we found a body?" Bree pictured it. "He appeared to be genuinely surprised."

"I'm sure he's a good liar."

"He didn't admit to knowing about the drugs, cash, or guns, but he didn't look surprised when I mentioned them."

"Angry, but not surprised." Matt shot her a look. "I'm staying at your house for the near future. I know you can handle yourself, but that whole family is violent and vindictive. I saw the way he was looking at you. He wants to hurt you."

"He does, and I won't take offense that you care."

"Good."

Also, she liked having him around all the time.

They reached the SUV and climbed in. Once in the vehicle, Bree took his hand. "Thank you."

"I'm not complaining." He squeezed her fingers. "But for what?"

"For wanting to be there," she said. "A year ago, I would have resisted. I would have pushed back and insisted I could take care of myself. But . . ." Bree couldn't put into words how she felt. "I'm not the same person I was."

"But you are. Remember when we met at your sister's wedding?"

"I do. I liked you back then, but I was too stubborn to see it. Too stubborn to think I could change my life and it could get better." Bree had been hanging on to her career as the most important aspect of her life. She hadn't wanted to make room for anything else. She hadn't been unhappy, but she hadn't been happy either. But then, she hadn't known what real happiness was, and now she did.

He grinned. "The first time I saw you, I was blown away."

Surprised, Bree said, "You never told me that."

"A man's gotta hold something back for the right moment." His blue eyes turned wicked. "Plus, it wasn't the right time. You're not the only one who would have resisted a deeper relationship a year ago. I wasn't ready either."

So much had happened since then. Grief rose unexpectedly in her throat, as it often did, blindsiding her. "I can't believe it's been a year since she died."

"I know." His face softened.

"I want the kids to move on but also not to forget her." She sighed so hard it hurt.

"They won't forget her."

"Luke won't. But Kayla's memories will be hazier. She's so young." It broke Bree's heart when she thought about all the milestones Erin was missing.

"She'll remember what she needs to, but maybe she needs that haziness to move on. Her loss can't be sharp all the time. Remembering is one thing. Living in the past is another. She's finding her way. You should be proud."

"Oh, I am. That kid is strong." Bree's eyes brimmed with tears. "I need to thank your parents for helping her with that. Luke is more independent. He looks up to your parents, but he has a job and sports and teammates for support. Kayla hasn't really developed her social circle yet."

"She's nine. Who had a social circle at nine?"

"Not her, but she needs people around her to feel secure."

"Well, my parents are thrilled. My dad was practically giddy at the chance to be a grandpa."

"Good. Then it's a win-win."

"Definitely." Matt rubbed the back of her hand with his thumb. "If we weren't in the jail parking lot, I'd kiss you right now."

She smiled. "I'd kiss you back, but I appreciate not having our PDAs recorded by the security cameras."

"You're so strict."

She loved that he could make her laugh at the most unexpected times.

"Time to see Ford?" he asked.

"It is." Bree shifted into gear. "Think someone notified him of Benjamin's arrest?"

"Probably. He has more cousins."

Matt plugged his address into the GPS, and Bree drove out of the parking lot.

Fifteen minutes later, Bree drove up to Ford's trailer. The park was crowded, with each unit squatting on a small patch of weeds. Like the family home, and Benjamin's house, the trailer's yard could have appeared on the reality show *Hoarders*. A kitchen sink leaned up against the trailer's foundation next to a stack of old tires. Why did people keep so much junk?

Matt pointed to the trailer next door. Flower boxes decorated its tiny front porch and the walkway had been neatly shoveled. "They must *love* living next to Ford."

Bree and Matt got out of the vehicle and flanked the front door. They stood on the ground, avoiding the cinder block that served as a front step. Wary, she kept one hand on her gun as she knocked. Ford opened the door, drinking a Coke. He was a little leaner than his brothers, but the family resemblance was strong, including soulless eyes that suggested killing and dismembering her would not keep him up at night.

Bree introduced herself and Matt. "We need to ask you a few questions."

"I know who you are, and I got nothing to say." He moved as if he were going to close the door.

"Not so fast." Bree put a hand on the door. "You agreed to warrant-less searches as a condition of your parole."

"Fucking cops," Ford muttered, moving aside. He stood still, arms crossed over his chest, glaring poison daggers at them as they stepped on the cinder block and entered a cramped kitchen and living room combination. The kitchen was filthy, covered in takeout containers, used plastic utensils, and various stains that looked vaguely sticky. Bree didn't intend to find out. She could see a bedroom through an open door to her left.

"You really have it out for my family," Ford said bitterly. "Some kind of cop vendetta."

"I'll look around. You watch him." Matt wandered into the bedroom, tugging on a pair of gloves.

"There's nothing in there," Ford called. "I know the conditions of my parole. I'm not taking any chances of having my parole revoked."

"Where were you Monday night about eleven thirty?" Bree asked.

"Here." Ford sulked.

"You're sure?"

"Positive." He ground his jaw. "I go to work. I come home. That's it. I'm not allowed to do anything else." He oozed self-pity. He wasn't remorseful. He was just angry that he'd gotten caught.

Bree had no sympathy. "What about Tuesday morning? Around eleven."

"I don't know. Probably here, sleeping. I work nights, but you know that."

"I do." Bree nodded. "I also know you were at Lily's Internet Café Tuesday morning."

Surprise flickered in his eyes. He shut it down. "Really?"

"You're on the surveillance feed."

"So I got coffee. That's allowed." His tone dripped with sarcasm.

"You didn't use their Wi-Fi to send any emails?"

"Not that I recall." He didn't bother to hide the lie in his eyes.

She held out a hand. "Let me see your phone."

"Don't have one." There was that belligerent chin lift the whole family shared.

"Really?" She didn't believe him. He probably had a burner stashed somewhere.

"Can't afford it. Being a janitor doesn't pay that well." The *dumb bitch* was implied by the twist of his mouth.

Matt emerged from the bedroom. "How does your parole officer contact you?"

"I have a landline." Ford nodded toward a cordless phone on the kitchen counter. "Or he calls me at work."

"Your employer doesn't mind?" Bree asked.

Ford sneered. "My parole officer got me the job. Dude hires felons because he can pay them shit, treat them like shit. They can't quit or risk going back to prison. He's got us by the short hairs. Soon as my parole is over, I'm outa there."

Matt opened kitchen drawers and cabinets. "And back to the family business?"

Ford didn't respond, but his eyes said yes.

"Can you prove you were here Monday night?" Bree asked.

"Can you prove I wasn't?" His tone was like a snotty teenager's. "I have to let you paw through my stuff, but I don't have to answer your questions. I got rights."

Matt tapped a pizza box with his foot. "Do you order a pizza every night?"

Ford shook his head. Matt lifted the top of the pizza box, then stepped on the trash can pedal. There wasn't much furniture in the living area to search, just a single recliner. A coffee can sat on the floor next to it, serving as an ash tray. The stink of cigarette butts filled the room.

Matt detoured to the bathroom.

"Do you know what happened to Benjamin today?" She watched his face for a reaction.

Ford clamped his mouth shut. But he knew. She could see it in the murderous look in his eyes. He was a seething font of anger. It bubbled inside him like black tar.

She moved a step closer. "Who told you?"

He stared back in silence.

"Did someone call you?" She glanced at the landline.

"If you weren't a cop . . ." He stopped, biting off the bitter words.

"What were you saying?" Bree stepped closer. She almost wanted him to hit her. Maybe she'd even let him. Then she could arrest him and put him back in jail, where he wouldn't hurt anyone. Because she knew deep in her soul that she was looking at a violent man. There were people in this world that could not be redeemed. People who were born with no empathy and an overload of selfish greed. They felt entitled to whatever they wanted. They dealt poison masked as drugs, abused dogs, and raped elderly women. They beat and intimidated their neighbors. Every Ekin she'd met so far made her soul cringe.

The tendons in Ford's neck stood out like steel cables. But Bree didn't yield. Finally, he looked away. Beneath his surrender, she sensed shame that he'd backed down from a woman and the desire to get even. But he wouldn't get his revenge like this. No. A man like Ford wouldn't be up front about anything. He'd set an ambush.

Matt emerged from the bathroom. With a curt nod, he said, "Nothing."

Ford smirked, another trademark Ekin expression. "Satisfied?"

"For now." Bree stepped back. "Stay out of trouble."

They left the trailer.

"Boots?" she asked.

Matt shook his head, clearly disappointed. "Several pairs. Size ten and a half, which might be close enough. Size can vary a little between different manufacturers, or he might allow room for an extra pair of socks, but they weren't Timberlands."

Damn.

"I'll bet he has a phone somewhere."

"Probably uses burners," Matt agreed. "Now what?"

"We go to the station. We need to regroup and check in with Todd about the search at the salvage yard."

"I have an email from Darcy," Matt said. "She pulled a thumbprint from the creepy diorama. Because it's a thumbprint, she can't compare it to the fingerprint from the spray can. I asked her to compare it to Benjamin, Ford, and Steve Ekin's official prints. No match. She's running it through AFIS."

"Then the paint can and box were handled by someone other than Benjamin, Ford, or Steve. Who's left?"

Matt shrugged. "It's a big family, but we're running out of possibilities."

"We know Ford Ekin bought coffee at the café the morning the email was sent from their Wi-Fi. So, I'm still betting the emails are from him."

"What about Louis Toland and his uncle?" Matt asked.

"I'm not sure. We don't have any evidence linking one of them either to the emails or physical threats."

"Do we have background info on the uncle yet?"

Bree checked her inbox. "Yes." She skimmed the report from one of her deputies. "His criminal record is clean. He's lived here and operated his business for decades."

"No criminal record means his prints probably aren't in the system," Matt said. "Stan Toland hates you. He could be your stalker."

CHAPTER

TWENTY-THREE

Matt scored a stale doughnut in the break room. He made two cups of coffee and carried them and the doughnut to Bree's office. Marge perched on a chair facing Bree's desk, a steno pad balanced on her knees. Matt set Bree's coffee on her desk and took the second visitor chair.

Bree shook a handful of pink message slips. "I can't believe we still use these."

Marge lifted a shoulder. "Some people will not use voice mail, and you are a public servant. It's your duty to respond." She referred to her notes, which appeared to be written in actual shorthand. "Madeline Jager called twice. She needs you to meet with the contractor to discuss the electrical issue."

"When?" Bree turned on her desktop computer.

"Monday. Ten a.m. I already put it on your calendar." Marge flipped the page on her pad and stood.

"Thank you." Bree tapped her "Enter" key as Marge left the office. Bree took a sip of the coffee and her lips curved. "Thank you."

He was always pleased to make her smile. "You're welcome." He lifted the doughnut in offering, but she shook her head. Matt ate it in three bites.

Her phone rang again. "It's Dana." She tapped the screen. "Hey. I'm in my office with Matt. You're on speaker. How did it go with Hanover?"

"You're not going to believe it." Dana told them a stunningly ridiculous interview story.

"You're right," Bree said. "I don't believe it. That's crazy."

Irritated, Matt shook his head. "He thinks you killed Kent?"

"Apparently. I felt like I was in an alternate dimension." Dana sounded exhausted.

"You need to call Morgan Dane right away," Matt said. "She'll feed Hanover his own balls."

"And she'll do it in heels and pearls," Bree added.

"I already did," Dana said. "She's calling him." Her next breath was a disgusted sound. "I shouldn't have let the interview go on that long, but he was sneaky, and my brain isn't working the way it should."

"I'm sure you handled it fine," Bree said.

Dana huffed. "I felt like an amateur. I know better, but I've never been on that side of the table."

"Morgan will handle it," Bree insisted. "Take a nap. You'll feel better. Have you eaten?"

"Nolan made me some french toast," Dana said.

"Good. Call me with any updates. We'll try to be home in an hour." Bree ended the call.

Matt wiggled his eyebrows. "He made her french toast."

Bree rolled her eyes at him. "Who are you? Cupid?"

"What can I say? It makes me happy." But Hanover's accusations did not. Matt hammer-punched the armrest. "I was wrong about Hanover. I thought he was an OK cop."

"Now we know." Bree shrugged. "Morgan will handle him the same way she handled Detective Ash from BCI."

"I hope so," Matt said.

A while back, Detective Ash had come after Bree for the murder of a former employee. He'd supported Bree after the truth had been discovered, and still . . .

"Ash, at least, did turn out to be a decent detective." Bree had apparently forgiven him. "What he did wasn't personal. He saw it as doing his job."

"He's still an ass." Matt held a grudge.

Someone knocked on her doorframe. Todd poked his head inside. His face was red from the cold. "I'm back."

Bree waved him in. "How is the search going?"

"We stopped for the night." He leaned on the doorframe. "We'll start up again in the morning. I hope we'll finish tomorrow, thanks to the dogs. We found the drugs and cash Tony ran with. He hid them in the wheel well of an old Chevy. Other than that, the most interesting thing we've found is a drawerful of burner phones. No financials on the *businesses* so far. We're confiscating electronics in case he kept digital records."

"Dealers usually keep track somehow," Matt said. "They like to know their margins."

Bree nodded. "Don't stay tonight. Go home after roll call. Get some food and sleep."

"I plan to. Cady is bringing me dinner." Todd gave them a tired smile and withdrew.

"So Benjamin's personal phone will likely be clean." Bree drummed her fingertips on her desk.

"I'm sure the whole family uses burners." Matt checked the time. "Do you want to go home for dinner and work there later?"

"Yes. I would like to have dinner with the family."

"Me too." Matt enjoyed family dinners as much as she did, something that surprised him. He'd always liked kids in the abstract sense, but he hadn't spent much time with any until now.

She tapped on her keyboard and squinted at the monitor, then fanned the pink message slips in front of her. "I need thirty minutes to answer emails and messages."

Matt stood, grateful that he didn't have to juggle PR and administration with a major investigation. "I'll work on reports."

Bree's phone rang as he started toward the door. "It's the ME." Bree answered the call. "You're on speaker. Matt Flynn is here as well."

Matt closed the door and turned to listen.

"We found something interesting when we were cataloging the body." Dr. Jones didn't bother with small talk. "There was no ID in the pockets, but I do have one interesting thing for you. The second GSW, the one in the torso, passed through the victim's flank just below the ribs. The bullet exited the body and was caught by a large cluster of keys on a ring in the victim's pocket."

"We have a bullet?" Bree's voice rose.

Matt wanted to high-five someone. They hadn't been expecting any evidence until the delayed autopsy was performed.

"I'll send it to ballistics," Dr. Jones said. "We sent the tarp to forensics, and I hope the victim's hands will defrost enough by tomorrow to be fingerprinted. I can't do anything else until the rest of the body thaws."

"That's more than I expected," Bree said. "Thank you, Doctor." She ended the call and turned to Matt. "Hopefully one of the weapons seized at the salvage yard or from Benjamin Ekin's house will be the murder weapon."

Less optimistic, Matt said, "That would be too easy."

With a quick trio of knocks, Marge opened the door. "You need to see this." She turned on the TV in the corner of Bree's office. "Chief Hanover is holding a press conference."

Matt sat back down. On the screen, Chief Hanover stood behind a podium. Two uniformed officers flanked him. To one side, a blonde woman hugged herself and clutched a tissue. Matt guessed she was the victim's family. Reporters clustered in the small space, which looked like the lobby of the station.

Hanover cleared his throat. "As you all know, Dr. Kent McFadden was shot in his home Monday evening. On Tuesday, Dr. McFadden succumbed to his injuries. The medical examiner has completed the preliminary autopsy report, and Dr. McFadden's death is officially being investigated as a homicide. At this time, we believe this to be an isolated incident and do not believe there is any danger to the general public."

A reporter called out, "Do you have any suspects?"

Hanover leaned into his microphone. "This is only day two of the investigation. We are talking to everyone in Dr. McFadden's life to understand why someone would commit such a terrible act."

"Was this an attempted robbery?" another reporter asked.

Hanover shook his head. "We don't believe that robbery was the motive behind the shooting."

"My sources say there was a woman with Dr. McFadden when he was shot," another reporter chimed in. "Is it true she was beaten by the intruder?"

Hanover looked pained at the question. Did he really think the reporters wouldn't already know two people went to the hospital Monday night? "Yes, there was a woman present, but please respect her privacy at this time."

The blonde woman stepped forward. Her face was ravaged and red, as if she'd been crying nonstop. Her eyes were so swollen, they almost looked closed.

Matt tensed. "Victim's family?"

"Yes." Bree didn't move, but her face went tight. "That's Kent's sister."

"Uh-oh."

"Yeah," Bree agreed. "This can't be good."

The blonde woman pointed a shaky finger at Hanover. "Her name is Dana Romano." Her voice was raspy and bitter. "She killed Kent! I know it. Why haven't you arrested her yet?"

While Matt felt bad for her, she had no right to slander Dana. How had she even gotten Dana's name?

Several uniforms encircled the sister. A female officer took her arm. But she was not going quietly. She yelled over her shoulder, "Romano used to be a cop in Philadelphia. It's a cover-up. There was no intruder."

Chaos broke out. Reporters all yelling at once.

"Is it true that Dana Romano is a suspect?"

"Why did she kill him?"

"Are you going to arrest Ms. Romano?"

Hanover's face shone with perspiration. He yelled, "No comment," into the mic and made a panicked retreat. The press conference was over.

"I hope Dana didn't see that." Bree reached for her phone. "She's not answering."

Matt called his brother. "Where's Dana?"

"Sleeping," Nolan said.

"Keep her away from social media and the news. Keep her off-screen completely," Matt said.

"Why?" Nolan asked, clearly alarmed.

"I'll tell you when we get home. We're on the way." Matt ended the call.

Bree grabbed her coat and purse. "Let's go." She turned to Marge. "I'll be working from home the rest of the evening."

"Go." Marge turned off the TV. "How dare she make accusations like that."

Bree slid into her jacket. "It's Hanover's fault."

"He shouldn't have allowed her in the room." Anger churned in Matt's chest. "She's clearly unstable. He lost control of the whole thing."

"Didn't look like he ever had control of the event." Marge huffed.

The goal of a press conference was to provide the community with accurate information and prevent rampant speculation. Hanover had done the opposite. He'd allowed misinformation to spread.

"It won't take the press long to learn who Dana is." Bree hurried toward the door. "And track her to the farm."

Thankfully, the farm was quiet when they arrived.

Matt opened the passenger door and climbed out. The only sound was the sweep of wind across the pasture. "Feels like the calm before the storm."

"Probably." Bree sighed.

The barn lights were on, and they made a stop to see who was inside. Luke was cleaning stalls. Kayla stood on a stool in the aisle, grooming Pumpkin. Her little Haflinger snoozed, one rear hoof cocked. He barely flicked an eyelid as Bree and Matt walked past him. Matt gave his own horse some neck rubs while they chatted with both kids for a few minutes before heading to the house.

The heat in the kitchen burned Matt's face. He took off his jacket and hung it by the back door. Bree did the same, and they washed their hands.

Nolan sat at the table, his laptop open. "The new camera is set up behind the barn. I also put one in the barn so you can check on the animals from anywhere."

"Great." Bree filled the teakettle. "Is Dana up?"

"Yes," Dana said from the doorway. She looked sick. "And I saw the press con. Morgan called. She already contacted Hanover. We have a meeting set up first thing in the morning."

"Where?" Bree asked.

Dana slid into a chair. "Hanover wanted us to come to the station, but Morgan didn't like the optics. It would look too much like a perp walk. I didn't want him here. We're meeting at her office. Neutral ground."

Matt filled a glass with water. "I hate that you have to worry about optics. You aren't a criminal. It's not right."

Dana propped her elbows on the table and dropped her head into her hands. "After the meeting with Morgan tomorrow, I need to stay somewhere else for a few days or the media is going to camp out front. The kids can't endure that again."

"You can stay at my place." Nolan lived in an apartment over his gym.

"I was thinking I'd go back to Philly until this is over," Dana said in a tired voice. "If it's ever over. Hanover isn't going to solve the case if he's fixated on me."

Nolan shook his head. "It's safer if you stay with me."

"Plus, you don't want to look as if you're running away." Matt sat down across from her.

"The kids are more important," Dana insisted. "They went through hell last year. I won't put them through that again. I'm going to pack a bag so I'm ready to go tomorrow."

"Hello?" Nolan stood and leaned on the table. "My place is very safe. No kids there. The gym has an excellent security system, and it's usually filled with fighters. No one is going to mess with you there."

Matt agreed. "Nolan's gym would be a great place to lay low."

Dana lifted her head and looked at Nolan. "The media will intrude on your life. Your students won't like news vans parked out front, and reporters shoving microphones into their faces."

"Eh. I could use the publicity, and the first reporter who shoves a microphone in my face will serve as an example for the rest of them." Nolan's eyes went cage-fight hard, a look Matt knew well. Anyone who crossed him would regret it.

Matt's brother was a marshmallow in so many ways, but he was also not a man to mess with. His students came to him because of his reputation as a professional fighter. Nolan was not under any pressure to bow to the media or anyone else.

"What time is the meeting?" Matt asked.

"Eight thirty," Dana said.

"I'll drive you," Nolan offered.

Bree pulled out her phone. "If Adam takes the kids to school again, I could go too."

"No," Dana said. "That'll just piss off Hanover and make me look weak. I am weak, but he doesn't need to know that."

Nolan's head snapped up. "You're not weak. You're concussed."

Anger swelled in Matt. "Hanover can't have a very strong case against you."

Dana said, "I wish that were true. Unfortunately, the way he presented the evidence, he made a very compelling case. He might convince me I'm guilty." She turned to Nolan. "If the offer is still open, I'll stay at your place for a couple of days."

"Of course," Nolan answered.

"Thank you. I'm going to bed. I'll pack a bag in the morning. I'm too tired to do it now. Hopefully, they won't find me until tomorrow." Dana got up and slumped from the room.

Normally, she was a resilient, take-charge kind of person. She wasn't the sort to give up, but tonight she looked defeated.

"I'll be back in the morning." Nolan shrugged into his coat and left.

"I'm still going to ask Adam to take the kids to school. I don't feel comfortable letting Luke drive himself. He's going to be disappointed, but I don't know what else to do." Bree frowned as her phone buzzed. "There's another email from RedBloodedMale03."

Matt moved closer to look at her phone screen. She opened the email and drew in a sharp breath.

There were two photos embedded in the email. The first showed Luke on the walkway in front of the high school. He was headed to the front door, his backpack slung over one shoulder. The second was a similar photo of Kayla.

Bree's face had gone pale. "I'm calling both schools in the morning, and I'll drive both kids to school."

Fury boiled in Matt's chest. "We are going to find this guy."

There was no text in the email, just the photos. But the message was clear. RedBloodedMale03 had been close enough to the kids to take photographs.

"I changed my mind." She met Matt's gaze. "Nolan and Dana should stay here. Even if the press hounds Dana, it would be too easy for RedBloodedMale03 to sneak up on an empty house."

CHAPTER
TWENTY-FOUR

Dana walked through the foyer of the converted duplex that housed Morgan Dane's office. The lawyer shared space with a PI firm, Sharp Investigations. At her request, Nolan waited outside in his truck. He wasn't happy about it, but she needed to appear and feel strong enough to handle this on her own. Weakness spread like weeds. Once it got hold, it took over.

Morgan ushered her into a neat office. "Coffee?" The attorney wore a deep-blue suit, pale-blue blouse, and single strand of pearls. Her hair was bound in a fancy twist.

Meanwhile, Dana needed an undertaker to do her makeup. "No, thanks." She eased into the chair facing the desk.

Morgan faced her, leaned her butt on the desk, and assessed her. "I'll get you some water. Did you take something for the pain?"

Dana nodded.

"Does it help?"

"A little. The headache isn't as bad today."

Morgan crossed to a mini fridge and took out a bottle of water. "Good, but you should be focused on your recovery."

"Tell Hanover."

"Don't worry. I will." The tone of Morgan's voice chilled as she handed over the cold bottle.

A hint of what was to come?

Dana twisted off the cap and took a small sip. "I appreciate you helping me out."

Instead of going behind the desk, Morgan sat in the chair next to her. "Can you tell me what happened the night Kent was killed?"

Dana lowered the bottle, her stomach wonky again. "I gave you a copy of my statement."

"You did." Morgan's voice turned sympathetic. "But I'd like to hear it in your own words." She paused. "Your statement is a little dry."

Dana snorted. "Just the facts, ma'am."

Morgan smiled. "My entire family either was or is in law enforcement. I know the evidence-based mindset, but I sense there are details—impressions—missing. Those details might make all the difference."

Dana closed her eyes for a second, then opened them again. She did not want to rehash the whole experience again, but what choice did she have? "OK."

"I know it's hard, and I'm sorry for what happened to you. And that Chief Hanover is amplifying your trauma and hampering your recovery." Morgan reached for a small recorder on her desk. "If it's all right with you, I'm going to record your recollection. The recording will be completely confidential. I will not play it for anyone without your consent."

Nodding, Dana wrapped both hands around the bottle to keep her hands from shaking. She took a deep breath and began with her arriving at Kent's house, her fight with the assailant, and going upstairs to find Kent bleeding out on the carpet. "I tried to save him, but he'd lost so much blood."

So much blood.

Morgan didn't interrupt or ask any questions. She just listened. Even her body language was quiet.

"Some parts of the night are foggy. I try to see details, and I just can't. Other parts"—like being up to her wrists in Kent's blood—"I can see every second like it's being played in slow motion." Over and over and over.

"You have a head injury. Your recall will not be perfect, and no one should expect it to be."

Dana sighed. "Hanover thinks I killed Kent." The thought still bewildered her. "I can't wrap my mind around that."

"He's just wrong. That's all." Morgan's quiet smile turned sharp. "Please let me handle Chief Hanover. It's my job."

Dana nodded and finished her story, filling in the details where she could and specifying what parts were hazy.

Hanover arrived a few minutes later. Morgan brought him into her office and directed him to the second guest chair. Then she went around her desk and sat. Hanover crossed his legs, then uncrossed them. He was uncomfortable. With what? His theory or being called out on it? He barely looked at Dana but focused on Morgan.

"Now, tell me why you have allowed my client's name to be slandered." Morgan pulled no punches.

Hanover didn't stammer, but his mouth opened and closed twice before he said, "I never accused her of anything. I can't control what Dr. McFadden's family thinks."

Morgan didn't respond in any way, her gaze steady, her body still and confident.

Hanover cleared his throat. "Elizabeth McFadden is distraught. She isn't thinking straight. She and her brother were close."

"She was standing with your officers. *You* allowed her into that press conference. *You* allowed her to slander my client. Ms. Romano is recovering from a serious injury. She was assaulted and suffered trauma in the same incident that killed Dr. McFadden. She should be home recuperating, not being accused of a crime in which she was a victim."

Hanover's lips twisted. "Is she?"

Morgan's head tilted an inch, and her eyes narrowed. "Please elaborate."

If Dana had been operating at 100 percent, she would have wanted popcorn for this show. Today, she was just relieved to let Morgan handle the questions. There was nothing wrong with Morgan's brain.

Hanover glanced sideways at Dana, then back to Morgan. "Ms. Romano claims she was assaulted. We have no evidence of that."

Morgan raised a hand and counted items off on her fingers. "The X-rays, CT scan, bruises—including a ring of them around her throat—and the diagnoses of the ER physician and a neurologist. Both doctors detailed Ms. Romano's injuries."

Hanover crossed his arms. "We don't know *how* she obtained those injuries."

"She has stated how she received these injuries," Morgan said. "In an altercation with Dr. McFadden's killer."

"So she says." Hanover shifted in his seat, the butt scoot a sign of additional discomfort. Was he lying or just unsure of himself? "But she could be lying. She could have received the exact same injuries in a fight with Dr. McFadden."

"That doesn't make any sense."

"They had an argument, and it got physical. McFadden was the one who choked her. She pulled a gun and shot him. It could have happened in the heat of the moment." Was he looking for a confession to a lesser degree of murder or even manslaughter?

"That's an interesting *theory*." Morgan's tone indicated her opinion of it. "If you like fiction."

Hanover lifted his chin. "Dr. McFadden had talked on the phone to his ex several times that week. He still had feelings for her." He turned to Dana. "Did you see the messages? Were you jealous of her? Is that why you killed him?"

Dana didn't even know how to reply. She started to say that was ridiculous, but Morgan said, "Evidence, Chief Hanover, where is your evidence?"

"His blood was literally on her hands," Hanover said.

"Because she gave him CPR. Should she not have tried to save his life?" Morgan asked. "I assume you tested Ms. Romano's hands for gunshot residue?"

Hanover frowned.

"They did," Dana offered.

Morgan nodded and returned that steady gaze to Hanover. "Was it negative?"

"Yes," he grumbled.

Morgan folded her hands on her blotter, as if she had this whole thing wrapped up. "The gunshot residue test on Ms. Romano's hands was negative, and her weapon was not the gun used to shoot Dr. McFadden."

"Correct." Hanover glared at her. "But blood or other moisture can prevent GSR from sticking to the test stubs. Her hands were covered in blood, so the result could be a false negative."

"But it *was* negative," Morgan pressed.

Hanover's silence was his answer.

"And her gun was definitely not the one used to kill Dr. McFadden, so I don't understand where this theory of yours even comes from."

He ground his teeth.

"In your scenario, why did Dr. McFadden access his weapon? He had a biometric safe. No one but him could have opened it." Morgan waited for two heartbeats before continuing. "Did he pull the gun before or after he tried to choke Ms. Romano? And why would he ever try to choke her in the first place? If he was choking her, why would he need a gun? You told Ms. Romano and Sheriff Taggert that Dr. McFadden was an easygoing man and loved by everyone who knew him. Him assaulting Ms. Romano definitely doesn't agree with your own witness statements."

"She could have attacked him first." Hanover's voice didn't project confidence.

Morgan lifted one eyebrow. "Why?"

"I already said. Jealousy."

"Your theory is that Ms. Romano, after a mere handful of dates with Dr. McFadden, was jealous enough to kill him over some phone calls with his ex?" Morgan made it sound ridiculous.

"It could have happened."

"Where did the extra gun come from?" Morgan asked.

Hanover nodded toward Dana without looking at her. "She could have brought it with her. She was a cop. She'd know how to get an unregistered gun."

Morgan gave him the slight head tilt again. "Do you have any evidence that she did that?"

"Not yet," he said.

"So, that's no." Morgan exhaled through her nose, the sound dismissive. "Earlier you said the crime happened in the heat of the moment. Now, you say it was premeditated. Which is it?"

Hanover didn't answer.

Morgan continued to roll over him like a backhoe. "What does the DA have to say about your *theory*?"

Hanover's jaw sawed back and forth. He hadn't taken anything to the DA, and they all knew it.

"You haven't even discussed this with Bryce yet, have you?" Morgan casually let him know she was on a first-name basis with the DA, Bryce Walters. "We both know he wouldn't risk his reputation on your *theory*." She pronounced *theory* like *feces*.

"All I need is a search warrant," Hanover said in a bitter tone. His expression suggested he'd tried and failed to get one.

Morgan shook her head and sighed. "We all know you don't have probable cause."

He sat and stared for a few seconds, grinding his teeth again.

Morgan continued, ignoring his obvious frustration. "You've already allowed Elizabeth McFadden to drag this retired, decorated police officer's name through the mud once. Irreparable damage has been done to Ms. Romano's reputation. Slander will not be tolerated without legal repercussion. In fact, we expect her name officially cleared and a full apology issued by you, publicly."

"Her name will be cleared when it's cleared." Hanover enunciated each word separately.

Morgan tsked. "So guilty until proven innocent?" She waited a beat. "That's not how this works."

Hanover stood. "I *will* get a warrant." The *somehow* was implied. He turned a scathing look on Dana before pivoting on a heel and striding out of the office without another word.

Dana suppressed a shiver. "He really thinks I killed Kent." The idea felt alien to her. "He's already decided I'm guilty. He won't look for anyone else. He's going to see any evidence they discover in one light." From her years of experience, she understood the danger of a detective formulating theories before having the proof to support them. "Instead of following the evidence, he's letting his preconceived theory lead the investigation. It's something an experienced detective knows can happen, so they intentionally suppress the tendency."

Still standing, Morgan stared at the empty doorway. "He's holding something back."

"Forensics found light rosin on my clothes and Dr. McFadden's. Light rosin is used on the bows of stringed instruments. Hanover doesn't know this, but Kayla has a violin in the back of her closet. She quit months ago. The case is probably covered in dust."

"But where there's a violin, there's rosin."

"Correct."

Morgan lowered herself into her chair. "How do you know this?"

"He told me." Dana's tired brain processed Hanover's statements, albeit slowly. "I don't like that he told us about the warrant he's trying to get. Did he tip his hand, or is he trying to set us up?"

"You mean he wants you to try and take something out of the house?"

"Yes. Maybe he's going to watch the house?" Dana rubbed her forehead. "This gives me a headache." She'd been having a better day—the pain and nausea had eased—until this meeting.

"Don't do anything. Don't touch that violin. Let it continue to collect dust. All you need to remember is not to talk to Hanover without me."

"I can do that." Dana stood. She needed this meeting to be over. "Thank you for everything."

Morgan rose and came around the desk, taking Dana's hand in both of her own. "I want you to go home and get some rest."

Dana nodded. Her head might be less painful, but the exhaustion remained. She could barely keep her eyes open. "I want to sleep all the time."

"Hopefully, you're on the mend, but we need to get ahead of any speculation. I'd like to call our own press conference."

"No." Dana felt better—but not that much better. "I'd underperform. My brain isn't up to it."

Morgan nodded. "A written statement then."

"OK."

"I'll work on one." Morgan wrote a note on a legal pad. "Keep me posted on anything else that comes up."

"I will." Dana left. Outside, the sky had darkened to steel gray, and the air smelled like woodsmoke and impending snow.

She climbed into the passenger seat of Nolan's truck. The seat was cold under her butt. She wanted to get into bed and stay there. Damn it. The Redhaven cops were adding to the trauma she'd already suffered.

He started the engine and turned on the heat. "How did it go?"

"It goes against all my years as a cop to love a defense attorney, but she beat him like a piñata. He'd swing in a different direction, and she'd smack him again."

Nolan laughed. "She has an excellent reputation."

"I have to call Bree and give her the lowdown." After the call connected, Dana summed up all of Morgan's evidentiary arguments. "The good news is his case has more holes than a golf course."

"The bad news?" Bree asked.

Dana leaned back and closed her eyes. "Morgan agrees that Hanover is up to something. Maybe trying to get me to react. We can't let down our guard."

Chapter Twenty-Five

In the cold barn, Bree ended the call with Dana, stuffed her phone in her barn coat, and called out, "Morgan thrashed Hanover."

Matt was grooming his horse, Beast, in the aisle. "Figured she would."

Bree swept a brush across her horse's shoulder. She'd driven the kids to school, spoken with both principals, then needed an hour to decompress. Worrying about their safety was making it hard to concentrate.

Cowboy arched his neck and nuzzled Bree's pocket. She pressed her forehead against his neck. The paint gelding had been her sister's, and Bree always felt more settled when she was with him.

Matt fussed with Beast. "Stand still, you big dope," he said affectionately.

The big dope nickered and snuffled.

Bree leaned over the half door of Cowboy's stall. Since Matt had bought the Percheron at auction out from under the kill buyer, Beast had filled out into a gorgeous animal. Matt was adjusting a new bridle to his huge head, but Beast just wanted scratches.

"Finally." Matt buckled the last strap and rubbed behind Beast's ears. The horse twisted his head and leaned into the attention.

An engine sounded outside. Bree left Cowboy's stall, went to the barn door, and peered in the two-inch gap between the sliding doors. A news van stopped on the shoulder of the road. A second crew parked behind the first. Van doors opened. People got out and hauled equipment with them. "The press is here."

Matt joined her, looking over her head. "I'll get rid of them." He turned his horse around. "Open the door."

Bree rolled the door sideways, and Matt led Beast out of the barn. Using the hitching post next to the barn, he mounted his horse bareback and rode him up the driveway, straight at the news crews. He didn't stop until he and the horse were less than five feet away. "Can I help you?"

People scrambled backward, staring at the giant black horse. At two thousand pounds, his size alone was intimidating as hell. His shaggy winter coat made him look even bigger. He snorted in the cold air, sending out plumes of foggy breath like a medieval warhorse. Feet the size of dinner plates pranced. Bree suspected Matt was making the horse dance intentionally. Beast chomped on the bit, raised his head, and neighed.

A man who appeared to be the on-air reporter stepped forward, craning his head to look up at Matt. "We're looking for Dana Romano."

"She isn't here," Matt said.

"But she lives here, right?" A woman stood slightly behind the first reporter, as if that would protect her if the giant animal charged.

Matt let Beast take another step. The horse snorted. More plumes of breath shot from his nose. He just wanted everyone to pet him, but the news crews didn't know that. The entire crowd moved back as a unit. At eighteen hands tall, jet black, and thickly muscled, Beast was quite a sight.

Someone yelled, "Would you answer a few questions about Ms. Romano?"

"No." Matt let Beast take another step.

"Can we talk to Sheriff Taggert?" the female reporter called out, now from the back of the crowd.

"She's busy. This is her home. If you have questions for the sheriff, contact her office. You all have the number." Matt's voice was polite but firm. The horse pawed the snowy ground. A cameraman folded his tripod and moved farther away.

"You may as well clear out. You won't see or learn anything here." Matt turned the horse and walked him back to the barn. He slid to the ground and led Beast inside. Bree closed the door behind them.

She greeted Beast with a neck rub. "Who's a good boy?"

Matt removed his bridle, and Bree gave him a carrot. Beast bobbed his head and rubbed his nose on her arm, smearing orange slobber on her barn coat.

"Do you think they'll come back?" She wiped a few slimy carrot crumbs from her sleeve.

"They might." Matt led Beast into his stall and put on his blanket. "But I enjoyed chasing them off. Don't come to a farm if you don't like large animals."

They closed the barn and set the alarm. After a washup and change of clothes, they headed for the SUV.

Bree paused as a Jeep turned into the driveway. She was about to stop the vehicle when she recognized Juarez behind the wheel. He parked next to her and lowered his window. Bree walked to the driver's side. Her deputy was dressed in cargos, boots, and a down jacket. A takeout cup of coffee sat in his center console.

"It's your day off," she said.

"Yes, ma'am." Juarez nodded. "Word's gotten around that you're being threatened. I'm here all day. Someone else will take over tonight."

A baseball-size lump swelled in her throat. "You don't have to do this."

"No, we don't," Juarez said. "But we will. You have our backs. We have yours."

"Well, thank you." Bree cleared her throat. "Matt's brother, Nolan, will be back soon. I'll let him know you're here. Feel free to go inside if you get cold."

"I can see better from out here. No worries, ma'am. Your family is covered." Juarez raised his window.

Bree turned and got into her SUV. This wasn't the first time her deputies had protected her family on their own time.

"Your deputies are loyal," Matt said.

"They are."

"And they know you won't strain the budget for your own protection."

"I can't. The board of supervisors would lose their minds, and the press would go ballistic," Bree agreed. Every time she questioned whether her job was worth the stress it caused, something happened that renewed her faith. If she didn't at least try to keep her office, she'd be letting her deputies down.

They were at the end of the driveway when Bree's phone rang. "It's forensics." She answered. "This is Sheriff Taggert."

"Rory here."

"Do you have word on who is sending me threatening emails? I want to find this bastard." Bree crossed her fingers. She needed one less thing to worry about.

"No, I'm sorry. I'm still working on that. RedBloodedMale03 was more careful this time. No public Wi-Fi. He used a VPN. I don't know if I'll be able to trace it. I'm still waiting for info from the email provider."

"I appreciate your efforts."

"Yeah, of course," Rory said. "He threatened your kids. We'll catch him."

"Thank you."

"But I do have news. Is Flynn there?" Excitement filled Rory's voice.

"He is. I'll put you on speaker." Bree touched the button on her phone screen.

"Two things," Rory began. "One, we found traces of rosin on the tarp wrapped around Trunk Guy."

"Rosin?" Matt asked.

"Yes! Do you remember me mentioning where else we found rosin?" Rory asked.

"On Dr. McFadden's and Ms. Romano's clothing," Matt said.

"Exactly!" Rory exclaimed. "But wait. There's more." He sounded almost giddy. "We asked ballistics to rush the bullet the ME sent over from Trunk Guy. The bullet was fired from the same gun that killed Dr. McFadden."

"I did not expect to hear that." Bree's mind whirled. "Thanks, Rory."

She ended the call and just sat there, her hands resting on the steering wheel. "Dr. McFadden was killed by the same person who killed the dead guy found in a drug dealer's salvage yard."

Matt stared out the windshield. "How is the home invasion of a cosmetic surgeon related to the body of a John Doe found on a drug dealer's property?"

"There must be a connection." Bree shifted the SUV into gear. "I'm going to have a deputy watch Ford, from a distance. I want to know what he's doing when he's not at work." She called Todd and asked him to make the assignment. "Send him in an unmarked car."

"You think the last email was a reaction to our visit to Ford?"

"Maybe," Bree said. "It can't hurt to keep an eye on him."

Matt rubbed his beard. "Now what?"

"Now I have to figure out what I'm going to do about Hanover. Kent's murder is his case."

"He's going to want Trunk Guy's case too."

"He is." Bree wanted to kick something. "Unfortunately, we need to set up a meeting. I also have another idea, something I want to do even less than meet with Hanover."

CHAPTER TWENTY-SIX

Three hours later, Bree sat in a conference room in the Redhaven Police Station. Frustration urged her to move. But she resisted, forcing her body to be still, channeling her energy to her brain. On the table in front of her was the murder book for the unidentified man found in the trunk. Behind the table, Matt paced the narrow space between the table and the wall.

The door opened and Hanover strode in, a file tucked under his arm. "Sorry to keep you waiting." He sat across from her, his forearms leaning on the table, and she couldn't help but envision a chess match.

Bree nodded. "I expect you've heard from Rory as well?"

Hanover frowned. "Yes."

Bree said, "Our murder cases are related."

"Yes." Hanover shuffled his papers. "I should take over both cases."

"No," Bree said. "That is not happening."

Surprise and indignation widened Hanover's eyes. "You've no right—"

"Stop." Bree used a quiet voice. She'd had enough. "The dead body in the trunk was found at the Ekin salvage yard. If they're involved, I'm involved. I've been investigating the Ekin family before either body was discovered."

"You have a conflict of interest," he reminded her.

"Which is why I want to bring in BCI to assist us in coordinating the investigation," Bree said. The Bureau of Criminal Investigation was the detective division of the New York State Police. BCI detectives handled cases initiated by state troopers and also supported local and county agencies with major investigations. "Your resources must be strained with one murder, let alone two. BCI adds value."

Hanover frowned. He hadn't wanted to call BCI, but there wasn't much he could do about it since Bree had already called them in.

Matt waved his hand over the murder book and Hanover's files. "Do you really think Dana Romano is involved with all this?"

Bree shot Matt a look. Diplomacy wasn't always his strength. She regulated her own voice. "Given this new forensic evidence that links the two murders, do you agree that Dr. McFadden's case needs to be reevaluated?"

Hanover cleared his throat. "She's still a suspect, but I'll admit, the new information will take the investigation in new directions."

A knock sounded on the door, and it opened. Detective Philip Ash from the New York State Police Bureau of Criminal Investigation, or BCI, walked in. He was a big, bald man who Bree had come to respect as a detective, even if she still didn't like him much personally.

"Sheriff." He dumped his overcoat and briefcase on a chair and extended a hand to Bree.

She shook it. Ash greeted Matt and Hanover.

A beat of silence passed before Bree took the reins. After all, she'd brought them all together. "Let's get Detective Ash up to speed. We have two cases here that we've discovered are related. Dr. Kent McFadden was shot in his own home Monday evening." Bree slid Dana's statement out of her file and passed it to Ash. "According to his date, Dana Romano, the intruder was still in the house." Bree summarized Dana's account of her encounter. "A frozen body we found at the salvage yard owned by a local drug dealer was killed with the same weapon. Ballistics made the match today, and forensics found traces of light rosin—which is used on the bows of stringed instruments—on Dr. McFadden's clothes, Ms. Romano's clothes, and the tarp wrapped around the body in the salvage yard."

Bree slid photos of the body in the trunk over to Ash, who pulled out a pair of readers to examine them closely.

Ash stared at the last picture. "He's frozen?"

Bree nodded. "The ME is thawing him out, but we likely won't have an autopsy for days. We got lucky with the bullet. It passed right through him. The ME will try to ID him sooner, as soon as his fingers thaw enough."

"The salvage yard is owned by local drug dealers?" Ash asked.

Bree detailed the criminal history of the Ekin family, including Travis's arrest and the threats she and Matt had been investigating when they walked in on the drug deal at the salvage yard. "We arrested four men involved in the drug deal, but the body had clearly been in the trunk long enough for him to freeze solid."

Ash nodded. "Lots of variables with that time estimate, but at least a few days, potentially longer."

"Right," Bree agreed. "Benjamin Ekin owns the yard and lives there, so he's the obvious suspect. His cousin, Steve, was also present. We don't know at this time how many other people have access to the property. Benjamin isn't talking, and his security leans to razor wire and guard dogs. No cameras. No alarm. No tech of any kind."

"Cameras and other security tech leave digital footprints," Matt said. "They're traceable and hackable."

Bree nodded.

Ash rubbed his face. "Can we tie Dr. McFadden to the Ekins family?"

Bree gestured to Hanover. "Redhaven has been handling the McFadden case. Both because the murder occurred in their jurisdiction, and because Ms. Romano is my former partner from Philly homicide and a member of my household."

"Ah, yes, the conflict of interest. I appreciate you being proactive about that." Ash turned to Hanover. "You have suspects?"

Hanover opened his file and slid a small pile of crime scene photos across the table. "Dr. McFadden has an ex-wife, whom he remained friendly with. She is out of the country doing some specialized plastic surgery for a medical charity group. Her background is clean. I spoke with her over the phone. She was surprised and upset about McFadden's death, but she couldn't think of anyone who would have harmed him. His business partner, Dr. Bhatt, was on a ski trip. He returned today. We have him scheduled for an interview tomorrow. I also spoke with him on the phone. He and McFadden were partners for more than a decade. They had no major disagreements. Their business was well established, with a steady income that satisfied both of them. Neither doctor had any unexpected debt or spending. Dr. Bhatt also has no criminal record and didn't know of anyone who would have wanted his partner dead. We spoke with neighbors, friends, and the staff at both his office and surgical center. Dr. McFadden was described as pleasant and friendly but mildly arrogant and superficial. He was particular about his appearance and liked to have the best of everything: clothes, cars, et cetera."

Ash went through the pictures slowly. "No other suspects?"

Hanover adjusted his collar. "None that we could find. We found no motive for Dr. McFadden's murder. No money problems. No irate patients. No squabbles with his business partner."

Ash tapped his fingers on the table. "What about family?"

"One sister, Elizabeth. Their parents are deceased," Hanover said. "Dr. McFadden spoke to and texted with his sister several times a week.

They met for lunch regularly, as confirmed by his phone records and calendar. We found nothing suspicious at all."

Ash set down the photos and slid them toward Bree. "I saw the sister at the press con. She looked . . . unhinged."

"She's definitely upset," Hanover admitted. "She did lose the key to her brother's house, but he routinely left the door unlocked when he was home. So I'm not sure the missing key is significant. Elizabeth is a dentist. We found nothing amiss in the financial statements of her practice. She's not as well off as her brother, but she's more than comfortable. Her personal financials are normal and boring. No significant debts, unexpected deposits, or unusual expenses."

"Does anyone else have a key to the house?" Bree asked, picking up the photos.

Hanover nodded. "He has a housecleaning service. We didn't find anything off with them either. It's a small company. The same two women have been cleaning his house for years."

"Life insurance?" Ash asked.

Hanover nodded. "He had a modest policy. His ex is still the beneficiary. According to the doctor's attorney, the bulk of his estate will be split between his sister and his ex with some nice chunks earmarked for various charities. His attorney said he refused to change his will after his divorce. His ex said she'd talked to him several times in recent weeks about this. She didn't think it was right, but she couldn't convince him. She's going to donate all the money to the medical charity she serves."

"So she's not short on money?" Matt asked.

"Not at all." Hanover shook his head. "She does a lot of pro bono work, but she still makes plenty. Plus, she's been out of the country for weeks."

"You can hire someone to kill your ex," Matt pointed out.

Hanover shrugged. "No significant or unusual transactions or cash withdrawals from her bank accounts. She's the one who initiated the divorce, and she has her own income."

"Did she say why she left him?" Bree flipped through the crime scene photos. The pics began with the bloody bedroom littered with medical debris. She didn't spot anything that didn't agree with Dana's statements.

Hanover flipped a page in his file. "She said they wanted different things in life. Kent liked his comfortable life, nice cars, and clothes. Jane wanted to spend the winter in Europe doing reconstructive surgery on Ukrainian soldiers and citizens with facial injuries. She said this without any animosity, just that this type of work felt like a calling for her."

"Does the sister have an alibi?" Ash asked.

Hanover sighed. "No. She was home alone Monday evening, but there's no evidence to suggest she had anything to do with his death. The only person linked to the scene by physical evidence is Dana Romano."

Bree clenched her jaw to keep from responding.

Ash did it for her. "Because she was there."

"Yes," Hanover admitted. "The only trace evidence that stands out at the moment is the rosin. There was no stringed instrument at the scene, and he was not known to play. His sister says she doesn't play either. No fingerprints taken at the scene turned up in AFIS. Ms. Romano stated the intruder wore gloves, so that's not a surprise."

"There seems to be no reason for anyone to kill Kent McFadden." Bree passed the first half of the photos, mostly of Kent's bedroom, to Matt. "What if he wasn't the target?"

Matt stroked his beard. "He lived alone. Are you thinking the killer broke into the wrong house?"

Ash's chair squeaked as he leaned back. "Might be worth checking into the neighbors."

Hanover wrote on a notepad. "We've already canvassed the neighborhood, so we can handle that."

Bree stared at a photo of Kent's street, her eye drawn to a yard sign near the corner of his driveway. She opened the magnifying glass app on her phone and zoomed in on the sign to read Stan's Landscaping

& Snow Removal. "Hold on." She passed the photo to Ash. "This company is owned by the uncle of a man I put in prison six years ago. He was recently released."

Hanover glanced over at the photo. "That company has been around forever. They do some work for Redhaven township in the summer. What's the nephew's name and what did he do?"

Bree gave him the information and explained about his presence at the café at the time one of the threatening emails was sent. "He won't talk to me."

"We'll handle it," Hanover said.

Bree didn't love passing off that lead, but she knew it was for the best.

Ash picked up the drawing of the tattoo. "Any leads on the tattoo?"

Hanover shifted in his seat. "Not yet."

Bree bet he hadn't done anything with it because he thought Dana had made it up. In the interest of forwarding the case, instead she said, "The ink is large and distinctive. I know something about tattoos. We'll ask around at local tattoo parlors and see if any of the artists recognize their work."

Ash turned to Hanover. "Let's get this drawing out to the media and see if anyone in the public recognizes it."

"Do we want to offer a reward?" Hanover asked.

"Everyone and their grandmother will call in." Ash shook his head. "We're not that desperate yet. Let's wait until we have an ID and an autopsy on the second body. If we still can't generate leads, then we'll consider the reward."

"It's going to be difficult to establish a link between the victims until we ID the second body," Matt said.

Bree cocked her head. "Dr. McFadden was a doctor. He could write prescriptions. Could drugs be the link between him and the Ekin family?"

"It's an idea." Hanover made a note. "His sister is a dentist. They can write prescriptions for painkillers as well."

Bree had another thought. "The drug link could go the other way. Any one of these people could use drugs. Addicts get really good at hiding their problem. The tox screen on McFadden's body won't be in for weeks, at best." The labs were so backed up; it could be months.

"I'll take the time to review all the materials for both cases." Ash stood and stretched his back.

"We'll take the tattoo drawing around to local parlors," Bree said. "And talk to Benjamin's business associates. The Ekin family isn't talking, but their customers might want to make a deal, since they're sitting in jail."

"Tony wasn't the bravest," Matt said. "He tried to run with the drugs and cash, then surrendered as soon as the dog found him. He might turn on the rest of them."

Hanover straightened his pile of photos. "We'll investigate the neighbors and question Dr. Bhatt and the staff at the office and surgical center again, find out if any drugs have gone missing. I already submitted the case to ViCAP and the NCIC. I'll forward any information I receive on like crimes or potential suspects."

The National Crime Information Center was a computerized index of crime information to assist law enforcement with locating fugitives, missing persons, and stolen property. The FBI's Violent Criminal Apprehension Program maintained a nationwide database of violent crimes, including homicides, attempted homicides, sexual assaults, et cetera. New York State also kept its own ViCAP system that worked in conjunction with the national database. ViCAP analyzed crime details and looked for patterns or similarities.

"Maybe we'll get lucky and find another random home invasion and shooting with no apparent motive," Matt said.

"Let me know when the forensic reports come in from the salvage yard." Ash slid into his overcoat, and they all filed out of the small room.

Hanover disappeared down a hallway. Matt and Bree made their way to the parking lot. Snow flurries drifted through the air.

"Did it get colder?" Bree shivered hard and quickened her pace.

"Yes, and it's going to snow tonight."

"The forecast is just for a few inches." It was only January, and Bree was done with winter. Unfortunately, winter in New York State wasn't nearly finished with her. A few inches of snow, however, barely registered upstate.

"Sheriff!" Ash caught up to them halfway across the asphalt. He matched strides with Bree. "I just wanted to tell you. I've known Colin Hanover for about eight years. He's a good cop. But he's blunt to a fault. If he's thinking it, he says it. He could never be sheriff because he doesn't have a filter. I'm sure it never occurred to him that Elizabeth McFadden would lose her shit on TV. It wasn't intentional."

Bree nodded, but said nothing.

"He'll learn he can trust you," Ash added.

"So, you trust me?" Bree grinned. The freezing air hurt her teeth.

"Do *you* trust *me*?" Ash echoed.

"I called you, didn't I?" Bree waved and climbed into her SUV.

Matt slid into the passenger seat. He closed the door. "I have to admit, Hanover ran out every lead I could think of, except for the tattoo."

"He did all the legwork." Bree started the engine. "I hate cases where every avenue of investigation leads to a dead end."

"It happens." Matt spread his hands in front of the heat vents. "Where are we going?"

"The station. I want to talk to Salvatore Orlando to see how loyal he is to the Ekin family. He already called for a lawyer when Juarez tried to take his statement, so we'll have to schedule that interview." Bree turned toward Grey's Hollow. "He isn't using a public defender. He has his own attorney."

"Or course he does," Matt said. "He has money."

They drove several miles, then the dispatcher's voice sounded over the radio. "A motorist reported an elderly man walking along RR18." Dispatch gave a mile marker. "Near Lonesome Hill Stables."

"That's near Mr. Pomar's estate. We're not far from there." Bree flipped on her lights. She grabbed the mic. "Sheriff Taggert responding. ETA four minutes."

She made it in three, slowing down as she neared the horse farm. She saw a Toyota Corolla parked on the side of the road, its hazard lights flashing. A woman stood with her hands on her hips. Twenty feet away, facing her, Mr. Pomar walked in a small circle. He wore a warm jacket this time, but was once again in his orthopedic sneakers. He wasn't far from home. And walking in the road was easier and dryer than crossing meadows ankle deep in snow.

Bree pulled up behind the Toyota. The sun was dropping, and she left the lights swirling for safety. The road wasn't busy, but the country was dark. Once the sun set, a motorist wouldn't see a pedestrian until they were upon him.

Bree and Matt stepped out of the vehicle. The woman turned toward them. She was in her sixties, with blonde-beige hair pulled back in a ponytail. She wore gray riding breeches and knee-high black boots. Her hands were shoved into the pockets of a bright purple puffy down jacket.

"I'm Sheriff Taggert." Bree stepped alongside her. The wind whipped down the road. Her ears burned with cold.

"I'm Ellen DiMarco. I board a horse at the farm over there." She pointed down the road. Lights glowed in a house that sat in front of a large barn. "I was pulling out of the driveway when I saw him. He was just walking down the shoulder of the road. I got out and asked him if he needed assistance. I could tell he wasn't OK. My dad is almost ninety. He wanders. I know the look. When I tried to approach him, he got upset. The best I could do was keep him here until you arrived."

"Thank you." Bree wrote down her name, phone number, and license plate for her report. Then she approached the old man. "Mr. Pomar?"

His head swiveled when she said his name. He froze, staring at Matt, who immediately stepped backward.

She smiled. "Do you remember me? I'm Sheriff Taggert."

He scanned her face. Then his gaze dropped to the badge on her jacket. "Air and walls red gone."

She remembered his random words from the last time she'd seen him and found them just as disturbing this time. She couldn't help but feel like he had something specific to say, but she also had no way of knowing what it was. "It's cold out. Let's get you home." Mentally crossing her fingers, she approached him. To her surprise, he allowed her to lead him to the vehicle. In the back seat, he ogled the inside of the sheriff's SUV like a kid. As Bree turned into the driveway of the estate, an SUV approached from the opposite direction. She saw the nurse behind the wheel.

They parked near the house and got out. Bree opened the rear door for Mr. Pomar. He scrambled out and lurched toward the house, his steps faster than she would have guessed he could move.

Nielsen climbed out of his SUV. "Where did you find him?"

"Down the road." Bree pointed.

Nielsen slapped his forehead. "I went the wrong way." He hurried to catch up to his patient and herded him into the house. Mr. Pomar had stuck to the paved and plowed road, so he wasn't wet. Nielsen steered him toward the kitchen, which was warm.

"What happened?" Bree took out her spiral notebook.

Nielsen checked Mr. Pomar's temperature with an infrared thermometer. Then he turned on an electric teakettle. "He was dozing and watching a hockey game on TV. I stripped his bed and put the sheets in the washer. When I came back, he was gone." He pointed to a doorway. "I was literally down the hall for ten minutes. After the last time,

I wasn't taking any chances. The doors were all locked, and the alarm system was turned on. He must have unlocked the door and turned off the alarm. Those must be rote memory skills for him." Nielsen dragged a hand through his gelled hair. "I'm going to call his son and have the alarm codes changed. He has to deal with the alarm company and anything that requires a major expenditure. I also want to order a GPS locator. It has to be something he can't remove."

After asking to use the restroom, Matt ducked out of the kitchen.

"Are you sure you have him secured for the night?" Bree asked.

"I won't let him out of my sight." Nielsen sighed. "I'll even sleep in front of his door. I wish the family had been more honest about the situation when I took the job."

"Do you have any additional help?"

"A little. There's another part-time nurse who comes two days a week. She'll be here on Saturday." He cast a doubtful glance at his charge, as if wondering how the hell he would manage him until then.

Bree didn't think that was enough.

CHAPTER TWENTY-SEVEN

Matt walked down the hallway. He went in the direction the nurse had pointed. At the end of the corridor, he found a half bath and a laundry room. He went into the laundry room. The front-loading washing machine chugged. He could see large swaths of wet fabric and suds churning in the window. A laundry basket full of towels sat on top of the machine. So the details of Nielsen's story checked out.

He walked back to the kitchen and found the old man drinking a cup of hot chocolate and eating a slice of pie. He looked up at Matt, his eyes startlingly clear. His mouth opened and closed several times, as if he wanted to say something but couldn't get it out. His hands balled up into frustrated fists and pounded his legs. Finally, he said, "Dead. Red." His gaze sliced through Matt for one long second before clouding over again.

The hair on Matt's forearms stood straight up, but the old man returned his attention to his pie and ate with enthusiasm. The moment passed as if it had never happened.

Bree was getting some information from the nurse. "Has a social worker spoken to you?"

Nielsen nodded. "The one at the hospital interviewed us both. She was going to call Mr. Pomar's family and discuss long-term care solutions and refer him to the county for follow-up."

Mr. Pomar couldn't get lost again. Matt didn't want a K-9 to find his frozen body in a snowbank. Bree obtained the son's contact information from the nurse before she and Matt left.

Behind the wheel of the SUV, she asked, "Can you verify Lyle Pomar's address and phone number?"

Matt accessed the dashboard computer. "According to his California driver's license, that is correct."

Bree put her phone on speaker. "I'm calling Mr. Pomar's son." She dialed a number. A man answered, and Bree introduced herself. "To whom am I speaking?"

"Yes, this is Lyle Pomar."

"Hello, Mr. Pomar," Bree said. "I'm calling about your father."

Lyle sighed. "What's he done now?"

Bree said, "He's wandered away from his home twice this week. With the current weather, the situation is quite dangerous. You know he was hospitalized for hypothermia?"

"Oh, that. Yes. I already spoke with his nurse and the hospital," Lyle said. "Dad wanders. That's why he has live-in care, and that's why I fired the last nurse. She couldn't keep tabs on one old man."

Matt and Bree exchanged a look.

"How many times has this happened?" Bree asked.

"It's a new problem that started a few weeks ago," Lyle said, sounding more annoyed than worried. "The first few times, he didn't go far. The nurse found him on the property. Now it seems he's wandering farther from home. I bought my father one of those chipped pendants with a button that called 911. He wouldn't wear it. We tried a bracelet. He picked his skin around it until he bled, so the nurse took it off. Other than having a microchip inserted under his skin, I don't know what to do."

"A social worker will be in touch," Bree said. "This isn't uncommon."

"Look. I know I sound uncaring, but I'm frustrated. If it were up to me, Dad would be in a memory care facility, but that's complicated. Dad has an advanced care directive that calls for home-based assistance, and his assets are tied up in a trust. I have to apply for any changes to his care and to have major expenditures approved." Lyle paused. "You'd think he would have trusted his own son more than a bunch of lawyers, but no." His voice turned bitter. "So this is where we are."

Matt sensed their relationship wasn't very *Father Knows Best*.

"Changes need to be made." Bree used her firm voice. "Your father needs more than one person to keep tabs on him. You'll need to do something to keep him safe."

"I'm working on it," Lyle snapped. "I talked to the home care company about adding home health aides round the clock in addition to the live-in nurse. Someone needs to have eyes on my father at all times. Until I can get the trust to approve the extra expenditure, I'm out of pocket for the additional cost." He sounded resentful. "I've booked a flight for Saturday. The current nurse just has to manage for two more days on his own. I'm changing the security system codes so Dad can't sneak out without setting off the alarm. Thank you for your concern, Sheriff. We'll handle Dad. He won't bother you again." The line went dead.

Matt glanced at Bree. "I sense there's some family drama we don't know about."

"Isn't there always?" Bree shrugged. "I've done everything I can do for today. The family is taking appropriate steps. It's a difficult situation, but it sounds like Lyle has it in hand."

Matt pictured the old man. "Mr. Pomar had a very *redrum* moment in the kitchen." Matt described the man's expression when he'd said *dead red*. "He looked momentarily coherent and frustrated, like he knew he couldn't say what he was thinking. Then it passed."

Bree frowned, the bridge of her nose creasing.

Matt continued. "I was thinking. He wanders pretty far and in all directions. The salvage yard is about a mile down the road. As the crow flies, it's even closer."

"And?"

"What if he saw Trunk Guy get shot?"

"Why would you think that?"

"I don't know." Matt thought about Mr. Pomar's expression. "It seemed like there was something dire that he wanted to say but couldn't. Maybe I'm reading too much into his behavior."

Bree tapped the wheel. "It's possible, but there's no way we can ask him. Mr. Pomar can't tell us what he's thinking. For his sake, I hope not. It would be hard enough to view a violent killing when one has all their faculties. In his state of mind, I can't imagine how he would process a sight like that."

"If he did see it," Matt said, "I hope he forgets all about it."

Bree nodded. "Let's go back to the station and meet up with Todd. We need to regroup."

Back at the station, Bree headed for her office. "I have some emails and phone calls to answer. Todd is on his way in. Let's meet in the conference room in thirty minutes."

Matt gestured toward a computer station. "I'll be here." He emailed Rory and typed reports while he waited. In a half hour, he grabbed a bottle of water and headed for the conference room. Todd was already at the table with his laptop open in front of him. Bree buzzed in behind Matt.

"Where does the search of the salvage yard stand?" she asked, taking her position at the head of the table.

"The physical search is complete. Forensics is working overtime to process the sheer volume of evidence, but it's going to take time." Todd scrolled on his computer. "I do have some preliminary information on what they didn't find. There was no indication someone was shot in the head in the house or workshop. No blood except for Mr. Orlando's.

No brains. No shell casings, except for the ones fired during yesterday's shooting."

"What about outside?" Matt asked.

Todd shook his head. "They found nothing, but we don't know when the victim was shot. We don't know if he was put in the trunk immediately afterward or if he was kept somewhere else for a time. He could have been killed at a completely different location and dumped at the yard. If he was shot in the yard, weather could have destroyed or washed away evidence."

"Too many unknowns," Matt said. "It'll be very difficult to make any traction on the case until we ID the victim and/or have the results from an autopsy. Even time of death would be extremely helpful."

"Let's work the tattoo lead. Send a deputy to local tattoo parlors and see if any of the artists recognize this." Bree handed Todd a copy of Adam's drawing.

Todd took the paper and stood. "I'll get right on that."

After he left the room, Matt's phone buzzed with a text from forensics. "Rory has some news for us." He called the tech. "Hey, Rory. You're on speaker. Sheriff Taggert is here as well."

"Matt, Sheriff," Rory greeted them. "I have some news on your stalker."

"Let's hear it." Matt wanted to make progress on something.

"You know that box you dropped off? The weird one with the doll?"

"Yes," Bree said. "Don't tell me you found more prints?"

"No, sorry. No prints. But I did find a small amount of fine dust. Guess what it is?" Rory waited a beat. "Light rosin."

The room went silent. Matt let the information sink in.

"Is it the same rosin that was found on Dr. McFadden's and Dana Romano's clothes?" Matt asked.

"It's the same type, yes." Rory sounded excited. He gave them some tech speak about the grade and color. "Light rosins tend to be used on violins and violas."

"Thanks, Rory. We appreciate the heads-up." Matt ended the call.

Bree's forehead furrowed. "Do we agree that isn't a coincidence? That light rosin is too unique of a substance to turn up in three cases without them being related?"

Matt's gut chilled. "It's extremely likely that your stalker is the same person who killed Dr. McFadden and the frozen guy."

The person threatening Bree had already killed two people.

CHAPTER
TWENTY-EIGHT

Bree sat back, stunned. How could the cases all be related? It didn't seem possible. "We need a conference call with Hanover and Ash." She sent emails to both. Her phone rang a minute later. "It's Hanover."

"This is a most unexpected development," Hanover said. "I messaged Detective Ash but haven't heard back from him."

Matt shook his head. "Connections could be made between two murders, but adding the sheriff's stalker to the mix . . ."

"We need to go back and take a harder look at cases the sheriff investigated previously," Hanover said. "Including those from Philadelphia."

"It makes sense that the stalker could be related to one of my old cases," Bree agreed. "But I don't see how Kent McFadden's death and/or the John Doe in the salvage yard can be connected."

"Did you work any cases similar to Dr. McFadden's murder?" Hanover asked. "Perhaps someone is copying a crime."

Bree searched her memory. "I can't think of any murders similar enough to make a direct comparison. Ms. Romano already inquired about a few cases during our tenure in homicide where prisoners had been released. One died since then. The other is back in prison for a brand-new offense."

"What about since you've been sheriff?" Hanover asked. "I'm sure you've angered people." His tone was full of confidence. "It's an unfortunate by-product of the job," he added, as if just realizing his possible faux pas.

"I haven't even been in office for a year," Bree argued. "Most of the people I've arrested for major crimes are still in prison. Some of them haven't even gone to trial yet."

Hanover sighed. "They have families. Anger and vindictiveness isn't limited to the person you arrested."

"He's right," Matt pointed out. "You've made a few enemies in the Ekin family."

"The frozen guy was found on Ekin property. Two family members made veiled verbal threats against me. Plus, we know Ford Ekin was in the café the morning their Wi-Fi was used to send me a threatening email," Bree said. "But we haven't established a link between the Ekin family and Dr. McFadden. Chief Hanover, did you have any luck investigating Stan and Louis Toland?"

"I personally went to see Mr. Toland," Hanover said. "He says he's been taking care of Dr. McFadden's property and three other houses in that neighborhood for years. His services include snow removal. No one from his company has ever been inside the house. Toland has no recent contact with McFadden. Bills are paid online. We've asked other customers. So far, we've come up with only good references. Stan and his company are clean, and the nephew hasn't been in any trouble since he came to live with Stan. This connection could be a coincidence, but we'll keep digging." Hanover paused. "We've also checked into the neighbors. The Katowski family lives a half mile down the road. Their nineteen-year-old son has a seventh-degree drug possession conviction for ecstasy."

Matt shuffled papers. "I don't see ecstasy on the list of drugs confiscated from the Ekin property. I suppose they could sell different drugs at different times."

"Or from different locations," Bree said. They were probably wasting their time, but they had to be thorough. She'd had important leads turn up in the strangest ways.

"Can we interview the kid and see if he recognizes anyone in the Ekin family from a lineup?" Matt asked.

"We can try," Hanover said. "He's already paid his fine. He can't be charged twice, so there's no risk on his part. I'd already planned to question him. I'll add a photo array."

"Seems like a long shot," Matt said. "But we don't have anything to lose at this point."

"We don't," Hanover agreed. "I forwarded the ViCAP query results, but I'm not sure how relevant they are considering this new development."

"Give me some time to review this information." Bree downloaded the file. "Let's touch base in the morning. Hopefully, we'll hear from Detective Ash and the medical examiner by then."

Hanover signed off and ended the call. Bree printed two copies of Hanover's list.

She leaned back, scanning the results. The list was long, as was typical in any database query without very specific parameters. "We need to thoroughly review this list."

Matt extended a hand in a *gimme* gesture, and she handed him a copy.

They settled down to read through the results, murders by firearms, where the killer broke into the victim's home and the motive for the shooting was unknown.

Bree stopped, her eye catching on a case from Philadelphia. "Here's a case from Philly. Break-in and shooting death of a male homeowner, no robbery, no sexual elements. It happened nine years ago. The investigating officer's name is listed as Detective Stuart Hoffman."

Matt blinked at her. "That name sounds similar."

"Stuart Hoffman was Dana's partner before me."

Matt sat up straighter. "Was the case solved?"

Bree scanned the case information and tried to remember how long Dana had worked with Hoffman. Several years anyway. "I think the time period is right for Dana to have worked the case with Hoffman. Gary Summer was convicted of the murder and sentenced to life in prison without parole. He lived one block from the victim. A witness—another neighbor—saw him leaving the house." Bree turned to her computer and pulled up the Pennsylvania Department of Corrections inmate locator. "He's not listed." Two phone calls told her why. "He died in prison six months ago. He hung himself."

"Shit. The box with the doll . . ."

"Yeah." Bree pictured the creepy diorama with the Polly Pocket hanging by its neck. "What if I'm not the target of the stalker? What if the target is Dana?" Puzzle pieces clicked into place in Bree's mind. "All the threats happened at the house. We assumed they were for me."

"They usually are."

"True," Bree admitted.

"And you were threatened in person by the Ekin family."

"Yes."

"The emails were sent to you," Matt argued. "Not Dana."

Bree considered them. "I get a lot of hate mail, physical and electronic. The email threats from RedBloodedMale03 could be unrelated. Ford Ekin could have sent those, and someone related to Gary Summer delivered the threats at the farm."

"So Dana is the link between the stalker and Kent's murder." Matt rubbed his beard. "But if Gary Summer is dead, who killed Kent?"

"I don't know, but the circumstances around the murder Summer committed and his hanging death in prison are too similar. He gained entry while the victim was at home. Killed him with a single gunshot wound to the chest. No known motive for the crime. It can't be a coincidence. If the Ekin family can want retribution for Travis's arrest, maybe someone who knew Gary Summer wants the same." Bree reached for her phone and dialed Dana's number. She didn't answer, and Bree left a message. "She's at the neurologist. She must have turned off her phone."

"I'll try Nolan." Matt lowered his phone a minute later. "No answer."

CHAPTER

TWENTY-NINE

Dana left the neurologist's exam room with a lighter step. Nolan sat in the waiting room, his phone on his thigh. He lifted and pocketed the phone as she approached.

"Well?" he asked.

"He says I'm recovering as expected." Her head had felt better that morning, but hearing it from the brain doc was reassuring.

"Excellent news." He opened the door, and they went into the hallway.

The office was in a large medical building. Dana tried to message Bree, but the text wouldn't send.

"I couldn't get any service in here," Nolan said.

She shoved the phone into the pocket of her puffy jacket and pulled out her gloves. They took the elevator to the lobby. She stopped to zip her jacket to her chin and flip up her hood before following Nolan outside.

Darkness had fallen while she'd been with the doctor, and the temperature had dropped with the sun. Tiny flakes of snow drifted in the pools of light surrounding the streetlamps.

She quickened her pace. The ground had been cold, and snow began to stick to the asphalt immediately. Her foot slipped on a hidden patch of ice.

Nolan caught her arm. "Let's not crack your head again, OK?"

"No kidding." Dana slowed down. "I'm finally starting to feel like myself."

They approached the truck and climbed in. A thin layer of snow covered the windshield. Nolan started the engine, then used the brush end of his scraper to clear the glass. After tossing it behind the driver's seat, he slid behind the wheel. He backed out of the parking space and left the lot. Traffic was steady but light, the constant flow of cars keeping the roadway mostly clear.

Nolan cruised at a moderate speed and turned onto Miller Road. A huge black truck flew past them. The driver honked the horn and flipped them off out the window. Nolan didn't react, but Dana had no doubt the other driver would have been more polite if he saw Nolan up close.

At the farm supply store, Nolan made a right. Her phone vibrated, and she pulled it out of her pocket. She had seven text messages and a voice mail. She opened her texts. The most recent message was a confirmation for the next neurology follow-up she'd scheduled for next month. Five texts were from Kayla and one was from Luke, a response to the checking-in text Dana had sent him on her way into the appointment. Luke's reply, a goofy GIF of an animated cat giving two thumbs-up, made her laugh.

She opened Kayla's barrage of texts and smiled.

WE MADE CAKE

BIRTHDAY CAKE

FOR LADYBUG

IN CASE ITS HER BIRTHDAY

ARE YOU DONE YET

Thinking of one year before, when no one would have missed her if she was late getting home, Dana smiled again and texted back: OMW. A year ago, Dana would have stopped for takeout and gone home to an empty apartment with a chronically ill heater. Or she would have gone to her parents' house, where the food would have been stellar, but her mom would have reminded her that she was alone by choice. She'd tossed away not one, but two husbands. Her mom, married for fifty years, did not understand that you could be both with another person and all alone at the very same time.

"Everything OK?" Nolan asked.

"Fine. Kids might be a little creepy, but they are also pretty awesome."

"That is a spot-on description." Nolan chuckled. He laughed with his whole self, the sound deep and rumbling.

And sexy as fuck.

Stop it.

Her head was feeling better, but still. He was her best friend's boyfriend's brother, which sounded like the title of a romantic comedy. He was hotter than molten lava cake. He was also ten years younger than her. He could still have his own kids, and that ship had sailed to fucking Bali for her. But she liked him, and not in the friends-with-benefits way she'd enjoyed Kent. She knew in her soul she could have something deeper with Nolan. Talking to him was effortless. When she was with him, she could just be her cranky and opinionated self. She knew what he was saying even when he wasn't actually talking. No games. No hidden agenda. No guessing.

He shifted in his seat, leaning forward to wipe fog from the inside of the windshield.

The truck shimmied. In the beam of the headlights, the snow had changed. Ice pellets bounced off the hood.

"Is that sleet?" she asked.

"Yes." He adjusted the defroster and slowed the vehicle. They left the four-lane highway and turned onto a country road. Nolan drove at a steady, slow pace. The truck slid when he touched the brakes. He straightened out the vehicle with a deft adjustment of the wheel. At an intersection, he eased the truck to a stop. Snow ground under the tires. Dana glanced back, but there were no cars behind them.

She clicked on the voice mail from Bree and pressed the phone to her ear. "Call me back as soon as you can, OK. We think the stalker might be after you, not me."

Dana couldn't process how this could be possible. She called back, putting the phone on speaker. "Nolan and I are on the way home."

"What do you remember about the Gary Summer case?" Bree asked.

"Home invasion and shooting." Dana's brain shifted into gear, another good sign. The memory clarified. She pictured the crime scene. "A middle-age male shot in the chest. The crime is similar to Kent's murder, but Gary Summer was convicted. We had a witness who heard the gunshot and saw Summer running out of the house."

"Did you find the weapon?" Bree asked.

"No," Dana admitted. "The house was down the street from the river. We figured he tossed it in the water. We sent down a diver, but no luck."

"But you got a conviction?" Bree asked.

"We did," Dana said. "His prints were in the house. He said he'd been inside a few days before to drop off a package that had been delivered to his house by mistake. But we found no evidence that happened. The witness knew him and recognized him. They'd all lived in the same neighborhood for years. You know how Philly is. People stay, raise their kids on the same blocks where they grew up."

"I remember," Bree said.

"Summer had been in low-level trouble in the past. He'd been associated with some local gang members. That particular gang was known for requiring potential members to commit a murder as part of their initiation, but we never had a confirmation. Summer's lawyer wouldn't let him take the stand. Why are you asking about Summer? He's in prison for life."

"Actually, he hanged himself in his cell."

And the reason for the call clicked in Dana's head. "Just like that doll."

"Yep," Bree agreed.

"But still, if he's dead, then he isn't the stalker," Dana argued.

"Did he have family?" Bree asked. "Anyone who might be angry about his conviction and death?"

Dana hesitated, the courtroom scene playing out in her mind. "There was a younger brother. He lost it during the trial. He claimed his brother was home with him at the time of the murder. The jury didn't buy it." She thought back to the night they served the arrest warrant. The brother had been there then too, watching his brother get dragged out of his bed and put in cuffs. She could still hear the mother wailing, the teen yelling, the father holding back his younger son. Dana and her partner had brought in a killer, but it had still been a horrible night.

"Do you remember the brother's name?" Bree asked.

"Jordan Summer." Dana did the math. "He'd be around twenty-five or so by now."

"I'll see if I can find any criminal records," Bree said. "Until then, be careful."

"Will do. Going home and staying there. The roads are slick. You take care too." Dana ended the call and turned to Nolan. "Did you hear all that?"

"Yes." Nolan turned up the defroster. The windshield wipers had iced up. Each back-and-forth stroke created smears instead of clearing the glass. He lowered the window, reached out, and pulled off a clump of frozen snow before raising the window again. An SUV approached, driving toward them on the same road. It stopped at the intersection opposite them, very slowly, then rolled forward at the same time Nolan released his brakes. The other vehicle's window was down. An arm extended. Gunshots *pop-popped*. The muzzle of a gun flashed orange. Bullets punched through the driver's-side window.

Dana reacted instinctively. Ducking, she drew her gun from its ankle holster. Before she could aim, the pickup lurched forward as Nolan punched the gas pedal. The back tires spun. He eased off and waited for the tires to grip the road before accelerating. The truck fishtailed through the intersection, slipping and sliding, the back end swinging toward the frozen snowbank left by the plow after the previous storm and a split rail fence that lined the road. As the truck spun, Dana braced herself for impact.

CHAPTER THIRTY

In Bree's office, Matt looked over her shoulder and read her computer monitor. "Jordan Summer doesn't have a criminal record."

"Not that I can find in the national database, or in the New York or Pennsylvania state databases." Bree tapped on her keyboard. "Let's see if he has a driver's license."

Her phone rang. "It's the ME." She answered. "Go ahead, Dr. Jones. Matt Flynn is also here."

"I have an ID on the victim from the salvage yard. He's not quite thawed enough for an autopsy, but we took his fingerprints. His name is Gavin Nielsen. He's a nurse who works for a home care service."

Shocked, Matt looked to Bree, but she looked equally stunned.

The ME continued. "I'll email the information. Just thought you wanted to know ASAP."

"I do. Thank you," Bree said. "Have you notified his next of kin?"

"Not yet," Dr. Jones said. "His family lives in Virginia. I'm contacting law enforcement there to do the notification in person. They can contact me with questions. Why? Did you know him?"

Bree said, "I met a nurse named Gavin Nielsen this week. I just saw him this afternoon."

The ME replied, "You didn't see this Nielsen today."

"That's the truth. Thank you, Dr. Jones." Bree ended the call. "Gavin Nielsen is the nurse who cares for Mr. Pomar."

"This case gets weirder and weirder." Matt's head spun with the implications of this new development. "If the real Gavin Nielsen is dead, who is with Mr. Pomar?"

"What are the chances there are two male nurses named Gavin Nielsen in this area?" Bree hit the "Enter" key and pulled up the motor vehicle record for Jordan Summer. She pointed to his photo. "He looks different now, but that's the Gavin Nielsen that takes care of Mr. Pomar."

Matt studied the photo of the young man. In his driver's license photo, Jordan had an unkempt *Duck Dynasty* beard, along with shoulder-length hair. "Face shape is the same. Eyes too. He trimmed the beard and changed his hair. The glasses are probably clear."

"So Jordan planned this." Bree also summoned the New York driver information for Gavin Nielsen. "Basic height and weight of the real Nielsen matches Jordan Summer."

Matt stared at the real Gavin Nielsen, who was in the morgue with half his head blown off. "I agree. Gavin Nielsen is actually Jordan Summer. Now what?"

"Now we go arrest his ass." Bree stood.

"He killed the real Nielsen and took his identity as Mr. Pomar's nurse. Then he killed Kent McFadden? And instead of killing Dana then and there, he let her go and left threats for her at the farm?" Matt turned back to Jordan Summer's photo on the computer screen. "Why would he do that?"

Bree stared at the computer. "From the threats he left at the farm, he blames her for his brother's death. If Gary hadn't gone to prison, he'd still be alive."

"Maybe Gary shouldn't have committed murder."

"I don't know why he didn't just shoot her after he shot Kent."

"She put up a fight. Maybe that was unexpected. He might not have known she was even going to be there. The night definitely didn't go the way he'd planned. That could have rattled him." Matt pictured the barn and then the box. "The graffiti read, *Dirty cops should die.*"

"The message in the creepy box was similar. *Dirty cops should die in prison instead of the innocent.*"

"He thinks his brother was innocent," Matt said.

"That's my guess too. The tattoo Dana saw on his arm was Lady Justice. He's getting justice for his brother." She shut down her computer. "Let's bring him in."

Bree's radio squawked. The dispatcher's voice sounded. "All units, 12-75 in the vicinity of Township Line Road. One injury reported."

Matt's belly went hollow. A 12-75 was a shooting. "That's the road Nolan would have taken home."

Bree turned up the volume. Matt held his breath. Neither of them moved—or breathed—as they listened to the dispatcher describe the incident and the shooter's vehicle. "Reported victim is driving a black Ford F-150 pickup truck."

Matt felt sick. "That's Nolan's truck."

"Maybe," Bree said. But her eyes spoke the truth. The F-150 might be the most sold vehicle in America, but a shooting involving one tonight in the same area where Nolan had been driving was too much of a coincidence.

Bree jumped to her feet. Over the radio, units responded, asking if dispatch had a more specific location. The dispatcher replied, "Negative."

"I can track Dana's phone." Bree grabbed her jacket and phone, and they rushed out of her office.

Matt retrieved his jacket from the workstation he'd been using earlier. Todd hurried into the squad room.

"We think the shooting victims are Nolan and Dana." Matt shrugged into the sleeves.

Bree was tapping on her phone screen. "I see Dana's phone near the Shady Creek Bridge." She used her lapel mic to give dispatch the location. Several units from neighboring PDs and Bree's own deputies reported ETAs of eleven to twenty minutes.

"We're fifteen minutes away." Matt ran for the rear door of the station.

Bree and Todd were behind him. She said nothing as they exited the building to a snow-covered parking lot. Todd headed to his own patrol vehicle. Matt's boots skidded on the slick surface. He froze, extending his arms for balance, until his momentum stopped. "Careful. The snow is mixed with sleet. The blacktop is slippery."

Bree shuffled to the SUV. "There was no ice in the forecast." The weatherman had predicted accumulation of three to five inches, not exactly an emergency in a region that averaged sixty inches of snow a year. "Would you drive? I need to make some calls, and navigating these roads is going to take full concentration."

"You got it." Matt slid behind the wheel. He fired up the engine and left the lot, lights flashing and sirens blaring. As they drove out of town, the roads became more and more slippery. Matt turned onto Miller Road, the SUV sliding through the turn and nearly slipping into the roadside ditch. The defroster ran on full blast, and the windshield wipers beat frantically to keep the ice at bay. "The road is like an ice rink." He killed the sirens. No need to announce their arrival to the bad guy. He debated the lights but decided the visibility was too poor to turn them off.

While he fought for traction, Bree made her phone calls, declaring the ice storm a special emergency for the county, issuing a travel advisory, and encouraging residents to stay off the roads. Nonessential county employees were sent home. Upstate New York residents were accustomed to rough weather. Most county employees—and citizens— knew what to do, and there was a standard protocol to implement.

The radio crackled with accident reports. "All units, 12-82 on Miller Road. Multiple vehicles involved. Tractor trailer overturned, blocking the northbound lane. Multiple injuries reported. Fatalities likely."

Bree used the radio to contact Todd, whose vehicle was behind hers, and send him to handle the accident. He responded and turned at the next intersection. In the rearview mirror, Matt saw his lights disappear, leaving the road behind them dark and empty.

"Some of the other deputies are on the wrong side of that crash," Bree said. "We'll be the first responders."

Frustrated, Matt banged a fist on the steering wheel. "I'm going as fast as I can."

"We can't help Nolan and Dana if we crash," Bree said, but her voice held the urgency he felt.

Several additional units responded with ETAs. Bree requested help from the state police, but they both knew assistance might not come or come too late. All law enforcement would be strained with the weather.

They were on their own.

CHAPTER
THIRTY-ONE

Dana's pulse scrambled as the truck slammed into the snowbank and wooden fence. The jolt sent pain through her skull like an arrow. She breathed, the nausea rising.

Nolan shifted into reverse and backed the truck away from the bank. Something clanged as he stopped and jerked the gearshift back into drive. The truck's tires spun, then caught. The vehicle lurched forward. Dana grabbed the armrest to steady herself.

She turned to look through the rear window. The SUV was trying to turn around. The vehicle was angled on the road, but its headlights weren't moving. "I think he might be stuck."

"Good." Nolan's voice sounded strained. The bullets had punched through the driver's-side window, leaving two holes and rings of spiderweb-like cracks level with his body. There was no way both of the shots had missed.

"You're hit?"

"Yeah. Shoulder." He hissed air through his teeth.

"How many times?"

Nolan hesitated. "Once, I think."

Dana dialed 911. "How bad?"

"Don't know, but it's not good." His face was as pale as the snow swirling across the windshield. He drew in a sharp breath but kept his eyes on the road. His left hand rested on his thigh instead of gripping the steering wheel. Blood dripped from his fingers.

Dana checked the rear window again but saw nothing but darkness.

The dispatcher answered, "911. What is your emergency?"

Dana identified herself and gave a brief description of the shooting. "The shots were fired from a dark-red Ford Explorer. License plate unknown. We are driving a black Ford F-150 on Township Line Road toward Grey's Hollow."

The truck hit a bump, and Nolan let out a grunt of pain.

She put the phone on speaker, set it on the seat, and loosened her seat belt. Hoisting herself up on one knee, she twisted around Nolan to get a look at his opposite shoulder. Blood already soaked the sleeve of his jacket. But it wasn't gushing or spraying, which would indicate the bullet had hit an artery. "The driver has a GSW in the shoulder, moderate bleeding."

"Are you being pursued?" the dispatcher asked.

Dana glanced behind them. No headlights. "I don't see the other vehicle, but visibility is poor. So, I don't know."

"Where are you? Do you see a mile marker?" the dispatcher asked.

Dana looked out the window, but she couldn't see anything. "No."

Nolan slumped, then shook himself. "I'm going to need you to drive."

"Let's switch seats." Dana reached for her seat belt to release it. The truck swerved.

One-handed, Nolan struggled to keep the vehicle on the road. He glanced at the dashboard. "The tire must have been damaged when we hit the fence. It's losing air. I'm going to pull over."

Dana looked behind them and squinted through the snow. Were those headlights?

She turned back. A bridge loomed ahead. Which one? Just before the guardrail, the tire blew. The truck jolted sideways and rolled down the embankment. The seat belt jerked taut, slicing into Dana's shoulder. She felt like a rag doll. Her limbs flopped. The world spun over and over. The truck jolted, lurched. Metal crunched and banged. Glass shattered and rained over Dana. Objects flew as if they were in a tornado. Something hard smacked her in the face. The truck landed upright and wobbled like a Weeble.

Then everything went still.

Shaken and dizzy, Dana breathed. When she turned her head to see Nolan, blood trickled into her eye. She wiped it away. The world spun again, but this time, she knew it was only in her head. She closed her eyes for a few seconds. "Nolan?"

He didn't answer for one terrifying breath, then said, "Yeah."

She exhaled. "You're alive."

"Yep. You too."

"Yeah." Dana opened her eyes. Powder from the side-curtain airbag hung in the air. The landscape had stabilized, and the pain in her head wasn't too bad. Adrenaline could be blocking some pain, but she'd take that. She needed to function. "We have to get out of here." She looked around the truck. The engine had died, and the dashboard was dark. Everything was dark. "Do you see my phone or my gun?"

"No."

"Where's your phone?"

"Dunno. It was charging in the console cup holder."

"Could be anywhere." Dana leaned over and felt around on the floor, but all she found were pebbles of tempered glass. The truck had rolled at least three times. The side windows were smashed out. Her hand found the charging cord still plugged into the USB slot, but the phone was no longer attached. Her fingers caught on a leather strap. Her purse! She pulled it to her. The zipper was still closed. Unfortunately, neither her cell phone nor gun had been inside it.

"I have my gun," Nolan said in a rough voice.

"Good." Looking behind them, Dana took stock. The headlights had gone dark, and they were below the road. Would their pursuer be able to see them from the bridge?

She reached for the door handle.

"Hold on." Nolan switched off the dome light. "Go."

The hinges squealed as Dana opened the car door and stepped out, shoving aside the deflated airbag. Her boots landed in shin-deep water. Shockingly cold liquid saturated her pant legs and flooded her boots. Her legs wobbled, and she put a hand on the truck to steady herself. The truck had landed at the edge of the frozen-over creek, breaking the ice on her side. Frigid water swirled around her legs. The driver's side was on dry ground.

"My door's stuck." Nolan released his seat belt with a click. "There's a flashlight in the glove compartment."

Dana fished it out. It was a metal, heavy-duty model. She handed it to him. Pieces of the driver's window were still in place, although the glass was a solid maze of cracks. Dana rounded the vehicle and grabbed the door handle. Bracing one foot on the side of the truck, she jerked the door open. Nolan shoved aside the dangling, deflated airbag. Clutching his left arm to his chest, he hoisted himself out the door. Dana tried to help him to the ground, but he was too big. The best she could do was control and cushion his fall as he landed on top of her.

He lay still, his breathing ragged, as she wiggled out from under him. Snow and bits of ice dusted his face and stuck in her eyebrows. She jerked her hood up. She didn't know what had happened to her gloves. Had they been on the seat?

"Do you have a first aid kit in the truck?" she asked.

He gasped. "Toolbox in the bed, but it's basic. Don't think Bactine and Band-Aids are gonna be much help."

Dana climbed into the truck bed and opened the box. The first aid kit was red and white. She spotted it even in the dark. She shoved it into her pocket. She risked using the flashlight for a few seconds, keeping the light below the top of the box. Then she grabbed a roll of duct tape and scrambled out of the bed.

Kneeling next to Nolan, she felt his arm. It was sopping wet with what felt sticky, like blood. The snow below him was stained dark. She lifted her hand and turned it over. Her palm was coated in thick, dark liquid. Definitely blood. In her mind's eye, she saw Kent, his eyes panicking, then going blank. Her fingers trembled. The shaking moved up her arms.

Nolan groaned, breaking the trance. Dana took two deep breaths of freezing night air. She turned her face to the sky and allowed the cold wind and sleet to pelt it for a minute. She could lose her shit later. Right now, she needed to act or they'd both die.

"I can't see your wound, but I don't want to risk turning on the flashlight. It'll make us visible."

He nodded. "Just tie something around it. Anything to slow the bleeding. If I pass out, leave me and get help."

Dana rolled her eyes in the darkness. She wasn't leaving him. She prodded his shoulder. His whole body flinched as her fingers found the wound in the meaty muscle at the top of his shoulder. Warm blood flowed over her fingers. An image of him, dead, flashed in her mind. She gave it a shove. It could be worse. If he were shorter, the bullet could have gone through his neck or head. "I'm not going to let that happen."

"You can't carry me," Nolan protested in a weak voice. "You can't even drag me. If you stay with me, we'll both die for sure. You should run—"

Dana cut off his ridiculous suggestion. "Fuck that. Give me your gun."

He used his right hand to remove it from his shoulder holster, wincing as he shifted his injured arm. The movement caused more blood to well.

She took the weapon, aware of a feral rage burning inside her. "You listen to me right now. If that motherfucker comes after us, I will shoot

251

him in the motherfucking face before I let him hurt you again. Am I clear?"

Nolan paused. Under eyes full of pain, his mouth quirked. "Yeah."

But he could still bleed to death, and she admitted silently that an unconscious Nolan would be very difficult to manage without a sled and a team of dogs.

"Good. Now shut up and hold still." Dana opened her purse and found the small zipped compartment. She pulled out a sanitary napkin, opened it, and pressed it over the wound.

"Is that a maxi pad?"

"Yep. It's clean, right?" She used duct tape to secure it the best she could.

"Smart."

"Did you know disposable maxi pads were developed from one of Ben Franklin's inventions?"

"I did not." He grunted as she pulled the tape taut.

"Yep. He created a disposable, folded bandage for soldiers' gunshot wounds. According to one account, his wife saw it and the rest is history."

That historical account was often disputed, but the story served to distract Nolan as she bound a final layer of tape around his shoulder. She ripped with her teeth and pushed the roll back into her pocket. "That's the best I can do for now."

How much time had passed since she'd spoken with 911? Five minutes? Didn't matter. The police didn't even know where on Township Line Road they were located, and the truck wouldn't be easily seen from the road. It would take time to find them.

An engine sounded, approaching, and it was way too quick for the vehicle to be a first responder. Dana's blood went colder than the water soaking her pant legs. She tugged on Nolan's good arm. "We have to move."

CHAPTER THIRTY-TWO

Bree communicated with her deputies and the state police. Todd was almost at the tractor-trailer accident scene. The state police were responding to assist him, but it would take time for them to arrive. Two of Bree's patrol deputies were closer. An ambulance and fire truck were also en route. As she divided her resources, dispatch reported a car in a ditch and two fender benders. The noncritical calls would have to wait. Injured people took priority.

They passed the farm supply store. The parking lot was dark.

"The power must be out." Matt turned right onto Township Line Road. "Not much farther. The bridge is up ahead."

He cruised through the stop sign with barely a pause. The vehicle seemed to crawl for the next agonizing mile, then he slowed near the Shady Creek Bridge. He scanned the side of the road. "Let me know if you see any tire tracks."

"There!" Bree pointed out the window. Two pairs of tire tracks led off the shoulder of the road. A dark-red Ford Explorer was parked next to the end of the guardrail at the base of the bridge. Bree typed the license plate number into the dashboard computer. "The vehicle belongs to Gavin Nielsen."

"If you're going to kill a guy and assume his identity, you may as well use his vehicle." Matt eased to a stop on the shoulder. He and Bree donned hats and gloves. Who knew how long they'd be out in the cold. Bree reported their location to dispatch, and then they climbed out of the vehicle. The wind had picked up. Snow and sleet slapped at Bree's face, making her eyes water.

She grabbed an emergency backpack from the rear of her vehicle.

"I'll carry that." Matt held out a hand. Ever practical, Bree didn't argue. He outweighed her by eighty pounds, at least. They'd move faster if he was carrying the extra weight. She handed it over, along with an AR-15. Their eyes met for two heartbeats, then Matt kissed her, his lips cold on hers. "Let's go."

She reported their location on her radio. "Sheriff Taggert and Investigator Flynn in pursuit of the armed suspect and searching for the shooting victims."

Standing on the side of the road, Bree shivered hard as the wind gusted, sending snow and sleet sideways. A cloud of snow blew across the landscape. Tracks wouldn't last long. Neither would Nolan and Dana if one of them had been shot. Were Bree and Matt already too late?

Pointing her flashlight at the ground, she followed the second vehicle's tracks. The ruts disappeared just behind the guardrail. One set of footprints led away from the Explorer. Bree aimed her flashlight down the embankment. A black pickup truck sat at the edge of the frozen creek. Deflated airbags hung from the tops of the open doors.

Clicking on his own light, Matt rushed past her to examine the vehicle. "Two bullet holes in the driver's-side window." He shined his light into the vehicle. "Blood."

Bree looked inside. Dark-red liquid streaked the steering wheel and stained the driver's seat. She didn't need to tell Matt that his brother had indeed been shot. She saw no blood puddles on the passenger side, but that didn't mean Dana hadn't been injured.

Grim-faced, Matt stepped back and scanned the exterior of the vehicle with his light. The roof was dented. Windows were smashed. "The truck rolled."

Bree shifted the beam of her light to the ground. Matt moved to stand next to her. The snow was trampled around the vehicle. "There's more blood." In the center of the flattened area was a bloodstain the size of a dinner plate. Three sets of footprints led away from the truck.

One pair were side by side and close together. Blood spotted the snow in random dots among the footprints.

"Dana and Nolan," Matt said.

Bree crouched next to the third set of tracks, which ran parallel to the others. She shined her light straight down. "These are fresh but the snow is filling them in fast." In another half hour, the storm would cover the trail. "We'd better move."

Matt broke into a jog, running parallel to the tracks, holding the rifle in both hands. Bree kept up. They didn't speak, but saved their breath for the chase.

CHAPTER THIRTY-THREE

"Which way?" Dana shivered. Even with her hood up, sleet had found its way into her jacket. She adjusted Nolan's arm, which was looped over her shoulder.

Sagging against her, he turned his feet to the right. "The farm supply store is the closest building."

"You can lean on me." Dana gripped Nolan's arm over her shoulder. How was he still on his feet? He was corpse-pale. If he passed out, what *would* she do? Adrenaline dulled the pain in her head. Without it, she'd never be able to help him. But she knew it was temporary. They were both injured. They needed to hole up somewhere and wait for help.

"I'm too heavy." He trudged, head down, one foot in front of the other, in a path parallel to the creek. They crossed an open field and entered a patch of woods.

Dana looked ahead. Their target was the farm supply store, the only building they knew was nearby. She'd been there dozens of times to pick up animal feed and other necessities for the farm. The creek ran about a hundred yards behind the parking lot. It should be on the other side of the trees.

"Any sign of him behind us?" he asked without looking.

She glanced over her shoulder. "I can't see very far." But their trail of footprints and blood was clear enough in the snow. No one could miss it. She focused ahead again. *Eyes on the prize, right?*

They continued in silence. She could tell Nolan was doing his best to keep his weight off her. But his steps were becoming less sure, less even. He stumbled. She tried to right him, but he was too heavy. With a groan, he tripped and went to his knees. His weight and size pulled her down with him. Something hard tore into her knee.

She adjusted her hold on his wrist. His arm was freaking heavy. Putting the sole of one boot solidly on the ground, she pushed to her feet. Her quads strained as she pushed. Nolan got one foot under him as well, and Dana was able to help.

"Sorry," he hissed, his voice harsh with pain as he regained his footing.

"I'm grateful for the thousand hours I spent in spinning class." She moved forward, half dragging him now. He'd been right. She wouldn't be able to carry him. She could barely be his crutch. If he went down, she'd never be able to move him.

They staggered around a bend. The woods opened, and Dana saw the farm supply store ahead. But instead of the lighted parking lot, the building squatted in darkness.

Nolan lifted his chin. "Power's out."

"Fabulous." Dana dragged him forward. She stepped off the curb into the lot. "Careful."

Ice and snow crunched under their boots. The sleet formed a crust on the snow. The lot hadn't been plowed. The two inches of snow over the ice helped with traction. They made it to the front door. A sign taped to the door stated the store was closed due to the storm. Now what?

Nolan sagged, then snapped his knees straight, as if working hard to stay upright. He wouldn't be vertical for long. They were both shivering. Her feet were wet and freezing, and her head throbbed.

Adrenaline—and fucking fury—were the only things keeping her on her feet and moving. Nolan was losing blood and probably going into shock. She needed to get him inside. The cold wasn't helping him, and her waterlogged feet felt like chunks of ice.

"Lean on the wall." She pushed Nolan up against the front of the store and went to the door. It was a standard commercial glass door. No tint, and hopefully no lamination, which would make it a bitch to break.

She swung the butt end of the flashlight at the glass, but it didn't break. She swung again, harder. The glass cracked. A third hit broke through. Seventy-five percent of the tempered glass door shattered, the pieces waterfalling to the concrete around her boots. She waited for the alarm to sound.

Nothing.

Shit. Most commercial security systems were equipped with battery backup so the essentials would function in a power outage. She'd hoped the alarm would call the cops. Maybe the manager had forgotten to set the alarm or the system was malfunctioning. Whatever. She didn't have time to dawdle.

She cleared the remaining pieces by running the flashlight around the metal frame and kicking out any remaining pieces. Then she turned to retrieve Nolan, but he was already swaying toward her. He turned sideways, and they slipped through the opening one at a time, taking care not to brush up against the edges.

Inside, the shelter from the wind was an instant relief. Dana stood Nolan against a support column. "Wait here." She ran to the side of the entrance and grabbed a wheeled dolly. By the time she returned to his side, he'd slid down the column and was sitting against it.

"We need to get you away from the entrance." She half dragged him onto the dolly. The wheels squeaked as she pushed it down the main aisle.

As they moved deeper into the store, the heat hit her skin. Dana's face burned. Emergency lights glowed above exits, but everything else remained dark. The farm supply store sold a little bit of everything, from livestock supplies to hardware and even clothing. Dana grabbed two battery-operated camp lanterns as they walked down the center aisle. She wheeled Nolan to the back of the store.

"The alarm didn't sound." He groaned.

"I'll try to call 911 on a landline."

His teeth chattered. "At least it's warm."

In the back of the store, Dana moved past the restrooms to an employee break room. She stuck her head inside. No windows. Perfect. She needed some light to assess Nolan's condition. "In here."

The dolly didn't fit through the doorway. Dana grabbed Nolan's uninjured arm. Nolan rolled off the cart to his feet and lurched into the room. Dana deposited him in a chair, left the lanterns next to him, and ran back into the store. She'd shopped here plenty of times and knew the basic layout. She snagged thick socks for herself, a warm blanket and hat for Nolan, the entire display box of hand warmers, and the biggest first aid kit on the shelf. She added a hunting knife on her way back to the break room, not that either of them was in any condition for a hand-to-hand confrontation. She detoured to a checkout and felt the underside of the counter and register for a silent-alarm button but found nothing.

Nolan was slumped over, unmoving, when she rushed in. She touched his neck and exhaled in relief when he opened his eyes. "I'm not dead."

"Glad to hear it." She examined the swinging door but saw no way to secure it. She tried the phone. No dial tone. She returned to Nolan. With no windows, she felt safe turning on the lanterns and using the flashlight to better assess his wound. The bleeding had slowed, but the bandage was more saturated than she would have liked.

"How bad?" he asked.

She evaded a direct answer. "Running through the woods didn't help."

He snorted. "We were hardly running."

"OK. Stumbling." Dana used an ACE bandage from the first aid kit to put additional pressure on his makeshift bandage. Then she covered him with the blanket and put the hat on him. She tucked some hand warmers into both their pockets. Finally, she pulled a chair closer to his, sat, and took a minute to change her socks. The insides of her boots were wet, but it was still an improvement.

Her eyebrow stung, and she swiped a hand across her forehead. Her eye was swollen. In the glow of the camp lantern, Dana saw a few small red splotches and lacerations on Nolan's face. She assumed she had the same. They'd both been wearing their seat belts, but there had been plenty of flying debris in the truck. His eyes drifted shut.

"Hey, wake up." She nudged him. "Stay with me. We need to find a better place to hide. Maybe an office. A room without windows and with a door that locks."

"I'm awake." He stirred. "Feeling a little better warmed up."

"Good, because we need to move." She stood and leaned down to help him. But his image morphed into two, her vision went fuzzy, and she heard the distant sound of footsteps crushing on glass. "Hurry. He's here."

Chapter Thirty-Four

Matt pushed them hard, moving at a fast clip despite the slippery terrain and darkness. His eyes adjusted to the dimness, but the landscape was still covered in shadows. Bree wheezed as she struggled to keep pace with his much longer legs, but he knew she wouldn't complain or give up.

"They're following the creek," Bree gasped. "Back toward Miller Road."

"They're headed toward the farm supply store. That's what I would do. It's the closest building."

They followed the tracks to the edge of the woods. They emerged and faced the farm supply store. The parking lot and building were dark and silent.

Breathing hard, Bree used her radio to update dispatch.

The dispatcher replied, "K-9 One is en route. ETA unknown due to the closure of Miller Road."

Collins and Greta would need to go around the long way. The detour was miles long.

Matt pointed to the three sets of tracks leading to the front of the store. "The shooter is in there with them. We can't wait."

Bree turned off the volume on her radio. "Let's go."

They raced across the parking lot, slipping and sliding, to the front door. Slowing, Matt and Bree flanked the shattered glass door. Matt spotted a half dozen large drops of blood near the exterior wall. He imagined Nolan standing there, leaning on the wall, while Dana broke in.

Matt went through the opening first, leading with the AR-15. Bree followed. In the dim glow of the red emergency lighting, they crossed the entrance and took cover in an aisle. Matt held still, catching his breath, listening. Except for the wind blowing through the broken door, the store was eerily silent. He heard a soft swish to his right, toward the back of the building. He nodded in that direction and tapped his ear. Bree tilted her head, as if listening hard. Thirty seconds later, she shrugged. The sound hadn't repeated.

Bree went forward. Crouching, Matt took her left flank. They moved as a team, stopping at the end of each aisle and peering around the endcap before hustling to the next. Bree nodded toward a spot on the floor. Blood. Matt scanned the pale-gray tile for another. He saw it, about ten feet away in the main aisle that ran through the center of the store.

Where would Dana and Nolan go? One or both of them was injured. The line of blood spots pointed toward the back of the store. He and Bree continued to creep down the aisle parallel to the main artery. Matt approached the last endcap. He could see the narrow hallway that led past the restrooms to the employee-only areas. To get to them, they had to cross thirty feet of space with three circular racks of outerwear and a snow shovel display. Jordan could be hiding behind anything, ready to ambush them. In the dimness of the store, Matt would never be able to see him.

What he wouldn't do to have a K-9 with him at that moment. Brody would have known where the bastard was hiding. How long would it take for Collins and Greta to arrive?

Bree crouched next to him. Keeping low, she peered left around the end of the aisle. Matt looked right. A display of horse blankets blocked his view. He shuffled ahead until he could see around it. Something moved about thirty feet ahead. A shadow, sneaking along the edge of the horse blanket display. The shadow took another step, and Matt could see his feet below a hanging blanket. The shadow's head appeared above it. Definitely a man.

Matt gestured to Bree, then chopped a hand toward the display. She turned her head and squinted into the darkness. Her posture stiffened, and he knew she saw the suspect. Matt leveled the AR-15 over the top of the endcap display, aiming at the approximate location of the shadow's center mass.

CHAPTER
THIRTY-FIVE

The shooter is in the store.

Dana squeezed her eyes shut. *Not now. One of us has to be functional.* But when she opened her eyes again, the room swam in front of her.

"Dana." Nolan's hand tapped her leg. "You OK?"

She wanted to say *fine*, but lying wouldn't help the situation. "Not really." She tried to focus on his face, but she saw two of him. "Double vision."

"That's a bad sign." His comment contained as much exhaustion as emotion.

Dana felt the same. She was drained. "Yeah." She pulled out his gun and set it between them. "You might have to do any shooting that's necessary."

"OK, but neither one of us is in any condition to run or fight. Our best chance is to find a room that locks and wait for help."

Run, fight, hide was the active-shooter advice given to civilians. Dana had never thought she'd need to use it.

Now that she was in the warm store, fresh pain bloomed all over her body. She was going to be a mass of bruises, again. No, still. The bruises from the assault hadn't faded. She opened her eyes. Single vision had returned, but the fuzziness remained. The pain in her head didn't seem too much worse, but the vision issues were wreaking havoc on her balance. Unsteady on her feet, she helped Nolan to his. They lurched like a couple of drunks toward the door, out of the break room, and into the hallway.

"What was that?" Dana whispered, putting her back to the wall and pulling Nolan with her. She squinted, closing the bad eye. The exit signs cast a red-light-district glow in the hallway.

"I didn't see anything." He slumped against the wall.

"Something moved at the end of the hall."

Nolan paused. "There's nothing there."

Her vision was getting worse.

"How's your head?" He breathed out the words.

"A little worse, but tolerable."

He assessed her. "Your eye is almost swollen shut. You need a hospital."

Dana cast a pointed look at his bandaged shoulder. Blood was seeping through the ACE bandage. "I'm not the only one, pal."

"Seriously, there's a thing called second-impact syndrome—"

Dana cut him off. "I've heard of it." In a recent hockey game, one of the players had suffered a serious concussion, and the sportscasters had talked about repetitive brain injuries. Dana didn't remember the details, only that the condition could be fatal.

Nolan didn't say anything else, but his eyes were worried. If Dana's head didn't hurt, she would have shaken it. The irony was so sharp it stung. The guy with the *bullet wound* was concerned about her.

"Can I do anything about it right at this moment?" she asked.

"No."

"Then I don't want to hear about it," Dana said.

"OK."

After passing two supply closets, they found three small offices. Nolan stopped. "They all have windows to the hall."

Dana tried a knob. "Locked." She tested another. Also locked.

"This one's open." Nolan held a door wide.

Dana hustled inside. Nolan stumbled in after her. The office was small, with barely room for a desk and a single chair facing it. Dana locked the door behind them. She pointed to the floor behind the desk.

Nolan checked the blinds on the glass, but they didn't close very tightly. With no exit lights inside it, the small space was darker than the hallway. It would be hard to see inside.

Dana went behind the desk. Her legs folded, and she sat on the floor. Closing her eyes helped her headache. Nolan sat beside her, pressing his uninjured shoulder against hers. She shivered. He shared the blanket. Bright side: even losing blood, he still gave off body heat. She couldn't see his expression in the darkness, but his body sagged against the wall. Without the support, she suspected he'd fall over.

Dana pulled the gun from her pocket and set it on her lap, hoping one of them was still conscious in case the shooter found them first. She must have dozed off, because she jolted when footsteps sounded in the hallway on the other side of the door. Fresh fear spiked her pulse into a nauseating staccato. She squeezed Nolan's forearm, but he didn't respond. She touched his wrist. His pulse throbbed against her fingertips. She exhaled. Unconscious but alive. How long would he remain so if the shooter broke in?

Dana slid out from under Nolan, easing him to the floor and covering him with the blanket. She picked up the gun and aimed it in the direction of the door, though she doubted she could shoot even remotely straight.

In the hallway, someone rattled a doorknob. More footsteps. Closer. Another rattle. The footsteps came even closer. The doorknob of their office turned. Behind the door, a soft voice called out, "Detective Romano. Are you in there? Come out, come out, wherever you are."

Another voice shouted, more distant and muffled. Dana couldn't make out the words, but there was someone else in the store. On their side? Or the shooter's?

CHAPTER THIRTY-SIX

Bree took cover at the end of the aisle. Peering around it, she raised her Glock. "This is Sheriff Taggert. Come out with your hands raised."

The shadow didn't hesitate. A man stepped out from behind the blanket, whispering, "Sheriff! Thank God."

He was wearing a store employee vest over a wiry body. A ring of keys hung at his waist and his hands were raised high in the air. Most importantly, he wasn't Jordan Summer. He was about fifty, with a receding hairline and a mustache that belonged in the 1970s.

"Who are you?" Bree stepped out from behind the aisle.

"Preston Rigley," he said in a very soft voice, looking around. "I'm the store manager. Someone broke in. I called 911. Isn't that why you're here?"

Bree had turned her radio volume off so the shooter didn't use the sound to pinpoint her location. "We'll find him."

From behind him, a voice said, "Too late." A man stepped up behind the manager and put a gun to the back of his head. "I found you."

Even in the dim light, Bree recognized the fake Nielsen a.k.a. Jordan Summer.

"Lower your weapon, Sheriff," Jordan said. "And tell the big dude with the rifle to put his down, or I shoot the manager."

Bree couldn't shoot. Matt wouldn't have a clear shot either, but he didn't move. She didn't want to relinquish her gun either. If Jordan was thinking straight, he wouldn't pull the trigger. Killing the manager would eliminate his hostage. He'd have no leverage.

"Look, Jordan," she began. "If you pull that trigger, the big dude will put a bullet between your eyes before you can draw one more breath."

"You know who I am." He sounded surprised.

"We do." And now Bree wondered, if Jordan was here, what had he done with—or to—Mr. Pomar? She put it out of her mind. She had to handle one crisis at a time.

"Then you know I have a score to settle." He moved closer to the manager, grabbing him by the back of the collar with his free hand. Then he shuffled backward and pulled the older man with him. The manager's eyes went wide, pleading silently with Bree. Tears streamed down his face. Jordan yanked on his collar and shouted, "Where's Dana Romano?"

Relief coursed through Bree. He didn't know where she was, so he hadn't killed her.

"I don't know." Bree kept her poker face intact.

"You're a fucking liar." Jordan prodded Preston in the nape of the neck with the muzzle of the gun. "I know she's here. I followed her into the building." Using the manager as a shield, he backed toward the hallway that led to the employee-only rooms. As he walked backward, Bree advanced. Matt held tight, his gun still leveled in Jordan's direction. Dana and Nolan were likely hiding somewhere in the rear of the store. Jordan was heading right for them. Bree couldn't let him out of her sight. She looked past Jordan, over his shoulder. The hallway went dark after the public restrooms. The corridor looked like it took a ninety-degree turn.

She couldn't let Jordan disappear around that corner. But how could she stop him? "You don't want to hurt anyone, Jordan. You'll only make it worse for yourself."

"Fuck you," he yelled.

"Let him go, Jordan." A figure appeared half in the shadow behind him. Dana. She stepped forward. An exit sign glowed over her head, casting her in a sickly red glow. She staggered a few more steps. "Your beef is with me. There's no need to drag innocent people into it."

Jordan spun a quarter turn, holding the manager closer to maintain his human shield. "What do you know about innocence? You railroaded my brother into prison."

Dana raised both hands in a surrender gesture. "Then let's settle this between us. Let the manager go. I'll trade spots with him."

Bree wanted to shout a protest, but kept her mouth shut. Maybe in the hostage shuffle, either she or Matt could get a decent aim on Jordan and take him out. Bree wanted to shoot him. He'd killed two people. He'd threatened her family. He'd been to her home.

He'd frightened Luke.

Her finger twitched on the trigger guard, and she had no doubt she'd pull it with no hesitation. Today, her murderous DNA didn't worry her. Instead, she'd put her inherited cold-bloodedness to good use.

She inched forward, taking care to stay out of Matt's line of sight. A long gun was much more accurate than a handgun. They needed a distraction. If only the lights would come on or backup would arrive.

Could one of them go around and surprise Jordan from behind? No. The rear doors to the store would be locked. Where was Nolan?

Jordan shifted his hold on the manager. "Fine. Come here." He gestured toward Dana with his gun. "Don't try anything. I don't care if I die, as long as I take you with me."

With hands raised, Dana moved forward. Jordan shoved the manager out of the way and grabbed her. The manager ran. Dana fell sideways, her balance clearly off. Jordan was careful to keep Dana between him and Bree. He didn't give Bree a clear shot, not for one second. Now he had Dana. He pressed the gun against her temple and murmured in her ear.

Bree took another step closer. She had nothing to lose. Jordan was going to shoot Dana right there in front of her. She knew it in her heart. His earlier statement indicated he was suicidal. He moved the gun, the muzzle almost stroking the side of Dana's face. In the quiet of the building, Bree heard him mutter, "We'll go out together."

Dana reached up and behind her with both hands. Her sudden motion knocked the gun sideways a few inches. She grabbed his face and shoved her thumbs into his eyes. With a scream he released her on reflex but pulled the trigger at the same time. The bullet went wide, striking an overhead fluorescent light. Glass shattered and rained down on them. Dana released Jordan's face and reached for his gun hand. She pushed his arm upward. They struggled.

In the darkness, Bree couldn't see whose body parts belonged to whom. She ran forward, aware that one of them could be dead before she could cover the distance.

Something streaked past her. Stunned, she caught a flash of a sleek black body. Greta leaped into the air, clamped her mouth on Jordan's gun arm, and took him down. He screamed, his words indecipherable, as the dog ripped her head back and forth.

Dana rolled away from the screaming man. Bree ran in front of her friend, facing the dog and man on the ground. Jordan's screams should have elicited some pity, but she felt no sympathy toward him.

Collins raced up the store's center aisle, breathing hard. She moved to her dog and barked out a command. Greta released Jordan's arm, and Collins hauled the dog off him. The dog's tail never stopped wagging. Bree moved in with handcuffs.

Behind her, Greta barked, and Collins praised her. "That's a good girl."

Bree rolled Jordan to his face, put a knee in the small of his back, and cuffed him. She patted down his pockets for weapons, then stood, leaving him facedown on the tile. Anger coursed through her veins, the heat of it blurring her thoughts as she stared down at him. She had wanted to kill this man. Not her fault, right? He'd been the one to make it personal. But still . . .

Bree glanced back to check on Dana. "You OK?"

"Yeah." Dana was bent double, her butt to the wall, her hands resting on her thighs. "Nolan is in the back. Shot. He's lost a lot of blood."

Matt rushed past them both.

"He's in the last office, behind the desk," Dana called after him.

"Ambulance is here." Collins pointed to the front of the store. Through the glass, several sets of lights swirled. "Miller Road is open. We have state troopers too."

Hallelujah.

"How did you get here?" Still dazed, Bree turned on her radio and listened to the chatter.

"We did a little four-wheelin'." Collins handed Greta her hedgehog. The dog took the toy and shook her head, just as she had with Jordan. As it squealed, bits of stuffing flew in all directions.

"Good work. Both of you." She turned to Jordan, breathing through her rage. "What did you do with Mr. Pomar?"

CHAPTER THIRTY-SEVEN

Matt ran down the corridor and opened the last office door. Afraid of what he was going to find, he held his breath. The room was dark. Matt shined his flashlight inside. "Nolan?"

His brother was on the floor, propped against the wall, a gun in his hand, aimed at Matt.

Relieved, Matt slid to a stop, heart thumping. "Don't shoot me."

Nolan lowered the gun, which seemed to use up the last of his strength, because he flopped sideways. "Glad to see you. Dana?"

"She's OK. Everyone is OK." Matt moved in, dropping to his knees beside his brother.

"Good." Nolan nodded. "Took your sweet time getting here."

Matt used his flashlight to assess the wound. Blood soaked the thick pressure bandage. "You'll be fine. This is practically a paper cut. Couple of Band-Aids and you'll be good to go." Banter aside, Matt's initial relief at finding his brother alive dampened. Nolan had already lost enough blood to weaken him, and the wound still bled enough to worry Matt.

Nolan snorted. An EMT appeared in the doorway, kit in hand. Matt moved out of the way, then slid the desk to the side to give him room to work. The office was tight, so Matt moved to the hall, where two ambulance attendants were hustling toward him with a gurney.

They wasted no time getting Nolan out of there. Matt followed them down the main aisle of the store. Near the entrance, Bree waved him away as he approached her. "Go with your brother. I'll come to the hospital later."

Grateful, Matt jogged to catch up with the gurney. Other deputies had arrived. At the front of the store, he paused and waited while they adjusted Nolan's IV and the gurney straps.

Juarez was interviewing the shaken store manager.

The man was impressively composed, considering he'd had a gun pressed to his head a short while before. "I closed the store and sent the employees home because of the weather. But my wife couldn't get to the store to pick me up because of the accident on Miller Road. So I didn't have much choice but to wait in the store. I locked up but didn't set the alarm. We have old motion detectors that are very sensitive. Plus, the alarm always acts wonky when the power goes out. It needs updating. I didn't want to listen to it screech for hours. I figured I'd set it when I left. I never expected . . ."

The attendants moved the gurney outside and loaded it through the double doors of the ambulance.

Matt caught sight of Collins and Greta a few feet away, playing tug with a fresh hedgehog toy.

"Thank you. Both of you," he said.

Collins walked closer and spoke in a low voice. "I hope I don't get the sheriff into any trouble. I didn't give a warning, but I thought if I did, the subject would shoot her or the hostage. He sounded like he was gearing up for a suicide by cop."

"I think you're right, and I would have done the same." Matt was happy with Bree's choice of handler for Greta. Collins weighed risks and variables in a split second. She put her K-9 partner's safety before her own career ambition. "I wouldn't worry too much. Your reasoning is sound. Those were definitely exigent circumstances. If anything, Greta showed how effective she is."

The dog brought her hedgehog over to Matt and squeaked it at him. Laughing, he gave it a tug.

Collins smiled. "I'm not worried about me. It's the program that concerns me. I don't want to jeopardize the department. The sheriff will have my back."

Nolan was loaded in the ambulance, and Matt moved toward the rear doors. He turned back to Collins. "I have no doubt she will, and you made the right decision. Don't let anyone make you doubt your choice."

CHAPTER THIRTY-EIGHT

Bree parked at the Pomar estate. Collins pulled up next to her in the K-9 unit. The rest of her deputies were tied up with the accident and hostage scenes. Plus, Bree was familiar to Mr. Pomar. If he remembered her.

She jumped out of her vehicle. The ground was slippery, and she half slid and half shuffled to the front door. It was locked, so she broke the narrow window, reached in, and opened the dead bolt.

The power was out, so the alarm didn't sound. She doubted Jordan had turned it on. The big house was deadly quiet, without even the hum of appliances. Jordan Summer had refused to say a single word after Bree had cuffed him. She had no idea what he'd done with Mr. Pomar.

"A scent object would help." Collins opened the rear hatch and pulled out Greta's working harness. The dog's tail wagged and her body wriggled as it went on.

Bree turned on her flashlight and went into the house. She called out Mr. Pomar's name, even though she knew it was likely pointless. She went upstairs to his bedroom and pulled a dirty shirt from his hamper. She brought the shirt down to the first floor, where Collins held it out to the dog. Greta knew her business. She inhaled deeply and began circling the house, sniffing the air in all directions. She walked the whole first floor, then stopped in front of a door in the hallway near the kitchen.

"Where does this lead?" Collins asked, juggling the lead and her own flashlight.

"The basement." Bree remembered from her previous search of the house. She opened the door. She'd been down there, but without the electricity, the darkness was stark. "Most of the basement is a big open space. Not much down there except for some boxes, the furnace, and hot water heater."

They descended the steps. The dog pulled hard. On the last step, a tread gave way. Collins stumbled. The leash ripped from her hand, and Greta took off.

"Shit." Collins recovered her footing and sprinted after the dog.

Bree was right on her heels, but there was no way they'd catch Greta. Dread spiraled in Bree's gut as she imagined the dog latching on to Mr. Pomar the same way she'd grabbed Jordan. Bree heard whining. She and Collins headed for the sound.

The beam of Bree's flashlight illuminated Mr. Pomar curled on his side on the concrete. Greta lay next to him, whining and licking at his face. Relief washed over Bree at the dog's gentle manner, but fresh fear bloomed at the old man's stillness.

Was he dead? The basement was damp and cold. Jordan could have drugged, strangled, or shot him.

Bree and Collins caught up. Collins moved to pull the dog away.

Mr. Pomar groaned. His thin fingers flexed. One hand lifted and touched the dog, stroking her fur and murmuring nonsense. Greta didn't care about his lack of communication skills. Her tail thumped on the floor.

"No, leave her." Bree knelt next to the old man. Clearly, the dog was giving him comfort and probably providing some heat. "Hey, Mr. Pomar. I'm going to check your pulse." She didn't know how much he understood, but he deserved her respect. She pressed two fingers to his wrist. His pulse was much stronger than she'd expected. She used her radio to call for an ambulance.

"He looks groggy," Collins said.

"I would bet he's drugged," Bree agreed. Jordan wouldn't want a wandering old man to garner any unwanted attention, and he wouldn't care if the old man died either. He'd already killed two innocent people: Nielsen and Kent.

Mr. Pomar opened his eyes and stared at Greta. His face softened. His tone and touch conveyed what his words could not. The dog, however, understood. She stretched her body alongside his, laid her head on his chest, and let him curl his hands into the thick fur around her neck. She didn't move even when Collins offered her the hedgehog.

Collins repeated Matt's K-9 mantra: "Trust your dog."

"She's a rock star."

"I'll get a pillow and blanket." Collins headed for the steps.

Bree swiped a tear from under her eye. The ambulance would take some time. The ice storm had knocked out power and caused accidents all over the area. But Mr. Pomar was safe, thanks to Greta.

The old man looked beyond the dog at Bree. His gaze seemed to zoom in on the sheriff department patch on her jacket. "Red. Boom. Gone."

He'd seen the murder. Bree knew it. He'd repeated those three words multiple times: *Red* stood for blood. *Boom* was the gunshot. *Gone* equaled dead. He'd seen his caretaker murdered. Had Jordan counted on the fact that the old man couldn't turn him in?

Pity welled in her throat. How horrible it must be to know you need to communicate and be unable to do so. She had no idea how well Mr. Pomar processed the trauma, but he must have been terrified. Bree bet that fear had driven his panicked and repeated flights from the house. He hadn't wandered. He'd fled.

The ambulance arrived within a half hour. Mr. Pomar cried when he was wheeled away from the dog. Collins promised to bring her to visit him, wherever he ended up.

CHAPTER THIRTY-NINE

At ten o'clock the following morning, Matt paced the hospital waiting room, waiting for his brother to come out of the recovery room. Bree sat in a chair, drinking her tenth cup of coffee. Matt's stomach had rebelled after number six. He glanced at the clock again. Time was ticking by in slow motion.

As he walked past her chair, Bree touched his leg. "He's OK."

Nolan had had emergency surgery during the night. He'd lost a good amount of blood, but miraculously he'd suffered no shattered bones or other debilitating injury. His shoulder should heal in time, though he would be out of commission for a few months. But Matt wouldn't rest easy until his brother was awake and comfortable.

In the chair facing them, Detective Ash balanced a notepad on his knee. "I interviewed Jordan at the jail. Hanover has a copy of the video at the Redhaven station. I expected Jordan to give me the silent treatment and demand a lawyer, but he wouldn't shut up."

"Ego or anger?" Matt asked.

"The latter. He was enraged, could barely hold it together to yell at me. In summary, he is a certified nursing assistant. He worked in a nursing home in the Philadelphia suburbs until his brother died.

Then he quit. His father died of a massive heart attack six months after Gary went to prison. His mother held on for a few more years, then got cancer. She passed four years ago. He's been alone since. According to prison records, Jordan visited his brother every week for his entire sentence."

Jordan's anger festered all those years, thought Matt.

Ash flipped a page. "We know that Jordan and Nielsen both interviewed for the job with Mr. Pomar on the same day. Their interview appointments were twenty minutes apart. The interviewer remembers the two talking to each other while they waited. Mr. Pomar's family wanted an LPN, not a CNA, so they chose Nielsen."

"Do you think Jordan recognized that they looked a little alike, at least superficially, and the resemblance gave him the idea to become Nielsen?" Bree asked.

"That's exactly what we think," Ash said. "His laptop was in his room at the Pomar estate. On it, we found saved web articles on Ms. Romano and her former partner, Stuart Hoffman, including Hoffman's obituary. It seems Jordan started building this file after his brother's death by suicide. He also has articles on the prosecutor and judge. We found a document where he brainstormed ideas on how to get to them after he'd taken care of Romano. His social media profiles are full of anti–law enforcement rants and his continued insistence that his brother was innocent."

"So he went to Mr. Pomar's house, killed Nielsen, and took his place?" Matt asked. "Did he shoot him in the house?"

Ash nodded. "Forensics is there now. They already found a few spatters of blood high on the wall in the back hallway. When the tech sprayed the wall with luminol, the whole hallway lit up. It was practically painted blue."

"I'll bet you find blood in the drains and washing machine too. Must have taken him some time to clean all that up." Matt had seen the hole in the back of Nielsen's head. There would have been brain matter as well as blood and possibly skull fragments on the walls and floor.

Ash continued. "We also found a pair of size eleven Timberlands. Forensics already confirmed the tread matches the footprints found at your farm. There was a violin and block of light rosin in Jordan's room as well, so that explains the rosin trace evidence that links the crimes." Ash glanced up.

"Does he play the violin?" Bree asked.

"He does." Ash nodded. "He planted the rosin and horsehair to implicate Romano. You're going to want to watch the interview for that explanation."

"Sounds like there'll be plenty of physical evidence against Jordan." Matt loved a tidy case, and so did the prosecutor.

Ash nodded. "He'd clearly been stalking Romano and getting the lay of the land up here. He'd missed work over the past few months. His gas purchases were way up, and he'd rented a few Airbnbs."

"Surveying the area," Matt said.

Bree tossed her empty coffee cup in the trash. "I believe Mr. Pomar saw him shoot Nielsen, and that's why he kept running away."

"It's possible," Ash said. "Unfortunately, he can't tell us."

Mr. Pomar had spent the night in the hospital, sleeping off the sedatives Jordan had given him. Luckily, the dose hadn't been lethal. The hospital was holding him one more night, and his son would arrive in the morning. The son didn't seem to care, but Matt hoped they found a safe housing solution for the older man.

Bree rubbed her eyes. "I stopped to check in on him. A therapy dog was in his room. The change in him was striking. I hope wherever he goes, there's a dog."

Matt nodded. "Collins says she'll sneak Greta in wherever he ends up."

Bree smiled.

"How is Ms. Romano?" Ash asked.

"Good." Bree leaned back. "Her CT scan was clear. No sign of a second concussion. She's waiting on a neurology consult, but the ophthalmologist thinks the localized swelling in her eye caused the vision issues. She struck her head on something during the rollover. Once the swelling subsides, he predicts her sight will return to normal."

"Excellent." Ash rose. "I'll keep you updated."

"Thank you." Bree shook his hand.

Matt nodded as Ash exited the room. Maybe he wasn't a complete asshat.

They had one minute of quiet, then Bree's phone buzzed. She glanced at it. "It's Rory." She answered the call on speaker. "Sheriff Taggert."

"I've got news!" Rory said. "The email provider finally sent the account information for RedBloodedMale03. The account is set up for Chevy Ekin, but the online payment service used to pay the monthly fee belongs to Ford Ekin."

"That's barely a fake name." Matt rolled his eyes. "What a dumbass."

"A dumbass who's going back to prison." Bree smiled. "Thank you, Rory. You're the best."

"I'm just happy to have helped catch the bastard," Rory said. "We can't let criminals target kids."

"No, we can't," Bree agreed. "You'll send documentation?"

"It will be my pleasure." Rory ended the call.

"Jordan is in custody. Ford soon will be." Matt sat down next to Bree. It would be his pleasure to see Ford back in prison, where scumbags who threatened children belonged. "The family is safe."

She rested her head on his shoulder. "Yes. They are."

"Still have doubts about your job?" He leaned his head on hers.

"No. Today was a good day. We need to appreciate those."

"That we do."

Within the hour, Matt visited his brother, who was loopy from the anesthesia, but his open eyes and nonsensical mumbling were enough to convince Matt that he'd survived. Leaving Nolan to rest, he and Bree left the hospital and drove to the Redhaven station.

"You're sure you don't want to sleep for a dozen hours and then watch the interview?" he asked.

Bree's lips flattened. "I want to see it now."

Matt supposed she needed to see Jordan behind bars with her own eyes, just as he had needed to see his brother awake.

Hanover looked as tired as Matt felt. His uniform was wrinkled. A dark blotch—probably coffee—stained the front of his shirt, and the bags under his eyes were big enough to hold a week's worth of groceries. He escorted them to a conference room and played the interview on a monitor. He fast-forwarded through the procedural statements.

A visibly agitated Jordan yanked at the handcuffs that secured him to the center of the table. In the short-sleeve jail uniform, the Lady Justice tattoo was clearly visible. A vein on his temple throbbed so hard, Matt could have counted his pulse just watching it.

Ash sat across from him, his expression neutral. "Why did you kill Kent McFadden?"

Jordan rattled the handcuffs. "To punish that bitch detective Romano. You were supposed to arrest her. I set it all up. I planted the violin rosin and the horsehair. You gave her a pass because she was a cop. You're all just as crooked."

"How did you get the rosin and horsehair?" Ash asked.

Jordan leaned across the table. "I was watching her. One day, while they were all in the barn, I slipped into the house. Animal hair was easy. It's all over the house. I found the violin in an upstairs closet. I figured it was specific enough to tie her to the crime. I know how rosin gets on your clothes."

Matt's blood turned to ice water. He'd been in their house. Matt wanted to reach into the monitor and take Jordan by the neck. He'd violated their home.

Except Dana's presence at the scene had never been in question. The presence of trace evidence that tied her to the body was easily explained, except Hanover had almost fallen for Jordan's ploy, hadn't he?

Ash didn't move, remaining impressively cool. "How did you know she'd be there Monday night?"

"The doctor left his door unlocked all the time. I actually sneaked into his place too, the week before, to check out the place. While I was there, I looked at his calendar." Jordan vibrated with rage. "I set it up to look just like Gary's case. She deserves to die in prison just like my brother. Gary was innocent, and she put him in prison anyway."

"Your brother was found guilty by a jury of his peers," Ash said calmly.

"He was with me that night!" Jordan screamed, the tendons on his neck standing up like anchor ropes on a tent. "He didn't kill anyone!"

Ash shifted backward just a hair, distancing himself from the intensity of Jordan's fury. "Dr. McFadden was collateral damage?"

Jordan seethed but didn't respond.

"What about Gavin Nielsen?" Ash asked.

Jordan shrugged. "I needed a place to stay close to Romano."

"How did you get rid of Nielsen's body?"

"That was easy. I drove to the back of the salvage yard and cut a hole in the fence. The place is huge. I figured no one would find it in that old car until the spring thaw. Just my bad luck that the junkyard is owned by a dope dealer." Jordan sagged backward. "You were supposed to arrest Romano. She was there when he died. Her fingerprints would have been all over the place. I waited for her to get there and made sure it looked like they'd had a fight. That's more evidence than the cops had against my brother. I guess the rules are different when you're investigating one of your own." Jordan went quiet and still, as if he'd finally run out of steam.

He didn't respond to Ash's next two questions, and the detective ended the interview. There would be additional interviews. Jordan would spend the rest of his life in prison.

Hanover turned off the monitor. "If you hadn't found Nielsen's body, his plan might have worked. I thought Romano did it." He scratched the stubble on his chin. "At least I wasn't willing to give her a pass just because she was a cop."

Matt stood. He was done. If he stayed any longer, he wasn't going to be able to keep his mouth shut.

Back in their vehicle, Bree stared through the windshield. "He was in the house. We have to be more vigilant about setting the alarm."

"No. You can't turn the farm into a prison."

Bree sighed. "You're right. Paranoia isn't going to make anyone feel more secure. It'll do the opposite, but we won't tell the kids Jordan was in the house. It won't serve any purpose. They don't need to be afraid all the time. The improvements Nolan is making to the security system should help."

"Agreed." Matt thought maybe another dog would be a better answer. Ladybug was not a watchdog, but he'd have to talk Bree into it. She was no longer instantly afraid of all dogs, but a guard-type canine still intimidated her. Maybe a puppy she could raise and help train . . . For now, Brody would stay at the farm. He didn't have an off switch.

Bree started the engine. "Hanover was totally going to arrest Dana if we hadn't found Nielsen's body."

"He's a tool."

"But not a corrupt one." Bree yawned. "Do you think Gary Summer could have been innocent?"

"It's possible, but it's more likely that Jordan was mistaken. Either way, Gary's dead, so there's zero chance of the case being reopened."

"You're right." Bree nodded once. "Let's go home."

"Sounds good." Matt took her hand, wondering if there had been a specific time during the past few months when her farm had become his home.

CHAPTER FORTY

Nine days later, Dana zipped her coat and stepped out onto the deck. A foot of snow had fallen the previous day. A clean layer of sparkling white blanketed the backyard and pasture. Streamers decorated the house, inside and out. A HAPPY BIRTHDAY, CADY banner spanned the back of the house.

Dana flipped up her hood. Today, winter was lovely. Though it was cold, the sun shone from the clearest blue sky, and the wind had abated. Horses dotted the pasture. Riot, the troublemaker, kicked up some snow and bit Pumpkin playfully on the butt. The littler horse flicked out a rear hoof in warning. Dana smiled. Pumpkin might be small and tolerant, but he wasn't a total pushover.

A vehicle door slammed. Dana looked toward the parking area. Morgan Dane climbed out of the passenger seat of a minivan. Dana recognized the big blond man with her as her husband, Lance Kruger. He opened the sliding door, and three little girls poured out, dressed in snow pants and boots. Dana could hear the excitement in their high-pitched chatter. Lance snagged the youngest around the waist. She squirmed as he carried her toward the house. Dana heard him reminding her of the "rules" they'd discussed in the car.

In the snowy backyard, Bree made the introductions between Morgan's three girls and Kayla. Morgan's oldest, Ava, appeared close in age, and the two paired off immediately. The middle child was enamored with Ladybug. Morgan's youngest, Sophie, seemed like a handful.

Matt's whole family was here. George was running the kitchen. He allowed Dana to perform light chores only, putting her in charge of the s'mores. Anna had organized activities for the children. She handed out carrots and large black buttons and put them to work making snowmen in the yard. The retired teacher stayed close to the smallest child, as if sensing she needed extra supervision. But Morgan and Lance didn't stray far either.

Dana leaned on the porch railing. Usually, she worked family events. Her headaches and exhaustion had eased, but she still benefited from an afternoon nap. Another two weeks, George had said, and she should be closer to normal. But she could see her old self returning, and she was grateful enough that simply watching was enough for today.

Luke led a saddled Pumpkin from the barn, and all interest in snowmen ended.

Morgan's littlest, Sophie, bolted for the pony. Lance scooped her up in flight. "Easy," he said before setting her down again.

Calmer, Sophie stared at Kayla in wonder. "You have a horse?"

"Yeah. Wanna meet him?" Kayla snagged the carrot nose from her snowman and skipped to her pony. "You can take turns riding him."

Lance gave Bree a questioning look. She nodded. "Pumpkin is very tolerant, and Luke will keep an eye on them."

Bree mouthed *thank you* to Luke, who grinned as if he were getting a kick out of the little kids. The lovely chaos made Dana wonder what she'd done with her weekends before she'd moved here. Slept in? Caught up on laundry? She'd been terribly inefficient. These days she could simultaneously do three loads of wash, feed pets, cook dinner, and supervise a social studies project.

Pushing off the railing, she went inside. After removing her coat, she hung it on a peg. "Smells great, George."

Matt's dad lifted the lid on a slow cooker and waved some steam toward his face. He smiled, as if satisfied with the aroma.

Dana continued to the living room. Nolan rested on the couch, propped on pillows, playing a video game with Adam. Two plates sat on the coffee table.

Adam stood and stretched. "I'm going to go see what's happening outside. Sounds loud." He left the room.

"The kids are having fun." Dana sat next to Nolan. "You look good."

"Dad is making sure I get the rest that I need."

Dana laughed. "I'm sure he is. When are you allowed to move back to your place?"

Nolan grinned. "Dad says five more days."

"Do you always do what your dad says?" she teased.

"Pretty much." Nolan's mouth turned up in a wry smile. "He's very persuasive."

"I've noticed."

Nolan snorted. "You're one of the family now."

"How hard is it staying with your parents?" Dana couldn't imagine.

"Actually, not hard at all. Dad and I had our moments when I was fighting. He understood the long-term health risks and was not pleased with me." Nolan paused. "But all his bossiness comes from love, and he does understand boundaries. He'll only interfere when it's serious."

"I love my parents, but I couldn't live with them," Dana admitted. "I haven't met their traditional expectations, and they can't get past that."

"I'm sorry."

"It's OK. I know they love me, and they really think I'd be happier if I'd made other choices."

"But?"

"But I'm pretty happy." She realized the truth of her statement as it came out of her mouth. "And I was happy when I was a cop too." She'd been lonely at times, but she'd had purpose. She'd made a difference.

She'd helped people. Now, her life had a different purpose, but one that felt just as important. "I have no regrets."

"Do you miss it?" he asked.

"No." The violence of the past week had convinced her that she was done with police work. Enough was enough. She eyed his plate. "Is that marshmallow?"

"It is."

"You ate a s'more?"

"I did."

She raised a brow. She had never seen him consume sugar. Ever.

He sighed. "I'm never going to be a professional fighter again. That's not to say I'm not going to stay in shape. Physical conditioning is important for what I do. But I don't need to be so strict. Life is short."

And it could have been much shorter for both of them.

"On that note." He took her hand in his. "Once I'm not living in my teenage bedroom, I'd like to take you out on a date."

Dana stared at their joined hands. "I don't know. You're ten years younger than me. That's a whole decade."

"But I have very high mileage," he deadpanned.

Dana chuckled. She really did like this man. "I hate to screw up our friendship."

He shrugged. "You have to risk it to get the biscuit."

She threw back her head and laughed. Neither of them was exactly timid. "You're right. OK. One date."

"Way to put pressure on a guy. Now I have to think of the perfect date." He gave her a pained look.

Dana turned and faced him. "Then let's take the pressure off the outcome." She leaned forward and pressed a kiss to his mouth.

He kissed her back, and she felt the potential between them to her toes.

There was going to be more than one date.

CHAPTER
FORTY-ONE

Bree surveyed the chaos. Hopped up on sugar and excitement, the kids raced in circles around the yard. George produced a birthday cake he'd baked from scratch. Cady, dressed in a parka, snow boots, and the birthday tiara Kayla had insisted she wear, blew out the candles.

Ladybug's snout was stained blue. Either the kids had shared some cake or the dog had helped herself. Bree let it go, crossing her fingers she didn't have to clean up vomit later or, if the dog did hurl, she did it outside. Blue food coloring would be a bear to get out of the rug.

The barn door opened, and Matt led Beast out. The draft horse pulled a shiny black-and-red sleigh through the snow. The thin jingle of sleigh bells sounded happy. The kids squealed.

Matt held up a hand to the kids. "The birthday girl gets the first ride."

Cady clapped her hands like a child. She stopped to pet Beast, who bobbed his head and snorted as if he couldn't wait to get started. Todd took her hand and helped her into the sleigh, which was funny because she was almost six feet tall.

Cady and Todd had both lived through their own personal traumas. They deserved to be happy. Bree couldn't have been more pleased to watch them snuggle up in the sleigh.

Matt climbed into the driver's seat. He shook the reins, and Beast started down the lane that ran next to the pasture. Beast broke into a jog, snow flying under his huge hooves. Matt looped around the pasture, then pulled up in the yard again. Cady and Todd exited. Bree loaded up the four little girls and climbed in next to Matt. She kissed him on the cheek. "This is an amazing surprise."

"I bought the sleigh last month. Then I had to learn to drive."

"Was it hard?"

"Only for me. The horse knows what he's doing. All the learning was on my end." He clucked, and Beast trotted on.

"Let me guess. All those solo trail rides you took while I was at work weren't just for pleasure."

Matt grinned. "Beast and I have been visiting that Amish farmer, Jacob Lapp, down the road. He taught me to harness and drive using one of his own carts. He's very patient." Pride shone on Matt's face. "Beast is very tolerant of my ineptitude."

Bree looked back at the four girls. Kayla's and Ava's heads were bent together. Sophie climbed on the seat to stand. Bree sensed the little one needed boundaries, firm boundaries, and pinned her with a look. "Sophie, either you sit or you and I will walk back to the house."

Sophie met her gaze, read her resolve, and made a calculated decision. She sat.

Bree felt like she'd passed a test, but also that there would be another one soon. The girls unloaded back at the house, and Matt took his parents for a ride. Bree noted that the elder Flynns held hands. She sighed. A year ago, she would have scoffed at the thought of two people being in love after more than four decades of marriage. But now, her eyes brimmed with sentimental tears.

After everyone had taken a turn, Bree started toward the barn. "I'll help you with the harness."

Matt shook his head. "Nope. Come for a ride with me."

Bree glanced toward the house. "The kids . . ."

Morgan and Lance were in the middle of the backyard with the four girls. Matt caught her eye, and she waved them off.

"Morgan can handle them for a bit," Matt said. "It's her little one who needs the supervision anyway."

"True." Bree laughed.

Matt extended his hand. She took it and let him help her into the sleigh.

"Want to drive?" he asked.

"Yes." Taking the reins, Bree felt like a kid. "I had a pony when I was little. I always wanted to get him a cart."

"I was thinking a cart would be fun. We could do hayrides."

"Beast seems to be enjoying himself."

"Jacob says he's bred to work. He offered to buy him."

"You'll never sell him, though, right?"

"Hell no!" Matt said. "He's got a home for life."

Bree looked over the snowy fields. "Can we stop at the oak tree?"

"Of course." Matt steered the sleigh toward the hill that overlooked the farm. He stopped the sleigh near the tree and waited patiently.

This was the place where they'd released Erin's ashes, where she could watch over all of them.

"Do you want to get out?" he asked.

Bree looked back over the snow-covered meadow. She could see the farm in the distance, the family milling about on the back lawn. Did Erin see? Did she know Bree was doing her best to make the kids happy? She knew, Bree decided. "No. This was enough. We can go back."

Matt clucked and Beast moved off again. Content, Bree rested her head on his shoulder. They returned to the farm. Matt drove to the shed, where he unhitched the horse and put away the sleigh.

Bree followed him into the barn. He removed the horse's bridle and put him on the crossties.

"Great party," she said.

Matt turned to her. "I think Cady had fun."

"A sleigh ride on her birthday? Who wouldn't love that?"

Beast nudged them both with his enormous head. Bree rubbed the horse's forehead. "You're a good boy, Beast. Thank you." She took Matt's hand and pulled him close. "And thank you."

"You're welcome. We need to remember to take a minute for us every once in a while."

She looped her arms around his neck. "Not just for this, though this was spectacular. But for everything."

This man gave everything to her, to her family, to his own. And all he asked for was an occasional minute.

"We should aim higher than a few minutes. I'm thinking a weekend, once everyone is healed. We've gotten past the anniversary of Erin's death. The kids are doing well. It's time."

Time for everyone to move forward. They would never forget Erin, but they would live—and love.

"I aim to please, ma'am." He grinned and kissed her.

She kissed him back. "And I want you to know you do. So very much."

With her lips pressed to his, Bree could definitely believe in four or five decades of love.

ACKNOWLEDGMENTS

Special thanks to the writer friends who helped me develop this concept: Rayna Vause, Kendra Elliot, Leanne Sparks, Toni Anderson, Amy Gamet, and Loreth Anne White. Cheers, ladies! As always, credit goes to my agent, Jill Marsal, for her continued unwavering support and solid career advice. I'm also grateful for the entire team at Montlake, especially my acquiring editor, Anh Schluep, and my developmental editor, Charlotte Herscher. As far as teams go, I am lucky to have the best.

ABOUT THE AUTHOR

Photo © 2016 Jared Gruenwald Photography

Melinda Leigh is the #1 Amazon Charts and #1 *Wall Street Journal* bestselling author of *She Can Run*, an International Thriller Award nominee for Best First Novel, *She Can Tell*, *She Can Scream*, *She Can Hide*, and *She Can Kill* in the She Can series; *Midnight Exposure*, *Midnight Sacrifice*, *Midnight Betrayal*, and *Midnight Obsession* in the Midnight Novels; *Hour of Need*, *Minutes to Kill*, and *Seconds to Live* in the Scarlet Falls series; *Say You're Sorry*, *Her Last Goodbye*, *Bones Don't Lie*, *What I've Done*, *Secrets Never Die*, and *Save Your Breath* in the Morgan Dane series; and *Cross Her Heart*, *See Her Die*, *Drown Her Sorrows*, *Right Behind Her*, *Dead Against Her*, *Lie to Her*, and the short story "Her Second Death" in the Bree Taggert series. Melinda's garnered numerous writing awards, including two RITA nominations; holds a second-degree black belt in Kenpo karate and has taught women's self-defense; and lives in a messy house with her family and a small herd of rescue pets. For more information, visit www.melindaleigh.com.